I0762162

SQUIRE ADAMSSON:
Or, Where Do You Live?

An Allegorical Tale from the Swedish Awakening
By Paul Peter Waldenström

Translation with Introduction and Notes by Mark Safstrom
Illustrations by Jeffrey T. HansPetersen
Foreword by Gracia Grindal

Seattle and Minneapolis

Squire Adamsson:
Or, Where Do You Live?

Pietisten, Inc., Seattle, Washington

SECOND REVISED PRINTING

Select paragraphs in the introduction and notes of this book were adapted from excerpts that earlier appeared in the article "Making Room for the Lost" in *Covenant Quarterly*, Aug-Nov 2013, and in *The Religious Origins of Democratic Pluralism* 2010 (see References, p. 36).

The illustration on page 138 is adapted from 'The Last Judgment' by Jan Van Eyck.

ISBN: 978-0-9913506-2-9

Till teamet som gjorde drömmen till verklighet,
Sandy, Jeff, Karl, Gracia, Steph, David,
Gud välsigne dig.

FOREWORD

The Narrow Path
by Gracia Grindal

My pastor father and mother, serving in the Lutheran Free Church, a small pietistic Norwegian American Lutheran Church, loved to tell the story of a new family in town. The family belonged to an even smaller Norwegian pietistic church body, and had to go shopping for another Lutheran church because there was no congregation in town from their denomination. As Lutheran Pietists they believed strongly that Christians were to separate themselves out from the world, and that to be a Christian was to stand firmly against it. The pastor of the largest Norwegian Lutheran congregation in town came to them and said, "You will want to join our church because everyone belongs to it!" The couple reacted in horror. Such a congregation was the last sort of church they wanted to join, they said, to the puzzlement of the pastor. It was a failure to understand another culture, but more than that, evidence of a great divide, unbridgeable, between the two pieties. (Of such misunderstandings came many jokes in our parsonage!)

They might as well have been speaking two completely different languages. The gulf between the pastor and the couple is the conflict that Waldenström and his readers know in their bones: Is one a Christian simply because one is Swedish and part of the state church? Ernst Troeltsch (1865-1923) described the difference in his morphologies of religious groups as a "sect type," since the sect type emphasizes faith as a decision, believing that the normal beginning of genuine Christian life is spiritual transformation through explicit commitment to

Christ and taking responsibility for one's life in moral terms. Lutherans historically have been both church types and sect types because of the pietistic traditions from which many of the Lutheran immigrants to this country tended to be, especially the Scandinavians.

I thought of that story many times while reading *Squire Adamsson*. For those who understand the "language of Canaan" this book will be easy reading—they will understand what is being said, almost like the secret code that tells everything when a believer in Scandinavia hears the answer to the question, "Are you a believer?" ("Er du troende?") If you answer, "Of course, I go to church," your inquirer will know exactly what you are saying, but you will have no idea that they have just heard you say, "I am not a Christian." I grew up in such a version of Norwegian-American Lutheran pietism, much influenced by Hauge's revival in Norway and softened some by Carl Olof Rosenius, whom my Grandfather Grindal read for daily devotions along with Bishop Laache, Norway's chief exponent of Rosenius' teachings. While I do know my grandparents read *Pilgrim's Progress* by John Bunyan, whom some could say was the inspiration for *Squire Adamsson*, I would not be a bit surprised if they had also read this book. Even though as Americans the Scandinavian state church was not our reality, it lingered in our minds. We knew people who practiced a kind of "churchianity," as we called it, rather than Christianity. They would be puzzled when a young person in their midst would return from Bible camp, Young Life, or FCA, with the testimony, "Although I was baptized and confirmed a Lutheran, it wasn't until [some experience] that I came to know Jesus as my personal Savior."

It is still a staple testimony of those who have come to faith through an experience of conversion or an awakening of their baptismal faith. Many Lutherans think that such a statement is somewhat unseemly, and yet it lurks in most Lutheran traditions in America, especially in my part of the Norwegian-

American Lutheran tradition. Even though we did not insist on an experience of salvation, we knew it well. We knew faithful Christians who had remained in their baptismal covenant, but also rejoiced at conversions. God could work in many ways, but talk of conversion troubled other Lutherans, especially those from other Lutheran traditions, like Eastern and Missourian Lutherans. Conversion? That's Baptist! It did not sound, nor look Lutheran to them. We Norwegians made our peace with each other as Norwegian Lutherans in the Madison Agreement of 1912, which said one could be an orthodox Lutheran and not resolve the argument, but value both orthodoxy and pietism as expressions of the faith. Although contested by some, it brought most of the Norwegian Lutherans in this country together in 1917 when they formed the Norwegian Evangelical Lutheran Church, later simply the ELC. The agreement and the tolerance of the theology of conversion that the Norwegians accepted have always stuck in the craw of the other Lutherans in this country as not being Lutheran. The Haugean pietist in me, however, understands the agreement in my bones. As does the Swedish Augustana Lutheran Pietist one would find at the Lutheran Bible Institute, or those among our best friends, Swedish Covenanters. We, after all, began our lives in this country together in the Scandinavian Augustana Synod (1860-1870) until the Norwegians and Danes broke away to form their own seminaries—Augsburg and Augustana. (My part of the Norwegian Lutherans always says, with regret, we merged with the wrong Swedes!) We have always understood, with Luther, whom we read with affection and delight, that faith is not knowledge or ritual, it is a living, breathing, active relationship with Jesus that sets one against the world.

Those Lutherans who understand the language of Canaan, most often Pietists, will know the city named World and the city named Holiness, the bookkeeper Conscience (a nice picture) and the city named Evangelium. They may even feel a slight needling at the Mission Society in one area of the City,

Sanctification, where the Workshop for the Redeemed keeps people busy doing good. They have met Shepherd-for-Hire, they grew up with Squire Adamsson, and will know why he changes his name to Abrahamsson and then Hagarsson. They know exactly why Mother Simple grows concerned for him, and even why she feels that Immanuel has abandoned her in what Luther would have called the dark night of the soul. They will hear biblical verses and stories referenced naturally as the way people spoke to one another of their common lives. People in these traditions uttered themselves biblically because it was the language they spent their time reading and speaking. And they knew when they were being reproved or upbraided. Waldenström's book has sharp teeth that cut at all religious and pious delusions. No matter whether one is a church or sect type, one is always surprised by one's own foibles, or sins.

Mother Simple, like many pious women in my background, is the voice of the true Christian, calling back, reproving, encouraging, speaking the truth. One thinks of Lina Sandell, whom the leaders of the Swedish revival knew would be a spiritual leader from her childhood on, or of Kristine in the first part of Bo Giertz,' *Hammer of God,* who is able to bring peace to the dying man when the young seminary graduate could not. They are, however, not without their own spiritual struggles and terrors, all of which devout Christians know and fear.

This is an edifying and cautionary tale for awakened Christians (and maybe for those church types trying to figure them out) to watch for all the ditches along the narrow way, from lukewarm Christianity that wants to sue for peace with the world to intellectualizing the faith, to works that try to hide the lack of faith, to other enthusiasms we delude ourselves with as we live both in and outside the church. There are dragons on all sides, and only Immanuel can save us. Mother Simple knows that and teaches us that the Christian life is not onward and upward, but daily ups and downs, lapses and successes, that turn us toward Immanuel. Faith in him assures that we are counted as righteous, nothing else. Waldenström knew where all the dragons lay in wait, and his book is an edifying guide on our way.

Paul Peter Waldenström

INTRODUCTION

It was in late 1862 that *Squire Adamsson* appeared as an eight-part series in the newspaper "The Stockholm City Missionary" *(Stadsmissionären),* and the following year as a best-selling novel, which would stay in print for decades, enjoying seven editions before the author's death in 1917. The novel also generated international interest, and in addition to the eleven Swedish editions, there were at least three Norwegian editions (in 1865, 1891, 1903), at least one Danish edition (1870), a Norwegian-American edition (1889, published by the Haugean Synod in Red Wing, Minnesota), and an English translation (1928, by the Mission Friend's Publishing Company in Chicago).[1] At the time of publishing, the author was a yet unknown, 24-year-old doctoral student at Uppsala University named Paul Peter Waldenström (1838-1917). His anonymity did not last long, for as soon as the cryptic signature "P.W." appeared along with the series, speculation began as to who could have written such a bold defense of the limitless and unqualified grace of God, challenging the doctrines of state Lutheranism of the time. After other famous people with the same initials had been ruled out and the true author was identified, a controversial career had been launched, one that would place Waldenström at the center of the wholesale transformation of Scandinavian religious practice through the beginning of the 20th century.

HISTORICAL CONTEXT & INTERPRETATION

Though this novel primarily addresses theological concerns, it had a remarkably wide appeal in its day. Literary scholar Harry

Lindström maintained that in terms of publication numbers, *Squire Adamsson* ranks among the most widely read Swedish novels of the late 19th century, building on the observations of literary historian Henrik Schück. In his inventories of Swedish literature in the 1890s, Schück was astonished to discover that Waldenström enjoyed a wider readership than either Oscar Levertin (1862-1906) or Verner von Heidenstam (1859-1940), two of Sweden's most popular authors at the time.[2] However, despite its wide readership, the novel has been all but forgotten within general Swedish literary history. Lindström identifies it as having attained the status of a *folkbok* (or a book with national significance), but speculates that the omission of this novel from literary studies, as well as its neglect by historians has much to do with the fact that it was embraced by lower- and middle-class church-goers rather than the bourgeois cultural elites, and that it also clashed with the later dominant Social Democratic ethos of the early 20th century. Another scholar, Gunnar Hallingberg, has marveled that a prominent academic like Schück would admit to having been ignorant of *Squire Adamsson*, and jokes that no self-respecting English literary scholar would confess to having been ignorant of *Pilgrim's Progress*.[3] Yet, Swedish scholars have done and continue to do just that. Hallingberg points out the remarkable fact that Waldenström's contemporary reading public initially dwarfed that of even the great August Strindberg (1849-1912), though Strindberg would win the contest of book sales in the long run.[4] Hallingberg also explains this historical amnesia as partly due to the conventions of literary studies, which he calls an "aristocratic science" that has often preferenced exceptional outliers and aesthetic innovation, but ignored the significance of popular culture and trends.[5] Nevertheless, contributing to the marginalization of the book in the consciousness of posterity is certainly its dominant religious themes, which have become increasingly foreign to the contemporary secular Swedish reading public.

In the context of the 1860s, however, Swedish society was steeped in the religious imagery that people learned from their membership in the Lutheran state church and from the religious instruction they received in the school system. National culture was inseparable from Christianity, and thus Waldenström's allegory was potentially of interest to everyone. The novel came as a radical exposé of misconceptions and hypocrisies in both high- and low- church circles, and provoked many clergymen in the state church. Although the author is rather even-handed in his critique of all parties, it is clear that this was a careful articulation of the theology of one group of dissenters in particular, the so-called "new evangelical" school *(nyevangelismen)* surrounding Carl Olof Rosenius (1816-1868),[6] as well as representing a dominant theme within the heritage of classical Lutheran Pietism overall. It is clear that Waldenström wished to make certain parallels between the characters in the allegory and the religious landscape as it existed in Sweden in the 1860s. Because of the comments that they make and their attitude toward the city of Evangelium, it is clear that The WorldChurch, the bishop, and Pastor Shepherd-for-Hire were intended to conjure up images of the Church of Sweden and its clergy. There are also several secular personalities who make cameo appearances. Since the book was revised and expanded over the course of the first five editions up through 1891, it is worth noting that this can be seen as a critique of real-life people who both served as the original inspiration for the characters, as well as later critics who also came to be conflated with the characters after the publication of the book. Thus, one can legitimately see reflections of prominent movers and

C. O. ROSENIUS.

shakers in Swedish society, such as Henrik Reuterdahl, Gottfrid Billing, Waldemar Rudin, Viktor Rydberg, S.A. Hedlund, or J.A. Posse, for instance. The various mission societies and sewing circles correspond to the revival activities of the Evangelical Homeland Foundation (*Evangeliska Fosterlands-Stiftelsen*, EFS), which was a wing of the Church of Sweden and the approved avenue for expressions of Pietism after 1856. In the allegory, however, the city Evangelium was not endorsed by the established WorldChurch, and therefore aligns with the more radical Pietists who were conducting their own private and sometimes separatist activities, at first in homes, but later in free-standing denominations. Some of these groups would gradually leave the Church of Sweden, such as the Baptists, Methodists, Salvation Army, and numerous mission societies, the largest conglomeration of these becoming the Swedish Mission Covenant in 1878 (for which Waldenström became a leading figure).

Although there are clear parallels between the allegory and this real-world confrontation between high- and low-church circles, it would be a mistake to conclude that this is the only interpretation that Waldenström wished to make. Certainly due to the complicated picture that he paints of the existential struggles of his protagonists, Adamsson and Mother Simple in particular, it can be concluded that this is not a simple salvation allegory. In other words, this is not simply a linear progression of characters transitioning from being lost to being saved; Adamsson in some respects could have been seen as "saved" already in chapter 4. Neither is the allegory suggesting that one ought to go from being "lost" in the Church of Sweden to being "found" in a Pietist mission society. The allegory instead has a largely circular or cyclical motion to it, in that the repetitive movements and crises of the characters reflect a quite modern existential search for meaning, moving from one paradigm to the next, oftentimes not in a straightforward, linear fashion. The reader is likely to find the plot somewhat repetitive or even find it frustrating to watch as the protagonists relapse and unlearn the lessons from previous chapters. This repetition is intentional, and hints at the complicated nature of relying on God's grace alone, which may be every bit as much of a challenge for the Lutheran reader as for readers from other traditions. Evangelium is a specific location in the allegory, but in the real world it can be found wherever this posture of faith is adopted. It is unlikely that Waldenström intended Evangelium to represent "true Christianity" as an institution, even if his sympathies are with these congregational mission societies.[7]

Finding one-to-one correspondences between the allegorical characters and their equivalents in the real world is elusive. On some levels, Justus All-Powerful and Immanuel are clearly intended to represent God the Father and Jesus Christ; their actions and their quotation of scripture make this unmistakable. However, if this correspondence were taken as a perfect equivalency, then this would actually threaten the integrity of the allegory. For this to be effective and challenge the reader, the reader must be alienated from the familiar biblical narrative just enough that he or she can re-evaluate long held beliefs or misconceptions. It may be for this reason that Waldenström has also included references to a "God" elsewhere, and this God does not go by the name of Justus All-Powerful (only in one place does he "slip up" by directly equating God with Lord Justus in the last line of chapter 16). Even the residents of The World reference God, and their God does not do business in the same manner as Justus All-Powerful does. There are also frequent inter-textual references made, reminding us that this allegorical world is not all that there is. The characters refer to Bible verses in both the Old and New Testaments, to St. Paul, King David, as well as Martin Luther, and several hymns from the Scandinavian and Anglo-American revival traditions, such as the hymn from the Wallin Hymnal, *"O Gud, som även räckt din hand,"* as well as *"Rock of Ages, Cleft for Me"* by Toplady and

Hastings *("Klippa du som brast för mig")*. Thus the reader has the opportunity to notice that the characters have an incomplete understanding of God based on limited information. By not demanding a perfect correspondence between the allegorical and real worlds, the novel allows the reader the opportunity to make the realization that he or she also has a fragmentary picture of the whole.

Because of this lack of correspondence, the reader may begin to suspect that Evangelium is perhaps not the definitive, end-all and be-all version of Christianity, but rather simply a paradigm of existence (actually, within Evangelium, the city is divided into various sections, so this could be seen as multiple paradigms or existential moments). Also, the characters continue to struggle after arriving in Evangelium, indicating a lack of uniformity in their experiences. Waldenström seems to be drawing on a similar notion of "tropes" that was articulated by his 18th century predecessor in the Pietist school of thought, Nicolas Ludwig, Count von Zinzendorf (1700-1760), leader of the Moravian Brethren. According to Zinzendorf, the various denominations and church institutions in the world were like so many perspectives on Christianity, and each had their own merits and shortcomings.[8] Even Luther's and Calvin's discussions of the "visible-" and "invisible church" can be useful to recall here. The fact that Adamsson does not live happily ever after in Evangelium (or anywhere, outside of Holiness) is an aspect of the allegory that demonstrates part of its genius and originality. Evangelium is not the destination, but a (recurring) stop on the way. This is a complicated presentation of the type of constant philosophical soul searching that is an essential part of thoughtful religious practice. Any faithful soul who has wrestled with God for more than a season will likely recognize himself or herself at some point in this story, and come to appreciate the complicated nature of discerning religious truth. It is perhaps this complexity that makes Waldenström's allegory, though delightfully embedded in its 19th century

Swedish context, truly timeless and relevant to contemporary existential restlessness everywhere.

On interpreting the significance of the characters and their intriguing names, the reader is faced with several choices. One could, for example, attempt to read every person as if they represented a type of person that exists in the real world. However, this causes problems when trying to understand some of the underdeveloped characters, such as the children of the Squire and Mrs. Adamsson. These children seem to have more to say about the condition of their parents; for instance, Hateful and Bitter are born while the Adamssons are in prison, suggesting that they are not representing anything other than the spiritual state of their parents. The same seems to be true of the other children of the Adamssons, Kind-Hearted and Complacent, who also represent two sides of the same coin. Furthermore, some of the antagonists seem to be no more than foils for the main characters (such as Bold, Dead-Sure, Self-Wise). It is a challenge to determine which of the other characters are meant to represent "whole" people, as it were. Certainly Adamsson is the focus of attention, as he is the most developed. Mrs. Adamsson, since she is often a shadow of her husband and subject to the consequences of his choices, only occasionally seems developed enough to be read as a whole person. Mother Simple, though she emerges as a heroine and even eclipses Adamsson as protagonist, can be read either as a type of person or as a state of mind. In some ways, Mother Simple and the other people Adamsson encounters, can be read as representing the present state of mind of Adamsson at a given moment. Beyond Mother Simple and the Adamssons, however, it is unclear how many of the other characters can be read as types of people. The Pastor Shepherd-for-Hire and the bishop can surely represent the clergy of the Church of Sweden, but more likely are an abstract representation of the mentality of the leadership of any established church, when it acts in oppressive and hypocritical ways to defeat the very faith it claims to endorse. In the end, it is perhaps not so important for the reader to come to a conclusion about the underdeveloped characters, but simply to remember that, collectively, all the characters serve to illustrate the fragmented quality of human states of being. The Adamssons and Mother Simple may be the main characters, but it is the reader who is the focus of this novel. The reader is to use the characters as a mirror, to ask the question of the subtitle of the work: "Where do I live?"

WOMEN IN THE ALLEGORY

There is an overwhelming gendered difference between male and female characters in terms of the frequency with which each represents wisdom. Despite there being more male characters overall, the balance swings in favor of women as most often speaking the truth. Waldenström uses the patronizing, but loving, term *"gumman"* ("little old woman" or "old girl") with great frequency whenever addressing Mother Simple. This term is most often used in Swedish as a familiar diminutive to refer to older women, beloved daughters and especially toddlers (who totter along like little old women). By contrast, the corresponding male term, *"gubben,"* is seldom used here and never used positively. The circle around Mother Simple also includes Mother Prodigal and Mother Wounded-Hip, two female versions of characters in the Bible who are male – the Prodigal Son and Jacob; a third character is Mother Penniless, who is reminiscent of the widow who donated her last two mites. The inner circle of protagonists is predominantly female. In understanding the reasons for this preference for women in communicating religious truth, it is helpful to keep in mind that Waldenström's own conversion experience was credited in large part to his aunt, Lina Benckert, and it is perfectly valid to conclude that Mother Simple represents some of the insights that Waldenström's aunt imparted to him.[9] Through her homespun, Socratic midwifery, Mother Simple's questioning is the centerpiece of the story, and she serves the role of a Lutheran catechist, posing questions for her confirmand to answer. Her naively-posed yet direct questions demonstrate that she is almost always at least one step ahead of Adamsson, but leaves it to him to make the conclusions himself (this is in stark contrast to the catechism scene in *Pilgrim's Progress,*[10] which represents traditional rote learning).

Lina Berg.

Elsa Borg.

Some of the real-life women who Lindström suggests inspired Mother Simple and her friends include Betty Ehrenborg-Posse (1818-1880), Amelie von Braun (1811-1859), Emelia Petersen (1782-1859), Elsa Borg (1826-1909), Cecelia Fryxell (1806-1883), Helena Sophia Ekblom (1790-1859), Maria Nilsdotter (*Mor i Vall,* 1811-1870), and Maja Lisa Söderlund (1794-1851).[11] What is more, in the circle around Waldenström, women often played influential roles. His wife Mathilda (née Hallgren, 1843-1937), like many women in that period, served in the role as unofficial secretary for her husband, managing his papers and corresponding with the press while he was on tour. Waldenström credited Mathilda with having influenced his theology on occasion. Also, a woman named Amy Moberg (1826-1905), who had served Waldenström's predecessor, Carl Olof Rosenius, as secretary for the journal *Pietisten,* also held considerable sway over Waldenström in the theological controversies of the 1870s. Moberg would notably urge him to restrain his combative nature during these debates, pointing to the irenic spirit of his predecessor, Rosenius.[12] William Bredberg points out several places in the letters between Moberg and Waldenström,

Cecilia Fryxell.

Amy Moberg.

Betty Posse.

which demonstrate that she was held in high regard by him, namely in a letter in which he assures her that, *"Despite the fact that you have not studied doctrine, I still place more value in your words than in the decree of an entire theological faculty."*[13] In a tribute to the 70th anniversary of *Pietisten,* Waldenström noted again that Moberg had kept the journal going, particularly in Rosenius's last months.

> *"Rosenius found an invaluable assistant in his work on* Pietisten *in Miss Amy Moberg. In those days he dictated to her most of what he was writing. Yes, in the end, it was in reality she who was the one who wrote* Pietisten. *He sat in his rocking chair and talked about how he wanted this or that text treated. Then she would write the commentary, and then read it back to Rosenius. He made only one or two additions or changes. She had so completely adopted his style that no one noticed the difference."*[14]

Yet another prominent woman, Lina Sandell-Berg (1832-1903), frequently had Waldenström's attention, demonstrated by his citations of her hymn texts in his devotional works (including *Gud är min tröst,* "God is my Assurance"), in which she keeps company with giants like Martin Luther and Johann Arndt. Mother Simple may be uneducated and dismissed by the learned in the novel, including Adamsson on many occasions, but this humbleness is representative of exactly the type of faith that Waldenström is prescribing, for both laymen and laywomen. The religious awakening in Sweden represented a dramatic democratization of faith practices, in which the lay person was exalted and given unprecedented opportunities to interpret Scripture and take decisive action as a disciple of Christ.

Waldenström stopped short of endorsing the appropriateness of women preaching from the pulpit. This is reflected by the way that Mother Simple is reminded by a certain Mr. Bible Bound to keep quiet in the assembly. Also, Mrs. Adamsson really does not have any agency of her own to speak of, and simply follows the decisions of her husband, without being able to influence him. However, Waldenström's statements at a preacher's meeting in Minneapolis in 1889 suggest a willingness to entertain this question. On that occasion, though he deferred to Paul's epistle texts that speak against this, he also noted that the introduction of women preachers in American churches might inevitably follow the example of the Salvation Army.[15] Furthermore, as early as 1866, Waldenström expressed support for the idea that women should be formally educated, and by 1913, he was even recommending that they be allowed to use their gifts in the church to do everything besides preaching (his argument was that the success of the Catholic Church was due in large part to its utilization of the gifts of women, which was in contrast with the situation in the Lutheran world at the time).[16] Furthermore, it is remarkable that from the pulpit of this allegory, Mother Simple has indeed preached and continues to preach to thousands of people. The question for Waldenström was not whether women should teach or whether they had valuable insights to contribute to theology. He appears to have simply been torn between deference to the letter of Scripture discouraging public preaching by women, and his own highly romanticized view of the layman, in which the ideal messenger of awakening could in fact be an uneducated, elderly lay*woman* who treads as close to this barrier as possible.

THE ALLEGORICAL TRADITION

The first impression that the reader might have when opening this book is that it bears strong resemblance to John Bunyan's *Pilgrim's Progress* (1678). That allegory would have been available to Waldenström in Swedish (first translated from German in 1727), and there are many moments in the text where character and place names, as well as aspects of the plot, resemble *Pilgrim's Progress*. He was certainly familiar with the

En

Christens Resa

genom werlden

till den saliga ewigheten,

framställd såsom sedd i en dröm

af

John Bunyan

Predikant i Betford.

Ny öfwersättning från originalspråket,

försedd med Plancher.

Stockholm.

Tryckt hos Isaac Marcus,

1853.

text, and even invokes it in his preface from 1907 when he mentions the "slough of despond," which is a location that exists in Bunyan's work, but not in *Squire Adamsson*. Not only was the text familiar to him, but he also promoted it. In March of 1916, *Pietisten* made a special offer to give away free copies of *Pilgrim's Progress (Kristen och Kristinnas Resa)* to subscribers who returned a mail-in form.[17] Rosenius had an even more direct connection to *Pilgrim's Progress,* when he led the effort to have the first direct translation from English to Swedish made, completed in 1853.[18] The translator recruited to complete the project was Betty Ehrenborg with Rosenius as the publisher.[19] Waldenström must have been aware of this interest of his predecessor in Bunyan's allegory. He was apparently also convinced that it was because of the success of *Squire Adamsson* that he came to be groomed as Rosenius's successor.[20]

If Waldenström took direct inspiration from any specific place in *Pilgrim's Progress,* it might be the moment when one of Bunyan's characters, Faithful, is offered employment by "Adam the First," who lives in the town of Deceit and whose wages are to be the inheritance of worldly delights. When Christian asks what Faithful had decided about this proposal, he replies: "*Why, at first I found myself somewhat inclinable to go with the man, for I thought he spake very fair, but looking in his forehead, as I talked with him, I saw there written, 'Put off the old man with his deeds.'*" Later, when Faithful recounts the harsh chastisement he received from the character Moses for his "inclination" toward Adam, Christian explains that Moses "*spareth none, neither knoweth he how to show mercy to those that transgress his law.*" [21] This episode bears striking similarity to the economic imagery that Waldenström uses to frame the spiritual outlook of Adamsson (who is a worldly captain of industry), as well as the unforgiving nature of Mosaic law and legalistic interpretations of Christianity. Whereas the pitfall of legalism is but one of the numerous themes that Bunyan entertains in his allegory, Waldenström focuses heavily on this dilemma, and in that regard *Squire Adamsson* could potentially be seen as a variation on this theme by Bunyan.

However, Waldenström's allegory is not a mere imitation of *Pilgrim's Progress.* In his own explanation, he indicates that the inspiration came primarily from Psalm 86 as he attempted to preach on this text in the summer of 1862. As he pondered the significance of the psalm, it struck him that the experience of reading it was like finding a "room for the lost." From there, he moved on to explain various other existential moments as houses in an allegorical world, and thus the tale was born. Some of the similarities with Bunyan also may have mostly to do with the fact that both authors have derived heavy inspiration from the Pauline theology in the New Testament, and have referenced the same biblical passages.

Harry Lindström also notes that there is a drastic difference between the main characters Adamsson and Christian, in that the way Adamsson speaks demonstrates that he is a modern human being.

> *"Christian is an anxious refugee from the world, the Squire is in certain respects a modern human being, conflicted, constantly searching for a spiritual identity, a participant in the new age of self analysis, reflection and restlessness. Waldenström's allegory is to a high degree a Swedish allegory, characterized by the complex of problems concerning faith in Swedish society."* [22]

Elsewhere, Lindström adds that the Squire grapples with pluralism to a greater degree than Christian, and points out that Waldenström's allegory lacks the closure found in *Pilgrim's Progress*.[23] The readers who follow Adamsson in his pursuit of the truth find themselves on a much less predictable and more troubling journey than that undertaken by Christian. Waldenström also presents enticing alternatives to the worldview that Adamsson attempts to follow, thus creating a far more realistic depiction of what the modern person's search for truth entails. Lindström identifies *Squire Adamsson* as having been fully engaged in the existential questions of Swedish culture of the period, and not at all isolated from the dominant culture.

> *"The book's presentation bears witness to a well thought out awareness of culture, an attempt to discern the alternative worldviews of pluralism and take a position on them. Not least interesting is the fact that the author provides the reader with so many objections to the culture of Evangelium and so many attractive arguments for alternative cultures."* [24]

The structure of Bunyan's allegory is also different than that of Waldenström's. There are two major differences; first, Bunyan often interprets the symbolism for the reader (via the dreaming narrator, the "interpreter," or the characters themselves) and makes direct references to biblical texts, rather than working these into the dialog; and second, the integrity of Bunyan's allegorical world is loose, in that there is little attempt to mask the identity of Christ with an allegorical figure, for instance. This is in contrast to Waldenström's allegorical world, which is far more self-contained (Christ and God have allegorical counterparts), and though he too has frequent references to external texts, these are often woven into the dialog, and thus seldom break this spell (this is most notable in the way that most of what Immanuel says are direct quotations from scripture, without attention being called to that fact). Also, Bunyan's allegory was especially suited to his 17th century audience, which had directed appeal to the Puritan and Baptist theological context of his readers. Waldenström's audience of 19th century "'new evangelical'" Lutheran Pietists found different messages directed at their own context. As a teacher of classical languages and literature, in addition to his theological training, Waldenström was also aware of a longer tradition of allegories and parables in the ancient and medieval canons, from which Bunyan is also drawing.

Furthermore, *Squire Adamsson* is rather innovative in this literary genre. Waldenström is not attempting to create a literary masterpiece, with sophisticated and oftentimes confusing symbolism, which seems to be the case in *Pilgrim's Progress*. Instead, the goal is to create a work that can make the existential struggles of Christianity easier to understand, endure and overcome. What the reader finds in these pages is a blending together of several narrative styles — the imagery and vocabulary of contemporary preaching, theatrical melodrama, and parody. One cannot escape the language and style of the low-church vernacular of the period, in which Waldenström imitates the charismatic and cathartic emotions that could appear in revival meetings and home Bible studies, or "conventicles." He himself was highly critical of preachers who toyed with people's emotions in order to bring about conversion, and thus many of the melodramatic statements made by his characters can be read as skepticism. In deliberate contrast, Waldenström's own sermons overwhelmingly demonstrate the same simplicity, reassuring tone and confident warmth expressed by Mother Simple. In fact, if there is any one character who can be seen as speaking for Waldenström, it is Mother Simple.

The drastic emotional swings of the characters were not limited to revival folks, and one can also see that Waldenström has playfully mimicked a dominant style of theatre performances of the 19th century, in which melodrama was the norm. When the characters are happy, they are enraptured; when they are sad, they are morbidly depressed; when they express their affection, they resemble hopeless romantics, sometimes achieving an uncomfortable effect for the critical reader. This use of melodrama is at times self-reflexive, in that characters like Mother Simple seem to look upon these emotional swings with knowing smiles or shaking heads. Melodrama can also serve a practical purpose for an allegory, in that by presenting exaggerations of these existential mood swings – instead of more realistic degrees of emotion – the reader is put at enough of a distance from the text that he or she is able to see the foolishness of these misconceptions and thereby arrive at a sensible conclusion (i.e. Waldenström's). As much as this is an allegory on a serious topic – the nature of God's grace – it is also has elements of parody, and is best read with a sense of humor. The melodramatic emotions are not to be taken at face value, and there are even several blatantly ridiculous moments, such as when Immanuel sits down to play a pipe organ, or when people decide to add pebbles to their bread to make it more "substantial." It is through this playful, light-hearted storyline that readers are invited to identify their own corresponding real-life struggles and crises and be able to see them from an exterior viewpoint.

PIETIST EXISTENTIALISM?

While melancholy, doubt, despair and anxiety have afflicted humans throughout history, these emotional states took on increased interest for authors and philosophers in the 19th century. In part, this was due to increases in standards of living and leisure time (which increased possibilities for boredom), the upheaval of industrialization and urbanization (which exacerbated poverty and social isolation from the village and family structures of agrarian society), and the fracturing of previously uniform religious paradigms (which demanded that people make their own exciting, yet stressful, decisions). All of this presented the average Northern European with an unprecedented level of independence and individuality. The chief dilemma facing Adamsson is that he cannot find peace and assurance, despite the efforts of Mother Simple to convince him of the trustworthiness of grace. The freedom of grace in Evangelium presents Adamsson with a dizzying experience of anxiety, such that he is repeatedly tempted *away from* Evangelium and toward other paradigms that promise a more regimented lifestyle and comfortable worldview.

The word for "assurance" that recurs throughout the text is *tröst* (this is also often a verb, *trösta*, and the nouns *försäkran, försäkringar, tröstare,* or the adjectives *tröstelig, hugnelig*). In all of these cases I have translated this as some form of "assurance." Much of the plot revolves around the characters' search for assurance, and the lack of assurance is what precipitates their troubles, not only for Adamsson, but also notably the residents of "the Hidden District" in chapter 12. This may seem like an obsession with assurance, and given the economic imagery that frames the plot, also as a sort of "commodification" of assurance. Through various transactions, the characters are attempting to acquire assurance, and often doubt whether "free" grace could ever buy this for them. The fact that so much effort is wasted in their attempts to purchase this commodity reveals the author's criticism of this commodification. It is right and good that the characters should be concerned about God's assurance, but they miss the point repeatedly that there is nothing that they can do to purchase it – it has to be believed, and comes only through faith. Furthermore, the goal should not simply be to achieve assurance, but to be able to distinguish between true and false assurance (for instance, there is a character named "False Assurance"), as well as to be able to trust grace even when one does not feel assured. The life lesson seems to be learning how to discern between having true assurance (coded positively), and foolishly mistaking assurance for "comfort" or "convenience" (coded negatively). For this reason, I have deliberately avoided the word "comfort," since "assurance" seemed to match the dynamic concept that Waldenström is trying to convey. Assurance was a central concern for him, evident in the fact that he would later go on to write a devotional book specifically on the topic, called "God is My Assurance" (*Gud är min tröst* – this originated as an article series in *Pietisten* during 1889-1890). One can benefit much by reading *Squire Adamsson* in one hand, while keeping *Gud är min tröst* in the other. Where the allegory examines the temptations that can *lead away* from trusting in grace alone, the devotional spends all its time assuring and tempting the reader *into* trusting grace, which is the role that Mother Simple plays in the allegory. It is the pull of both of these temptations that creates the state of tension that causes Adamsson so much anxiety.

The world in which the allegory debuted in 1862 was, thus, one of modern individuals facing a uniquely modern existential dilemma: how to trust traditional claims of Christianity in a now pluralized religious market, in which one had not only several religious firms to choose from, but also the option of choosing none of them. Waldenström's solution to this modern anxiety is an exhortation to "simplicity" and to straight-forward scripture reading, and he projects a confident faith that theological controversies can be solved by discerning "what is written" in scripture alone (without the constriction of the Lutheran creeds). One of the historical criticisms of Waldenström's theology in general, and this allegory in particular, is that his emphasis on scripture alone and grace alone has erred on some extreme: he has either been characterized as being a fundamentalist or a universalist. Lutherans have tended to see his theology as naïve biblical literalism, and one recent history of Lutheranism has even dismissed Waldenström as contributing to American fundamentalism, for instance.[25] Evangelical Covenant historian Karl A. Olsson has suggested that *Squire Adamsson* borders on presenting a one-sided view of grace in which the believer can never be confident that he is saved, and also that the allegory served to cast doubt on seminary education.[26] Scholars from the Mission Covenant Church in Sweden have also been conflicted in their assessment, such as William Bredberg's conclusion that Waldenström's "Christianity of misery" *(ömklighetskristendom)* was in contrast to the spirit of Rosenius and new evangelicalism. However, Harry Lindström has offered a corrective to both of these assessments, explaining instead that Waldenström was simply building on themes of human depravity and *anfäktelse* (crisis of temptation) that had long been pronounced themes within classical pietism and new evangelicalism, and furthermore can be readily found in both Rosenius' and Luther's writings. Lindström presents Waldenström's theology as having dual emphasis on *uselhet* and *sällhet* (wretchedness and blessedness), in which human experience is suspended between these two poles. One need only look as far as Waldenström's hymns to see that these are in balance, says Lindström.[27]

O, vad sällhet det är / i all uselhet här
att ha Jesus till broder och vän,
att få vila med tröst / vid hans trofasta bröst
att få tro att han älskar mig än.

Oh, what sweet blessedness
In my poor wretchedness,
To have Jesus as brother and friend.
To be resting assured
By his strong arm secured,
To have faith that his love has no end.[28]

It should be noted that Waldenström's (and Mother Simple's) constant recommendation of simple faith in grace is a rhetorical strategy as much as it is a sincere belief. As an ordained minister and a doctor of philosophy, he was plenty aware of the historical developments of theology, of the biblical basis of the Lutheran creeds, in the diverse manifestations of Pietism, and the fact that biblical and textual criticism and interpretation are indeed not always straightforward. His task was not to ignore any of this extra-biblical material. Instead, he can be seen as compensating for the over-emphasis on objectivity within Swedish Lutheranism, and instead advocating a lifestyle of repeated first-hand encounters with biblical truths, one that is grounded in the subjective experience of the believer (or doubter). By watching the repetitive failures and successes of the main character in the allegory, the reader is able to "try on" various perspectives, and may recognize his or her own past experiences. This preference for personal experience is reflected in the school that Adamsson is forced to attend, "the class of the wretched" taught by Father Experience. Here he learns a more reliable form of knowledge than that possessed by the Theologians, who have no first-hand experience living in Evangelium, but merely view the city from above. This emphasis on learning spiritual truths through first-hand experience is evident in the philosophy of Count Zinzendorf, and there is also a long tradition in Pietism of learning by proxy, through observing and sympathizing with other people's experiences. This can be seen as early as Johann Arndt, when he notes in *True Christianity* in 1605/09: "*The trespasses of your neighbor are your mirror, in which you are to learn to know your weaknesses, and that you, too, are a man.*"[29] Waldenström is continuing in this long tradition as he makes his case for an experientially-based model of faith. His chosen task is to assert the priority of subjective experience over objective knowledge, in an ecclesiastical environment in which the latter is dominant. In order to reverse this imbalance, overstatement may be required, and in that light, Waldenström's rhetorical strategy of insisting on "simplicity" may be easier to appreciate, and also avoid being mistaken for either fundamentalism or universalism.

In this light, Waldenström's attempt to "clear the air" on theological matters in Swedish Lutheranism begins to resemble that of another 19th century Scandinavian theologian. Søren Kierkegaard also asserted the primacy of subjective faith, and also, coincidentally, was informed by Pietist thought via the Moravian circles in Copenhagen. Squire Adamsson faces a similar dilemma as Kierkegaard's character Johannes Climacus, in the narrative of the same name written in 1843. Climacus strives to become a philosopher, but struggles to understand how his subjective experiences with doubt can ever lead to mastery of the great corpus of philosophical knowledge that has been generated by philosophers since the dawn of time. That same year, another book with an allegorical dimension was published, *Fear and Trembling*. Here Kierkegaard's pseudonym, Johannes de Silentio, portrays the character of Abraham in a way that reflects a similar struggle to understand theological truths objectively. Kierkegaard's Abraham takes a subjective leap of faith by trusting in God's promise to make him the father of many nations, despite the fact that this would ironically be canceled out by God's demand for him to sacrifice his long-awaited only son, Isaac. The pseudonym explains that Abraham is worthy of being called the "father of faith" not because he has objectively understood theology, but precisely because he *did not* understand and nevertheless trusted in this absurd promise. Abraham's reward will come as result of this subjective movement of faith. Systems of knowledge, be they philosophical or theological, are secondary to an experientially-based perception of truth, suggests Kierkegaard.

Like Kierkegaard in *Johannes Climacus* and *Fear and Trembling,* Waldenström approaches his analysis of the topic at hand by lining up a kaleidoscope of possibilities for interpretation and treating them one by one. In *Squire Adamsson,* the various chapters are experiments, in which variables have been changed, sometimes only slightly, and the characters who previously had arrived at some certainty, are now faced with a changed context that forces them to re-evaluate their situation and concede that they did not know as much as they thought they did earlier. One recurring theme is that the characters vacillate between confidence, doubt and despair regarding their current situation, their ability to grow and reform, their self-image, and the worthiness of grace.

Although it is unclear just what kind of an influence Kierkegaard can have had on Waldenström (he had at the least read one small "tract" and a history of Kierkegaard's life[30]), there are similarities in how each presents the movement from unbelief to faith. One key area is in their understanding of temptation. In both Waldenström's Swedish and Kierkegaard's Danish there are two terms that are used when discussing temptation, *anfäktelse (anfægtelse)* and *frestelse (fristelse)*. While *frestelse* is used in a more straight-forward way as "temptation," *anfäktelse* is more difficult to translate, and can be variously translated as trial, tribulation, testing, vexation, or temptation. I have settled on temptation for both, in following the example of Kierkegaard's translator, Alastair Hannay.[31] In analyzing the way that Waldenström uses these terms (in *Squire Adamsson,* as well as in *Gud är min tröst*), there is a clear difference between them. Whenever the temptation in question is to commit a specific sin, *frestelse* is used. However, *anfäktelse* is used for macro-level temptations away from faith in general. In some ways, *anfäktelse* is more than just temptation, but is a profound state of tension and an existential crisis, in which the individual is tormented by the realization that he or she has the possibility to fall away from faith or even deliberately choose to leave faith. Thus, *anfäktelse* becomes a moment of despair, as the individual is tempted away from (or sometimes even toward) faith, and overwhelmed with anxiety in facing all the possible consequences of this freedom of action. Grace in *Squire Adamsson* is celebrated for being "free," but it is this very freedom which causes the traumatic encounters with temptation experienced by the Squire, Mother Simple, and other characters like Fallen and Evangelist.

For Kierkegaard, this kind of temptation occurs as the soul makes the "leap of faith," in which he or she is forced to abandon objective reason in order to arrive at religious faith. Faith is a completely exposed, momentary, and vulnerable position, one in which the subject is often unsure of his situation and tempted by the security offered by lower states of being (reflected in Adamsson's temptations away from Evangelium to the several surrounding towns). In both Kierkegaard's and Waldenström's presentations, this temptation is a severe and often recurring spiritual crisis, but a crisis that is essential in order to experience the truths of faith. Even John Bunyan ventures into this territory, as despair ("despond") is a frequent pitfall and obstacle to his protagonists, one that is sent by the devil to test faith. In all these cases, it is in facing this despair head on that it can serve a productive purpose in refining one's faith. In the face of anxiety and despair, one might be tempted to rely on one's own intellectual powers to understand faith, but as these three allegorists point out in their different ways, the only option is to subjectively trust God's promises, try out one's wings and fly...which entails falling repeatedly.

Returning to the critique of Waldenström's allegory – that it represents the naïve idea that one can never be sure of one's salvation or security before God – it is fair to say that Waldenström is in fact explaining that there can be no certainty in this life. Adamsson dies and is transported to Holiness without ever having arrived at any certainty regarding his situation. Even as he is transported into Holiness, he encounters Evangelist, who has missed his chance, which casts an ominous shadow over the otherwise happy ending of the tale. Also, the character Conscience sometimes guides the others to the truth, but frequently adds confusion to their deliberations. However, in the light of Waldenström's great corpus of devotional works, such as *Gud är Min Tröst,* it is clear that this allegory is part of a lifelong desire to communicate the conflicted reality of modern Christianity: the assertion that God's promises are constant and true, as in ancient times; and the acknowledgement that it is no easy task to believe and be confident in these promises in modern times. The only thing one can do is to choose to exist in these promises – or, to follow the allegory, to choose which city we are going to live in, over and over.

Suicide is a theme that may catch readers off-guard, since it appears in contrast with the otherwise light-hearted nature of the narrative. But this inclusion demonstrates an awareness on Waldenström's part that extreme despair and contemplation of suicide is part of modern existence, even for believers like Mother Simple in chapter 9. It is interesting what he has to say about suicide in the beginning of *Gud är min tröst.*

> *"Even the richest of the rich have often been the most unhappy of people; yes, they too are plagued by economic worries. It is very common, that the poor are jealous of the rich and imagine that they live especially good days. But they may not feel this way deep down, and 'good days' – days that can truly be called good – do not have their basis in external circumstances, but in the heart. The rich are often far more unhappy than the poor. Many a proud factory owner* [brukspatron] *is far more unhappy than the poorest of his workers; many country landowners are more unhappy than their poorest tenants. […] Near Brooklyn, N.Y. in America there is an unusually striking burial place, called Greenwich Cemetery. Once, when I passed through there, the coachman pulled to a stop near one hill that was full of graves and said: 'Here there are buried seven millionaires, and all of them took their own lives.' Directly afterwards, I bought the day's newspaper. The first thing I noticed was an article reporting that a millionaire in New York had, that very night, ended his own life with the shot of a revolver."*[32]

It can be no coincidence that the first example he gives is that of a *brukspatron,* which is the occupation and class title of Adamsson in the allegory. Readers of *Gud är min tröst* will likely keep Adamsson in the back of their minds, as Waldenström proceeds to make his case that a "life without God is a life without assurance," as well as to acknowledge that even in a life spent with God, there can be a recurring temptation to abandon faith and its assurances (here again using *anfäktelse,* rather than *frestelse*). One also remembers that John Bunyan, too, included the discussion of suicide in *Pilgrim's Progress* in that poignant scene where Christian and his companion Hopeful are locked up in Doubting Castle by the Giant Despair, who recommends that the only way out is for them to end their own lives, by "knife, halter or poison."[33] Waldenström seems to side with Bunyan on the solution to this dilemma, and just as Christian realizes that the key to his freedom is "in his bosom," similarly, Mother Simple greets the Adamssons in their prison cell in Sinai by asking how long they are "intending" to remain there. The solution presented in both is to believe in and own the assurances of God before they may be visible, and despite current circumstances that would say otherwise. So, while the allegory has its melodramatic and light-hearted spirit to it, underneath all of that runs a profound awareness of just how difficult it can be to actually have faith and trust the assurances of God.

UNITY IN DIVERSITY

Readers unfamiliar with the religious context of Lutheran Pietism may wonder why Waldenström has seemingly overstated his case for an unqualified view of grace, at the same time as he has avoided granting certainty to his characters and leaves their anxious speculations unresolved. This allegory reflects the reality typically faced by Pietists, which was that theological controversy often followed in the wake of the religious awakenings within German and Scandinavian Lutheranism. In this climate of perennial controversy, Pietists were forced to justify their strange and subversive activities to the state church clergy, as well as compete with other revival movements for members from the same pool of disaffected Lutherans. For one group of Pietists, the Moravian Brethren, this was of particular concern, such that they adopted the motto *"In essentials, unity; in non-essentials, liberty; in all things, charity."* What this slogan had meant for the Moravians and their leader, Count Zinzendorf, was an assertion of the importance of truth regarding a core set of agreed upon values, and a relaxation on peripheral matters, and a preference for dialogue when various opinions clashed. In the allegory, Waldenström is articulating his support for this "unity in diversity" principle, at the same time as he is modeling, through the tribulations of his characters, how difficult it is to actually live by this.

Waldenström inherited this outlook from several currents within Swedish Pietism, and also actively passed this heritage on to the institutions he played a formative role in founding, namely the Mission Covenant Church of Sweden (1878) and the Evangelical Covenant Church (1885) in North America. Perhaps as a natural result of his own combative nature and the theological controversies that seemed to always surround him, Waldenström developed early on a strong interest in ecumenism and in understanding the implications of pluralism for congregational life. This effort to reconcile conflicting sides of theological arguments began early. According to William Bredberg, Waldenström reacted against the evangelical orthodoxy that had swept across his home province in Northern Sweden in his childhood.[34] This aversion to dogmatic conflict was no doubt in play as Waldenström was drawn to the circle around Carl Olof Rosenius, whose "new evangelicalism" featured an irenic ecumenical message and a commitment to keeping the Pietists united *within* the Church of Sweden and avoiding separatism. In 1872, however, Waldenström himself became responsible for generating conflict after his atonement theory sparked vigorous public debate and culminated in the exodus of the "Waldenströmians" from the Church of Sweden. Even though the allegory predates these controversies, one can see a striking resemblance between Waldenström and Adamsson.

So, how successful is Waldenström in translating this principle into an allegory? Is he tricking the reader into agreeing with him, or is this truly an exploration of the nuances of truth? One area in which religious allegories have been criticized is in their linear construction, which has been mentioned before. Stanley Fish is one literary scholar who has pointed out this weakness, notably that the main characters in allegories move on a one-directional journey from ignorance to understanding, from being "lost" to being "found," and other binary poles. In his explanations of John Milton's *Paradise Lost*, Fish linked this linear construction to the inherently linear nature of pursuit of the truth in the Judeo-Christian historical worldview and the scientific method of the Enlightenment. Experiential readings, like allegories, are designed to pull the reader on a journey of discovery, with the final destination being truth. However, there are pitfalls along the way, which have the potential to distract and mislead the main character. Fish claims that rhetoric has often been situated in the role of "distraction," while reason and rationally defended theology have been given priority of place. In Western intellectual history, there has been a persistent belief that truth is discoverable and absolute, which only increased with the Enlightenment and the emphasis on the scientific method. According to Fish, the belief that truth is ultimately knowable has created a blindness to the limits of the paradigms created by rational, linear discourse, whether used by scientists or theologians. While theologians and philosophers have traditionally assumed that their fields were moving vertically toward absolute truth, they were in fact simply moving horizontally from one paradigm to the next.[35]

This assertion that Western audiences have been ignorant to how these rational narratives can, in fact, be deceptive rhetoric is supported by another philosopher, Richard Rorty, who explains the dilemma thusly: *"There is no activity called 'knowing' which has a nature to be discovered, and at which natural scientists are particularly skilled. There is simply the process of justifying beliefs to audiences."*[36] What is objectionable for both scholars is that this linear understanding of world history creates an inherently static conception of truth, and Fish in particular finds fault with the bias against rhetoric that he finds in religious allegories like *Paradise Lost* and *Pilgrim's Progress.*

Whether this evaluation of Milton's and Bunyan's allegories is valid or not is beyond the scope of this introduction. However, it is worth the reader's time to ask whether this is the case in *Squire Adamsson. Squire Adamsson* seemingly confounds the notion of a linear salvation allegory. Truth remains unresolved at the end, and therefore cannot be seen as static. In this regard, the allegory demonstrates a significant departure from the tradition in the way that they have been defined above. Rather than demonstrating a completely linear pursuit of truth, the path of discovery for Waldenström's protagonist is decidedly circular and lacks the resolution found in the other allegories. The salvation narrative is secondary to the main task, which is to explore the nuances of what it means to exist as a Christian.

The novel's circular structure is underscored by the inclusion of the same scripture verse as both a foreword and epilogue (Romans 4:4-5). Adamsson must repeatedly grapple with the meaning of the free gift of divine grace rather than trusting his own good deeds and his intellectual powers. In the end, Adamsson is redeemed, but not due to his arriving at a perfect understanding of the truth, but simply because his life has run its course and at the time of his death he is found trusting completely on God's grace. What has changed about Adamsson by the end of the novel is that he has accumulated various experiences with grace. His learning takes place through experience, symbolized by the name of his teacher, Father Experience. Even though the residents of Evangelium attend the same school, none of them has exactly the same experience, and it is significant that Waldenström denies full insight to any of his characters. When it comes to Justus All-Powerful, the narrator says, *"In short, everyone had their own ideas about him, but no one truly knew him."* Not only do the residents of The World have incomplete and even false understandings of truth, but the residents of Evangelium also argue among themselves as to the truth. Ultimately, there is no one who has arrived at complete knowledge, and even the constant Mother Simple is shaken in her trust in grace. Even so, this experiential learning is preferenced by Waldenström, in contrast to his negative portrayal of the academics and theologians. This pietistic mistrust of scholarly and scientific approaches to faith comes through loud and clear. It would be easy to argue that Waldenström is demonstrating anti-intellectualism, which was also a current in the Pietist movement. However, it should be remembered that Waldenström's challenge is aimed at the false confidence regarding truth that can arise in both theological and secular academic circles.

A climax in the novel is the discussion of "the hidden district" in chapter 12. A complication with unconditional grace arrives in Evangelium when the residents have to decide how to address people who are suffering from illnesses (sins) that are not healed before their arrival in Evangelium. Miserable, Fallen and Depraved are three people who have been convinced by a missionary to move to Evangelium, despite the fact that they have not first overcome their illnesses. There is room for speculation as to what Waldenström intended their sin to be, but it is described as a taboo that is not appropriate for public discussion and must be kept secret, even from parents. Harry Lindström has suggested that the sin that the characters are hiding is meant to be reminiscent of the debates about sexual health in the 1860s. Notable here is the speculation within medicine at the time that masturbation was linked to insanity and deviant lifestyles, and which was also condemned due to scriptural taboos against it.[37] Waldenström was engaged in this discussion and wrote on the topic of sexual health and youth, *Ungdomens farligaste fiende* ("The most dangerous enemy of youth"), so this is entirely plausible. However, the genius of this chapter is that there are only hints at what the sin might be and it is left unnamed. As such, the allegory bears eternal relevance because this unnamed sin can symbolize absolutely any sin that people attempt to hide from public view and the judgment of the congregation. It also astutely identifies the perennial problem that congregations have in deciding how and when to accept people as members; do people need to have overcome their sins and non-normative behavior before entry, or afterward? What happens if they don't improve? Should they be allowed to stay? Is this a defense of sin? Mother Simple's response to questions like these is to assert that she is defending grace, not sin, and this is the conclusion that Waldenström invites the reader to entertain.

Squire Adamsson is a vivid representation of the way in which some Swedish Pietists attempted to pursue truth. They were dissenters who had been punished for their dissent, and as a result developed a philosophy that left room for other dissenters and protected their rights. Essential in this philosophy was the freedom for discussion and disagreement. In order to enter this discussion, certain assumptions about the truth had to be accepted (such as the concepts contained in the Apostle's Creed). However, when lesser doctrinal issues came into question (such as the specifics of how and when to baptize a believer), the practice of these Pietists was to keep this discussion open and agree to disagree. Despite (and perhaps because of) his role in the theological controversies of the 1870s, Waldenström preferred to be a minimalist in terms of doctrine. On the issue of baptism, for instance, his mission societies chose to observe both infant and adult baptism, a practice that is unthinkable in many Christian denominations. This acceptance of the necessity of pluralism, without conceding to relativism, shaped his career as a religious leader and profoundly influenced the way he participated in politics as a member of the Swedish parliament.[38] Waldenström's view of biblical interpretation was to attempt to navigate somewhere between the extremes of fundamentalism and universalism, with the idea that complete understanding of truth was elusive to the human mind, that subjective experience was a better schoolmaster than objective rationalism, and that in all these disagreements, discussion and debate on these matters allowed for a nuanced view of truth. This is most directly articulated by Mother Simple in her advice to Adamsson:

> *"There are many different opinions that hold sway here in this city, the Squire is well aware of this. This is something one has to tolerate. For we all understand in part; and we all in one way or another make our mistakes. But everything will go well, as long as everyone is* standing on the foundation. *But those, who tear away at the foundation, those people are not to be tolerated."*

ON THE TRANSLATION

To undertake the translation of a work that has already appeared in English, a translator usually has some reasons to give as to why the earlier translation alone is not sufficient. In addition to the fact that I have found it enjoyable and personally rewarding to closely read Waldenström's monumental work and give it new expression, there are also matters of theological interpretation that are at stake in the reading of this allegory. Given that some of the central theological currents of the 19th century Swedish Pietists found expression in this work and were widely disseminated in its publishing over many decades, it is indeed important to try, as far as possible, to both "get it right," as well as present this tale in fresh, contemporary English. As with the Bible, having multiple translations of the same work can help, rather than hinder, the interpretation of the original. Such is the intention here. Ruben Nygren's 1928 translation published by the Chicago-based Mission Friend's Publishing Company served the desire to make this book available to the second generation of immigrants who were drifting away from the language of their parents.[39] In this service, it certainly accomplished its goal and then some.

However, upon the close reading of the original and comparison with the 1928 English text, it became clear that it was time for a new translation. For one, the vocabulary used 80-plus years ago is not the vocabulary used today, as words and expressions tend to shift and sound stilted over time. Moreover, there was nothing historically sacred about the language used in 1928, since the work was originally written in the 1860s. It was thought that a new translation could present the story in more contemporary English, although still preserving the fairy tale language of the original. One aspect of Waldenström's prose that made his books so popular was his remarkable simplicity in choosing words and crafting illustrations that were approachable, yet profound. Every effort has been made to capture the voice and cadence of Waldenström's storyteller prose, which in some cases has meant preserving a certain Germanic tendency for run-on sentences and (from the English perspective) an inverted word order. These have been maintained in some places, wherever it does not detract too much from readability. The scripture passages are based on the King James and the New King James Bibles, to maintain the tone of Swedish Bible that Waldenström is quoting. There are places where key words in Waldenström's Swedish differs from English translations of the Bible, and in those cases I have made a composite of the two in order to maintain his meaning. I have compiled scripture references and allusions in the footnotes. In only three instances did Waldenström himself include footnotes, which are indicated as such. All the other footnotes have been included here by me as a study guide. Specifically, I have attempted to include as many pertinent references to Harry Lindström's extensive research on *Squire Adamsson* as possible, since that work is only available in Swedish.

In addition to considerations of form, there were also issues of interpretation that the 1928 edition seemed to confuse rather than aid in the understanding of the original. Readers of the earlier edition will notice that some of the major differences have come in the translation of the characters' names. Here are some examples:

Mrs. Praise *(Beröm)* – instead of Mrs. Flatterer; the former being positive or ambiguous, the latter being only negative.

Pastor Shepherd-for-Hire *(Legoherde)* – instead of Pastor Mercenary, since *Legoherde* is a made-up word, referencing Christ's parable about the hired shepherd.

Mother Simple (*Enfaldig*, adj.) – instead of Mother Simplicity (noun).

Mother Wounded-Hip (*Mor Höftlam*) – instead of Mother Invalid, which misses entirely the allusion to Jacob wrestling with God.

Heart-For-Children (*Barnkär*) – instead of the unfortunate "Child-Lover," one of the more extreme examples of how words have changed or become obsolete since 1928.

Mother Prodigal (*Mor Förlorad*) – instead of Mother Forsaken, which misses the logical comparison with the prodigal son (*den förlorade sonen*).

Bankrupt Faith (*Utfattig Tro*) – instead of Poverty-Stricken Faith; by pairing bankruptcy with faith, this name underscores the desirability of not having assets, which is in contrast to Adamsson's economic worldview.

The complete list of names and their equivalents in the Swedish and the 1928 edition are included as an appendix, with the idea that scholars using this text may find inspiration in considering multiple interpretations of these names.

The socio-economic context of this allegory was also somewhat obscured in the 1928 translation. Perhaps in an effort to Americanize the story, some of the occupations and class titles were generalized, such as the use of "peasant" instead of "cotter" *(torpare)*. Waldenström chose to make the main protagonist of his story a "squire" *(brukspatron)*, which is a decision that is loaded with potential for discussing the economic and class dynamics of the Swedish religious awakening. A *torpare* was at the very bottom of the social hierarchy in Sweden, and a *torpare's* widow like Mother Simple would have been even lower. A *torpare* was a tenant on someone else's land, in this case the land of the *brukspatron*. A *brukspatron* was often the main employer in a given village, in charge of some factory or ironworks *(bruk)* or agricultural enterprise. Though not (necessarily) a member of the nobility, a *brukspatron* was considered among the highest of the five classes of people in 19th century Swedish society.[40] A *brukspatron* could also become a "patron" of religious activities and public works in the community, filling a role as an economic, spiritual, and civic authority all wrapped up into one. Lindström suggests three real world examples of this dynamic type of *brukspatron* who might have inspired Waldenström: Hans Henrik von Essen of Tidaholm (1820-1894), Olof Gabriel Hedengren of Riseberga (1812-1870), and Count Gustaf Lewenhaupt of Hällefors (1791-1873). The last example is most likely, and Lindström even goes so far as to speculate that Waldenström may have been tempted to imitate the entrepreneurial lifestyle and philanthropic ideals of Lewenhaupt, but ultimately chose instead to allegorize this temptation in the adventures of Adamsson.[41] The deference with which the members of the estate address Adamsson and his wife (including the avoidance of the informal pronoun "you"

– *du*) reflect the extremely formal, patriarchal agrarian context of Sweden in the 19th century, which was in stark contrast with the more democratic contexts of the American and Canadian societies that many Swedish Pietists entered after they emigrated. From a theological point of view, the reflection on this economic and class hierarchy can do much to critique the posture of deference that appears in many forms between Christians, perhaps even the imbalance that often exists between wealthy Christians in the West and the activities they "sponsor" among people in developing nations. Certainly Adamsson's economic standing and class were no random choices, and Waldenström has included this deliberately in order to provoke our notions of religious hierarchies of all kinds, not least the economic ones.

Olof Hedengren.

H. H. von Essen.

K. G. Lewenhaupt.

Echoing Waldenström's own hopes for this novel, it is my hope that new and old readers of this allegory will continue to be delighted, to be inspired to lively (but not too intense) discussion, and find it to be a much-needed refuge and message of assurance.

Champaign, Illinois,
Reformation Sunday, 2012
Mark Safstrom

SELECTED REFERENCES

Johann Arndt. *True Christianity* (New York: Paulist Press 1979).

Oloph Bexell. *Sveriges kyrkohistoria vol. 7; Folkväckelsens och kyrkoförnyelsens tid* (Stockholm: Verbum 2003).

William Bredberg. *P.P. Waldenströms verksamhet till 1878; Till frågan om Svenska Missionsförbundets uppkomst* (Stockholm: Missionsförbundets Förlag 1948).

John Bunyan. *The Pilgrim's Progress; From this World to That Which is to Come.* Introduction by W. Clark Gilpin (New York: Vintage Spiritual Classics 2004).

Arne Friztson. "En Gud som är god och rättfärdig" in *Liv och rörelse: Svenska missionskyrkans historia och identitet.* Hans Andreasson, et al. (Stockholm: Verbum 2007).

Gunnar Hallingberg. *Läsarna: 1800-talets folkväckelse och det moderna genombrottet* (Stockholm: Atlantis 2010).

Søren Kierkegaard. *Fear and Trembling.* Introduction and notes by Alastair Hannay (New York: Penguin Classics 1985).

Karl A. Olsson. *"Paul Peter Waldenström and Augustana."* in *The Swedish Immigrant Community in Transition; Essays in Honor of Dr. Conrad Bergendoff.* Ed. J. Iverne Dowie and Ernest M. Espelie (Rock Island, Illinois: Augustana Historical Society 1963).

Harry Lindström. *I Livsfrågornas spänningsfält; Om P. Waldenströms Brukspatron Adamsson – populär folkbok och allegorisk roman* (Stockholm: Verbum Förlag 1997).

Mark Safstrom. "Defining Lutheranism from the Margins: Paul Peter Waldenström on Being a 'Good Lutheran' in America" in *The Swedish-American Historical Quarterly.* April-July 2012, Vol. LXIII, Nos. 2-3.

Mark Safstrom. "Making Room for the Lost: Congregational Inclusivity in Waldenström's Squire Adamsson" in *The Covenant Quarterly.* Aug-Nov 2013, Vol. LXXI, Nos. 3-4.

Mark Safstrom. *The Religious Origins of Democratic Pluralism: Paul Peter Waldenström and the Politics of the Swedish Awakening 1868-1917.* Dissertation. (University of Washington 2010).

Ragnar Tomson. *En Hövding; Minnesteckning över P. Waldenström till 100-årsdagen av hans födelse* (Stockholm: Svenska Missionsförbundets Förlag 1937).

P. Waldenström. *Gud är min tröst.* Fifth edition (Stockholm: Svenska Missionsförbundets Förlag 1938).

von Zinzendorf, Nicolas Ludwig. "Thoughts for the Learned and Yet Good- Willed Students of Truth" in *Pietists: Selected Writings* (New York: Paulist Press 1983).

PREFACE TO THE FIFTH EDITION 1891

It was the summer of 1862. I was staying in Sundsvall, visiting with friends and preparing to preach for the guests who were staying there at the baths. The text for one day was Psalm 86. While I was preparing my sermon, the thought came over me: "This psalm is like a room for the lost." It came like the voice of God; and my heart rejoiced.

It was with these words that my sermon began. "But," I added, "before we enter into this room for the lost, let us take a look at how the people are doing in the house next door." And from there I went on to paint a picture of a man who had just gone through a bankruptcy and who, with his entire family, found himself in the most dire straits – until he found refuge in the room for the lost.

That was the beginning of "Squire Adamsson." When I came home from Sundsvall – I was staying that time in a parish parsonage outside of Härnösand – I prepared to write down the parable and send it in to the newspaper *Stadsmissionären* ("The Stockholm City Missionary"). As I was writing, it began to grow exponentially. Not until three days later was it finished. From that point, it was run in *Stadsmissionären* over the course of several issues. In the spring of 1863, the question came as to whether it could be published as a book of its own. This happened, yet not before undergoing a significant revision and expansion, which made it about three times as long as it had been originally. It was published by the Stockholm City Mission to benefit its orphanage, and enjoyed three editions without any further revision. In 1874, there was a fourth edition that was published, with some changes, which were prompted by the contemporary debates over the doctrine of the atonement.

The attention that this book gained after its first edition was not insignificant. Many were delighted by it. But there were also strong reactions by those who unsheathed their swords. But the debate was neither all that long, nor was it intense.

Now “The Squire” is coming out for the fifth time. He has not been significantly revised or expanded this time, but will resume the same free evangelical perspective as he always has. He preaches grace for the lost following the rule of Paul: Where sin abounded, grace abounded much more. This message is certainly needed. It unfortunately seems that it gets pushed into the background in all too many places.

May God now bless this little book to the instruction and spiritual upbuilding of the souls who read it. May it be a means by which many people are pulled up out of the slough of despond, as well as guarded against loose living, worldliness and self-righteousness, and that, in all things, God and the Lamb might receive the glory.

Gävle,
17 October 1891
P.W.

PREFACE TO THE SIXTH EDITION 1907

It was in 1891 that the preface above was written. The book has now been absent from the bookshops for several years. But requests for it have not been rare. For this reason, it is being published once again. It tells the story of a man, whose name is Adamsson. He lives in the city called The World. After being ruined financially, he moves to the city Evangelium, where he receives a new name, Abrahamsson. After some time, he grows weary of life there and travels to the city Loose Living and goes by Adamsson. He returns to Evangelium, but soon moves to the city Self-Righteousness, where he adopts the name Hagarsson. However, he becomes unhappy and returns again to Evangelium, where he remains, until he is able to move home with Justus All-Powerful in the city called Holiness.

I know that many people have in fact been helped up out of the "slough of despond" from reading this book when they were on the verge of despair. For this reason, I am publishing the book once again, with the wish to God that it might once again come to the assistance of many. May God make it so.

Stockholm,
August 1907
P.W.

SQUIRE ADAMSSON
OR
WHERE DO YOU LIVE?

Now to him who relies on works, the wages are not counted as grace but as debt. But to him who does not rely on works but believes on him who justifies the ungodly, his faith is accounted as righteousness.

Romans 4:4-5

FIRST CHAPTER

Adamsson's Estate, Family and Enterprises

On the outskirts of a great city called The World, lay a vast and reputable estate, or country manor, which due to its stunning beauty was widely known by those who lived in the surrounding region, and even from many miles away. The estate was called Industriousness and properly belonged to the city and fell under its jurisdiction, even though it lay outside of it. Everyone believed this estate to be a very productive and profitable holding. For, besides the fact that it included enormous acreage, with all the barns and other trappings that accompany such estates, its income was also significantly increased by the fact that a great ironworks was situated there, which provided the owner with many advantages and a considerable profit. The estate was, furthermore, replete with all the architecture, gardens and other attributes that so often contribute much to intensifying the beauty of nature. At the ironworks were produced Good Deeds of many kinds. Though there were some people who were unkind enough to suggest that the goods that the ironworks produced were made from poor material. Nonetheless, everyone was in agreement that they always had a beautiful, eye-catching appearance. They were also usually packaged with handsome labels.

Flowing right through the heart of the estate was a beautiful river, named SELF-CENTERED-PIETY, which supplied the inhabitants and livestock with water, as well as watered its vast fields, which also gave an uncommon yield. Yet, this river was most essential to the ironworks. For on the one side, the waterwheel of the ironworks was driven by this water, as it had been dammed up to create a waterfall. On the other side, this same river was used to carry all of the goods produced in the fields and ironworks alike down to the city and surrounding areas. It flowed up against a hill, which was called SELFISHNESS, and even flowed through the better neighborhoods of the city THE WORLD. All along this river on the grounds of INDUSTRIOUSNESS there were small parks, which provided the people with a pleasant spot for rest and refreshment. There were also excellent swimming beaches situated here, which were frequented religiously. People were of the opinion that the water of this river was most refreshing and good for the health. On the surface the water was quite clear, but it had a polluted and muddy bottom. This did not matter though, since at every swimming beach, people had laid out smooth boards over the sludge, so that the swimmers could avoid feeling the bottom.

It was the custom among friends from the better classes to congregate here in these little parks so that they could chat with one another about their business, their work and other important concerns, during which everything proceeded in a proper and decent fashion.

On this estate there once lived a rich and well-to-do country squire by the name of ADAMSSON.[42] His house was remarkable in many respects, and the people in the neighborhood had many good things to say about this gentleman. Personally, Adamsson was a stately man with a good education – he was a doctor of philosophy, to be specific – decent and respectable, honest in his conduct and measured in everything that he said. He also possessed an ability to inspire confidence and respect among his fellow human beings, partly through his genius, partly through his way of being, his hospitality and thoughtfulness. Moreover, he was the chairman of a mission society, which he himself had founded out of zeal for the glory of God and for spreading the word of God among the heathen. Of all of the members of the society, he was the most eager and open-handed, and every month without fail great sums were regularly donated by him to an even larger mission society. He was also regarded and praised both privately and publically as the strongest advocate of mission. For his own part, he subscribed to a number of mission publications, and did not hesitate to circulate these among his servants, employees and friends. These publications he read with a passion. It was with uneasy anticipation that he waited for the arrival of these publications each month. When they came, his habit was *first* to look to see if there was anything mentioned about him or his last contribution. There was one time that he himself had explained to his wife his reasons or motivation for doing this. On that occasion, he had not been at home and it had namely been she who had been the one to receive the day's mail, with which had come the mission newspaper. Upon his arrival home, he found her reading through it, and he requested to borrow it for just a moment. Immediately he began to flip through the pages.

"Why are you reading like that?" asked his wife, "or, what are you searching for?"

"Well," he answered, "I wanted to check to see if that measly little mite that I had the grace to be able to send in two weeks ago had in fact arrived at the society."

His wife did not say a thing, but in her heart she admired her husband for this humility, which expressed itself in words like these. About his humility there were many stories that could be told. It was a frequent subject of discussion at the estate and among the neighbors.

On the estate there lived a poor old lady with the name Mrs. Praise, who was in good standing with the Adamssons. The kindness that they had shown toward her was truly remarkable. One evening like many others, she came calling. Adamsson had just finished reading the freshly delivered mission newspaper. Mrs. Praise was one of those who received the paper as a gift from the squire. When she came in, she asked: "Has the Squire seen what was written today in the mission newspaper about him?"

He smiled with kindness and grace, and raising his glance toward heaven, he answered:

"Oh, dear Mrs. Praise – about that we had best not speak, but instead pray to God, that the little bit that I have had the grace to be able to do, might bring some blessing to the miserable heathen. Consider this – these unfortunate people live in ignorance and grave ungodliness, such that it is rather the case that we ought to be doing far more for them than we actually are." At this, a tear appeared in his clear eyes, which were still fixed toward heaven.

"But..." answered Mrs. Praise, deeply moved by the squire's tenderness and humility, "...but the Squire is still worthy of much praise, for there is hardly anyone who works for these people as much as the Squire does."

"Yes. But we *may not* give the glory to ourselves, for if we become conceited, then we sin."

"Well, yes. The Squire is certainly right about that. Nonetheless, he is still remarkable."

As Mrs. Praise was about to depart, Adamsson told her that she should feel welcome to visit anytime, "For," he added, "I appreciate your honesty, and would gladly hear from you more often."

At this they parted company. When Adamsson rejoined his wife, he said:

"It is remarkable what nice, pleasant people there are in this world. MRS. PRAISE was just here. She can be a tad bit over the top, of course, but she only means the best. She always makes such a good impression on me, and I feel so good inside after she has been for a visit."

"Yes, she is exceptional," answered his wife.

Both Adamsson's example, as well as the words of praise that he received, were an encouragement to many to forge on ahead in this same beautiful cause, for everyone wished to be good, just like him. It was for this reason that one of his closer acquaintances, who had the name MR. ADMIRER, would often declare about him: "Of all the men I know, I do not know anyone who has worked for the kingdom of God with the same diligence and self-sacrifice. And," he would add, "it is remarkable to see the endurance and patience, with which he suffers through the most bitter mockery[43] of his work by the children of THE WORLD, as well as to observe the great spiritual light, with which he is gifted, and through which he has exposed false prophets and driven out foreign teachings from these parts."[44]

MR. ADMIRER was also the father of MRS. PRAISE. His motto was:

Thou shall think and speak well of thy neighbor
and present everything in its best light.

At his ironworks, Adamsson had employed a certain preacher to look after the spiritual well-being of his tenant employees. This preacher's name was SHEPHERD-FOR-HIRE,[45] and each evening and morning he conducted a prayer meeting in the chapel –

one that the squire himself had built – and also preached there at the ironworks for a great crowd every Sunday. It was at the squire's own orders that no one could work at the ironworks on Sundays, no matter what the production schedule demanded. Thus everyone had plenty of time to go to church. And the workers were quite industrious church-goers. How this came to be can be best explained by the following story.

One Sunday, Mother Pious came home from church looking jubilant, her eyes sparkling with joy. Her husband, who because of an illness had not been able to attend the service that day, asked what had prompted her great joy.

"Well," she answered, "you will never believe what a marvelous sermon the pastor gave today!"

"In that case, what did he speak on?"

"Well, he preached about the eternal Sabbath rest.[46] And then he said that, if we are diligent and upright and God-fearing, we will be able to reach it. And everyone knows that I have always been upright and God-fearing, and have carried out my service to God just as diligently and properly as any of the rest of my duties. And then he said that up there in Zion we will be able to lay down our tired heads under the shade of palms and by sweet gurgling springs, and, for all eternity, enjoy the fruit of our labor in blessed rest and peace. This is exactly what he said, I remember it word for word. And then he read a hymn verse, where it was written:

If we've lived by God's command,
we shall there in heaven stand.[47]

And this just went on and on. It was so splendid, that even the pastor himself began to weep, and so we all just sat there with tears in our eyes."

Mother Pious was similarly moved as she gave her enthusiastic and stirring account of this sermon for her sick husband. When he had dried his eyes, he answered with a sigh: "Well, it is no wonder that we are so eager to go to church, when one can hear such priceless words spoken there. Oh, I do hope that I will be well enough next Sunday!"

After a while, SHEPHERD-FOR-HIRE received a large city pastorate in THE WORLD. For his installation he held a lavish banquet, where wine and strong drinks were served. The bishop raised his glass several times to the new pastor, to THE WORLDCHURCH,[48] to the council, and so on. Adamsson also gave a speech. When everyone headed for home, they were all rather euphoric. One member of the council said to the bishop:

"The morning's service was impressive, the meal was delicious, and this evening has been a delight."

His sentiment was confirmed by the bishop.

With an indefatigable zeal, Adamsson tended to the needs of the sick and the poor. Never was anyone so diligent as he was in visiting the cottages of the destitute and miserable. Wherever he went, he was always welcomed with jubilation and greeted with eyes that sparkled with joy, by old and young alike. Once, marveling at this, his faithful friend MR. ADMIRER jokingly said about him:

"I dare say that it was a mistake that Adamsson came down here to earth, for he seems to have been created for a higher world."

This judgment was shared by everyone who knew him at all. There was only *one* person who was known for hesitating in sharing this praise. Whenever she heard it, she chose instead to shake her head and mutter her suspicions. Often she said, quite plainly:

"With the Squire, things are not as well as they seem."

When someone asked her what she thought of this 'remarkable' man, she generally kept silent, but one time when she answered, she said quite succinctly and with a sigh:

"That poor man. It will never go well for him."

It was clear that words like these, coming from a 50-something, decrepit old bird (she was namely the widow of a cotter), would rain on everyone's parade and cause much annoyance. People thought, quite wisely:

"What does she understand about such things? Does she think that her words can possibly matter more than all those words of praise that Adamsson has received from distinguished men, both privately and publically? Or is it not as the old proverb says:

You will know them by their fruits[49]

In particular, comments like these had been prompted by the "shameless slander," as people called it, that she had once leveled at Adamsson, when she had accused him of being false-hearted. The incident had played itself out in the following way:

Mrs. Praise had just lauded Adamsson for his great zeal.

"One must work while the sun shines," answered the Squire.

The little old woman, hearing these words, said with a gentle and still voice:

"Things are not as well as the Squire might believe. The Squire is false-hearted. All his Good Deeds and his practice of Godliness is simply an attempt to escape *the sorrowful realization that things are not as they should be with him.*"

It should not come as a surprise to anyone that this was difficult to tolerate. Soon everyone knew what this little old woman had said. Because of this, no one was able to completely be on good terms with her again. People gave her their scorn, which they called pity. But they commonly referred to her as "that poor old cotter-woman." Her proper name was Mother Simple.[50]

Adamsson's good reputation only continued to grow. Naturally he was a representative in the above-mentioned mission society. And as he had a more prominent social standing, his name was printed in the report of the membership with a larger font than the others. He had risen to being chairman of the board quite quickly, as well. In this role, just as in all the others, he was exceptional. With one word, one could say about him that he in all things belonged to other people. His accounts and business he never administered himself. Instead they were taken care of by a taciturn treasurer and bookkeeper, who had the name CONSCIENCE. This man had previously been a councilman and civil secretary in THE WORLD but had been ousted from that office as a result of the anxiety that he often had voiced and caused.

Such was the nature of this Squire Adamsson, and though much more could be said about him, what has been said so far are the most characteristic and important details.

SECOND CHAPTER

Adamsson's Family

If Squire Adamsson was remarkable, his family was a perfect match. His spouse, whose maiden name was EVASDOTTER, was a loveable woman, generally admired and appreciated for the services she provided. A mother to the defenseless and a champion of the downtrodden, she lived just as her husband did, almost exclusively for others – or at least appeared that way. That she in this way would come to be loved by everyone was only natural, and the poor addressed her as: "Gracious Lady" or even "Your Grace." Like her husband, she was very pious and godly and diligent in her prayers. One time when she had been reading a short passage of GOD's WORD to the poor MOTHER CAPRICIOUS, who was ill, and then said some prayers, the little old woman asked her, teary-eyed and filled with wonder:

"My dear Gracious Lady, from which prayer book was this marvelous prayer taken?"

"None…" was the answer.

"Oh, can that be possible? Where did Your Grace find it then?"

"Well, my dear old girl, this was just something that came out of my own soul."

"Doesn't Your Grace ever use a prayer book?"

"No, for I am of the opinion that it is best to pray with one's own words."

At this, tears streamed from the eyes of Mother Capricious, which also caused the squire's wife to be deeply moved, and she experienced a moment of holy reverence. But then this little old woman dried her eyes and said:

"Yes, My Gracious Lady – Oh, that I could pray as beautifully as that!

"Oh, dear mother, you may well have to be satisfied with less, as not everyone is able to do this."

"No, no. That's just it: not everyone is able to be satisfied with less."

"No, dear mother, I did not mean it like that. I meant: it is not everyone who can pray that way – as I can," answered the squire's wife hastily, while the flash of redness in her cheeks betrayed that the little old woman's misunderstanding had touched a sensitive point.

"But, hear this, Your Grace," continued the little old woman, "they say that Mother Simple also shares this habit of not using a prayer book."

"Yes, she is conceited, and imagines she can do things that she cannot."

"Well, well. I can easily believe that."

One factor that contributed greatly to making Adamsson and his wife remarkable was that the things people praised as "remarkable" about them were things that were seen as completely normal when other people did them. If the estate foreman greeted one of the cotters nobly and cheerfully, or his wife said a few heartfelt words to the cotters' children, no one paid any particular attention to this. This was what people are expected to do. But if the squire gave a word of greeting and appeared cheerful, or if the squire's wife curtsied and nodded to the wife of a cotter or gave her children a delicious *skorpa* to eat, then this was something so remarkable that one could not say enough good things about it. It was ultimately as if people did not expect as much from the squire and his wife as they did from the foreman and his wife.

Mrs. Adamsson was a quiet and serene woman. With exceptional competence she took care of and presided over her household. Mild and gentle toward her servants, tender toward her beloved children and with an intimate love bound to her husband, she was perhaps among those rare women, mothers or matrons, who truly excel at spreading peace and cheerfulness around her. In addition to her general liberality and openhandedness, there is one of her charitable causes in particular that deserves mention. This was her famous sewing society, which was devoted to supporting the mission to the heathen. She had established it and she herself remained its heart and soul. The members she recruited for this society included many distinguished ladies and young women from the city THE WORLD, in addition to her good friend and neighbor MRS. ADMIRER, who lived not far away on the beautiful estate of SELF-ACTIVITY. Moreover, it was always her motto:

"The more hands we have, the more money we make, and the greater the sum, the greater the blessing."

In this way, she had quite a few workers under her direction, for these worthy ladies from the city could not deny that it was "beautiful" and proper that they worked and accomplished something for their neighbors in distress – so as long as they did not get carried away and forget their own needs. Above all, they reasoned, one ought to be on guard against appearing self-righteous. And although they thought that Mrs. Adamsson was slightly caught up in a desire to be just a little bit superior to others, all the same they still participated in her sewing society. One thing that had caught everyone's attention was the fact that Mrs. Adamsson provided all the materials for the work herself, which cost her quite a large sum. But this was necessary for her to do, for if everyone had been burdened by providing the materials themselves, then there would not have been many who would have bothered to join her society. At the moment she always seemed to have plenty of seamstresses. That these worthy ladies always came to the gatherings in proper form and fashion had much to do with the fact that they always knew that Mrs. Adamsson would treat them to an afternoon coffee hour and even a nice supper.

This is how the society's gatherings were regularly conducted each month. Everyone was generally in full agreement – with the exception of MOTHER SIMPLE – that this was a model for all the other societies, and that it was the society that brought the greatest blessing. Whenever MOTHER SIMPLE heard talk like this, she remained quiet and distant, for the most part. This greatly disturbed everyone. Yet, what provoked them most was one conversation, which MOTHER SIMPLE had engaged in with the wife of MR. ADMIRER.

"Now, MOTHER SIMPLE," asked MRS. ADMIRER, "which sewing society do you like the best?"

"I like MOTHER WOUNDED-HIP's little society," the little old woman answered.[51]

"Oh, my poor old girl, how can you be so dense? At each of their weekly gatherings they bring in just one *öre* per person. In addition to that, they have very few workers there. Of the profit that comes from their hard labor, the lion's share goes toward purchasing materials – since they are so poor, of course. And I can hardly believe that what they bring in for missions would amount to more than 10 *kronor* over the course of half a year. Now we in Mrs. Adamsson's society pay 50 or 25 *öre* each month, based on what we can afford. Plus, there are more of us, and Mrs. Adamsson provides all the materials, so that each month we can send in more than 50 *kronor.* Besides, the other societies, when they get together, spend nearly the entire time reading and praying. We are diligent workers and find other opportunities to seek out spiritual upbuilding, so that the chaplain at our meetings only offers a short prayer at the opening and closing."

With this, Mrs. Admirer said her goodbyes. But Mother Simple thought in her heart: "Poor souls! Oh, if only someone would read to them about the widow's mite!"[52]

In addition to these things, Mrs. Adamsson had opened one home for orphaned children and another home for poor, aging widows. The former was run by a well-liked widow by the name of Heart-For-Children, and the other was run by Mrs. Adamsson herself. And it was truly moving to see the greeting Mrs. Adamsson received whenever she entered either of these establishments. When she came to the old ones, every eye lit up with joy; when she came to the little ones, every foot sprang into motion, every child bounced all around her, each tiny fist trying to grab hold of some part of her skirts, each child trying to tell her something, and so on. No one paid any mind to what Mother Simple said, but instead, as has been mentioned already, "the poor old cotter-woman" received everyone's scorn. Mr. and Mrs. Adamsson were celebrated for their Christian zeal and spiritual insight, so much so that people had ascribed to them the right to teach and correct everyone else. As such it was unthinkable to allow their standing in the community to be challenged by this pitiful little old woman, whom everyone considered to be so misguided and presumptuous, *that she would take it upon herself to find fault with people who had far more understanding, insight, gifts and experience than she did.* What is more, Mother Simple often held her tongue. She was rather reserved, so much so that people often became oblivious to her. But whenever she did make one of her pronouncements, everyone would listen, even if they were angered by it or thought that what she said was nonsense. Also when anyone was praised or criticized by her, it would affect that person more than when such words came from others. And when she praised someone, the recipient always considered the little old woman to be quite a good judge of character. Her own true friends, with whom she confided and who understood her, were Mother Wounded-Hip and her two sisters, Mother Prodigal and Mother Penniless.

The squire and his wife enjoyed this blissful existence for many years. They were of one heart and mind; their household was considered to be so peaceful and pleasant that anyone should certainly be able to thrive there. "They have it so good and are such loving people," was the general consensus about this household. Their marriage was blessed by several children, which they loved dearly as their delight and joy. The people of the estate were also fond of these children. But two of them were distinguished and loved above all the rest. These were two lads, the one named Kind-Hearted and the other Complacent.[53] The former was of a strong build with an uncommonly handsome face and sturdy frame, though he was somewhat chubby. He was everyone's darling, and everyone hoped he would be around for a long time. But Mother Simple, who understood a thing or two about medicine, could see that the lad was affected by tuberculosis, poor digestion and a latent case of leprosy. Though Complacent was smallish and insignificant in stature, he was unusually healthy and strong. He also had a peculiar upbringing, completely different from that of the others. He was born in secrecy, and no one was told his true name. Only the bookkeeper Conscience and Mother Simple had any idea of what his name was. But this they shared with no one. Mother Simple once explained to Mother Wounded-Hip that the Adamssons were too close of friends for her to say a disparaging word about them, "For," she thought, "such talk brings no nourishment to the soul, and if we can at all avoid it, there are far better ways for us to spend our time when we get together."

The little lad was his brother's shadow everywhere he went. Never were there such devoted brothers as these two, who never were apart, never fought. Wherever Kind-Hearted went, there went Complacent as well. But he was almost always a closed-lipped, silent listener to whatever his brother said. His father had, to be specific, strictly forbidden him to ever express himself. He just nodded his head, with beaming countenance, and looked around at those present whenever his brother was speaking or doing something, as though to say "Wasn't that a splendid thing to say?"

But since he was not able to *express* himself or *say* anything in the presence of others, he was all the more able to *see* and *hear*. Never was a person as perceptive to other people's gestures, expressions and words as he. Whenever he would return home to his father after these encounters, he was in the habit of telling him everything that he had observed, every good thing that the people of the estate had said about their "good and gracious squire." Should he happen to have heard some evil complaint, then he would usually keep silent about these things, since he considered such comments to be mostly unfair and inappropriate. This he could prove, furthermore, by naming all the thousand Good Deeds that his father produced, as well as all of the praise that his father received from everyone else. He also thought that these unfavorable judgments were largely the result of jealousy or their failure to discern the *noble* intentions of his father. For this reason, he would often look upon his father – sometimes with deep sighs and great tears in those clear eyes – as a martyr at the hands of these cruel people and their misunderstanding and bitterness. His father usually liked to listen to what the son had to say, but from time to time he would also ask him to keep silent. That was in vain. Such was the case one day, for example, when both brothers had just come home from Mrs. Praise. Right away, Complacent started listing everything she had said.

"The dear old girl thanked God that there was such a man – such an angel – like our papa. She said that he is truly walking according to the words of the scripture: 'Let your light so shine before men, that they may see your Good Deeds.'"[54]

When their father heard this, he said:

"No, that is going to far; don't speak of such things."

"But, dear papa, why should I keep quiet?" answered the son, "it is *true* after all, these things that I say. And my intention is only for this to be a great encouragement to papa."

To this, Adamsson was not able to object. Complacent continued his story, and it did do his father good to hear it. Such occurrences were not rare. This dear child seemed to become more talkative with every command to keep quiet and every time he was forbidden to open his mouth in the presence of other people.

Since people did not know what he was called, but still needed to call him something, they thus came up with a nickname based on his appearance. They had, for instance, noticed that he was very silent and reserved, to the extent that most of the time he would creep behind his brother's back when they were out. Besides, they had seen how he would occasionally blush or hide his eyes in his hands, whenever someone either praised him or his brother. For this reason, people generally referred to him as "the Gracious Master Squire's little Humble," a name that had been thought up by Mr. Admirer.

It was remarkable to see how much Kind-Hearted loved this brother of his...yes, perhaps even more than his brother loved him in return. For anytime Complacent was not allowed to go along, then his brother would refuse to go outside. Their father often tried to send Kind-Hearted out on his own with some message of joy or gift for some poor person or the like, but strictly forbid Complacent to accompany him.

Despite all of these efforts, that was simply impossible, for Kind-Hearted always would say:

"If my brother is not allowed to come along, then I am not going either."

This happened one time in particular, when Adamsson was going to send him to bring medicine to a factory worker who was ill. In the end, the father had to resort to shutting COMPLACENT up in a room by himself. But this resulted in him being forced to send MISS UNWILLING in KIND-HEARTED's place. She was a maidservant in his household, and was usually put to use whenever he was making a delivery to the kind of people from whom the squire knew he could not expect any other response than ingratitude.

These two brothers were as one, and so time floated by in this way for the next several years. And this is how we will leave them for now, and let them live in peace for a while.

THIRD CHAPTER

Imprisonment

In a city called HOLINESS,[55] there ruled at that time a mighty king by the name of JUSTUS ALL-POWERFUL.[56] There were many peculiar rumors circulating about him among the citizens of THE WORLD. Many considered him to be an inhumanely strict man, which is why they feared him tremendously. Others were of the persuasion that he was a good-natured master, of whom there was nothing to fear. Some even wondered if he really existed, or if he wasn't just some kind of saga hero. In short, everyone had their own ideas about him, but no one truly knew him. Because of this, it often happened in THE WORLD that one could hear people mock his name, as well as mock anyone "who was foolish enough to believe all those fables about him, spread by that former councilman CONSCIENCE and his kind." At the same time, there were others who were at a loss for how they were supposed to be able to praise and exalt him for his "goodness" and "mercy" and "leniency toward their faults and weaknesses." There were also plenty of people to be found who, out of fear of him, lived an arduous life, expending all their energies in an attempt to escape his wrath. While there were still others who gladly and with a cheerful spirit worked to make themselves right with him, in the expectation that they would earn some reward by this service.

Even Mr. Adamsson's household had dealings with LORD JUSTUS in certain matters. To be specific, Adamsson owed an enormous amount of debt to this man. All these debts had been carefully recorded by the bookkeeper CONSCIENCE in the squire's account books. After some time had passed, JUSTUS ALL-POWERFUL sent his faithful servant MOSES to demand payment on the entire amount. Mr. Adamsson was just then sitting at home with his wife, peaceful, glad at heart, and with his mind completely at ease. KIND-HEARTED had just returned from his rounds, and COMPLACENT had started in with reporting on all the day's activities to his parents, especially all the remarkable things that his brother had accomplished. With steamy eyes, his father blessed this "precious treasure" of his (a nickname he had for KIND-HEARTED), and declared himself happy beyond measure to call such a child his own. All the while, he humbly admitted that he was not worthy of such an altogether enormous grace.

It was into this scene that MOSES had intruded and delivered his master's certificate of debt. Astonished by this, Adamsson curtly replied, saying that he did not believe himself to be indebted to LORD JUSTUS at all, "beyond a few small trifles, which he well knew LORD JUSTUS did not keep such close accounting over, but instead would gladly remit." He therefore did not understand how MOSES could come in his name with a demand of 10,000 talents[57]; neither could he acknowledge that such a debt existed, nor believe that this demand had come from the *good* and *righteous* LORD JUSTUS. Instead he kept insinuating that "this must be some fraud or mistake."

With this response, MOSES made his journey back home. Enraged, LORD JUSTUS sent him out again with the same certificate of debt, threatening this time that if he was not immediately compensated, that then Adamsson should expect to have all his assets promptly seized and himself thrown in prison.

This all occurred on a dark and chilly fall evening. Adamsson felt nervous and even a little bit sick to his stomach. Earlier that day, he had been out on his customary rounds among people of the estate. While he had been on his stroll, he had run across MOTHER SIMPLE, with whom he had struck up a conversation.

"How do you do?" he asked.

"I am getting along the same as ever," had been her reply. "Wretched and miserable as I am in every way, I cannot seem to accomplish a single thing. But despite this, I am still content and glad, since the gracious LORD JUSTUS has just offered me a refuge and dwelling place in his holy city, EVANGELIUM. There I will have everything that I need, at no charge. And though I am so old, poor and feeble, nevertheless, I am not above living on grace. But how is the Squire?"

"Well, thank you. Very well!"

MOTHER SIMPLE turned away and dried her eyes with her apron.

"Why are you sad?" asked Adamsson, bewildered.

"Oh, dear Squire – but why is the Squire out and about in this nasty weather?"

"Well, you know one has to work while the daylight lasts. But tell me this, at least – why are you crying and depressed?"

"Oh, because I am deeply concerned for the Squire. He has always been so good to me, that I guess it just brings me to grief when I consider his situation."

"Brings you to grief? My dear old girl! Why should that be?"

"Because I worry that the Squire will not take advantage of the great grace that is available to him, before it is too late – I mean, to leave his property and move to EVANGELIUM. I have heard from his bookkeeper, CONSCIENCE, that the Squire's affairs are not standing on as firm a foundation as one might hope."[58]

"Oh, don't you go on worrying about my affairs! Each of us will have to answer to his own master; so, you can stick to worrying about yourself. My affairs, I trust, are secure enough. And I have my debts, just as well as I have debtors."

After this they parted company. Adamsson continued on his rounds. At first he was somewhat bewildered by the little old woman's unusual behavior. Although he well knew that she sincerely cared for him and wished him the best, while he walked along he began to feel himself become all the more troubled by her words.

"My affairs," he said to himself, "my affairs…how…could they be that bad? I say, Conscience!" he called out, when at that same moment he caught sight of his bookkeeper in the distance, "my affairs *surely are resting on a firm foundation, right?"*

After his fashion, Conscience said nothing; for he usually never answered *half* questions of this sort, which *more expressed a wish to be set at ease, rather than to receive a true answer.* Thus when his squire did not ask him straight out how things actually *stood,* but instead if they were not *really* right, he acted like there was nothing wrong and went his way.

This struck Adamsson as peculiar and increased his state of alarm. In order to find some assurance and to calm his nerves, he sought out Pastor Shepherd-for-Hire. And he began to confide with this man, explaining his troubles and the conversation with Mother Simple. In turn the man, puzzled, asked how something like that could bother him.

"The Squire," he asked, "isn't thinking of leaving Industriousness? Why? In order to move to Evangelium? In order to be lazy? Whatever for? No, no. Christianity calls for more seriousness, for more life and activity, than exists there. One cannot help but be filled with zeal when observing how often – sad though it is – people can be tricked and led astray by sanctimonious preachers of falsehood like this. Such preachers are talented in the art of hiding their sloth, incompetence, and idleness under a mantle of beautiful talk about grace. No, dear Squire, remember that beautiful verse:

If we've lived by God's command, we shall there in heaven stand.

Furthermore, the Squire can always speak with the bishop. He lives on Pious Street in the city The World. He certainly knows more about these things than a cotter-widow."

A few moments later, they parted. Adamsson felt himself somewhat comforted by Pastor Shepherd-for-Hire's words, but not entirely set at ease.

"The bishop," he thought, "yes, the bishop! Did not Luther once say: if the devil takes the Pope, who then will take you?"

He felt a chill come over him, and so he hurried his steps in order to warm himself up. On the way he met Mrs. Praise.

"Can it be that the Squire once again is out delivering blessings, even in weather like this!?" she exclaimed.

At this the squire was once again overcome by anxiety, for he was well aware that on this trip he had hardly accomplished one good thing. But just then, he also met his son Complacent, who reminded his father that when one is producing Good Deeds, one should not so much look at the outward results, but instead concentrate on the good will and noble intentions behind them. Once again he felt partially calmed down, yet not fully at ease. Mother Simple's words weighed heavily on his heart. As he walked and pondered them, he happened to have the misfortune of tripping and tumbling into a mud puddle, so that he ended up soaking wet and managed to catch a cold.

He had no sooner returned home from this worry-ridden outing and taken out his best clothes in order to change, when Moses came calling for the second time, bearing with him his master's stern and threatening certificate of debt. One can easily imagine Mr. Adamsson's horror when he read this letter, especially since his bookkeeper had also arrived with the account books, and verified that the debt really was as great as it said.

"Why have you never shown me this before?" the deathly-pale squire asked his bookkeeper.

"This is the Squire's own fault. For he has paid so much attention to other people's accounts that it has never crossed his mind to review his own. Every time I have wanted to show these to the Squire, he has been preoccupied with matters pertaining to the mission, or visiting the poor and sick, or prayer, or the study of God's Word and the like. Lately, I have, for this reason, considered it pointless to try to bring any of this to the Squire's attention."

Horrified and shaken by this answer, Adamsson immediately set to writing a *humble* petition to this harsh moneylender, explaining that if the payment of the principal could be deferred, he would be willing to make annual payments on the interest. His letter sounded like this:

"Most austere and mighty Lord Justus!

With all my heart, I humbly confess that I have dealt dishonestly with you and have incurred all of the debt that you have demanded. But, Lord Justus, *as much as I wish that I had not done all these things, and as much as I sincerely wish that I could pay my debt, it is nevertheless impossible. Therefore I beg you, that you would look with grace on my distress, my prayers and my tears, and allow these old debts to be deferred. In the future I shall strive to improve myself, and will offer to pay the yearly interest. Have compassion on your miserable, but honest, servant,*

–Adamsson"

In response to this petition, Adamsson only received a renewed threat to seize his assets and send him to prison if he failed to pay the entire sum immediately. What was he going to do now?

Well, he tried once again, with the *greatest* humility, to write another request that LORD JUSTUS might reduce the principal in some way, just as much as would allow him to pay.

"Is it your will to altogether ruin me and cast away your servant?" he wrote. "Oh, master, I stand before you and promise that I will, with faithfulness and diligence through your grace, work and strive to make right the wrongs I have done. And I beg you, that you, in your mercy, would reduce or remit that which I cannot pay."

But to his horror he received an even harsher answer than before. Now there simply was no way out of this, other than to pay. He tried in vain, partially through work, partially through loans to come up with the requested sum. His property was sold, and he and his wife and children were thrown in the prison SINAI. Oh, to hear their cries of distress! It was here that they would sit like this, until everything was paid. And how could any payment ever be made when they sat there with chains bound fast on their wrists, and without any means of earning a single crumb? But that was hardly the extent of their sorrows, for it was in that prison that KIND-HEARTED would die.

That poor father who sat there, bound hand and foot, was in utter despair. His suffering was only worsened by the fact that in this prison his wife bore two twins, HATEFUL and BITTER, seemingly to take the place of their lost child. At the same time, a strict order was issued from LORD JUSTUS, that he would pay his debt or else risk being thrown into an eternal prison, GEHENNA.[59] Oh, that poor man! He begged that someone would remove his chains, but no one did. And now he realized that he had no other way out, but would face an eternity of imprisonment.

"Oh," this poor prisoner thought, "if only I could bring MOTHER SIMPLE here as an advocate! She is on good terms with LORD JUSTUS, and I am sure that she would be able to give me advice."

"Wouldn't it be far better," answered his wife, "to call for Pastor Shepherd-for-Hire, instead? He is certainly a good helper, and surely he knows Lord Justus better than Mother Simple does."

"Do not speak like that," retorted Adamsson, through his tears. "Shepherd-for-Hire has misled me long enough. He has preached peace where no peace was to be found, and by this he has lulled me and others into the false belief that everything was fine. Oh, that I had just listened to Mother Simple earlier! Then I would not now be sitting in this prison. But perhaps even now she has some advice, if only I could bring her here."

"Well," sighed his wife, "that would certainly be good. But we have offended that little old woman to such an extent, that she can't possibly ever want to see us again." And so they sank back into their despair.

Poor Adamsson! He had never experienced distress like this. He had certainly read and heard much talk about Sinai, but never had he been able to imagine that it could be as bad as what he now experienced. All of the great spiritual knowledge that he had absorbed from his reading, was of no use. In this prison, he met many companions for his misery, and every one of them was just as in need of advice. The cells echoed with their lamentations. Every day, new prisoners arrived.

"Oh, how is all of this going to end?" he asked his wife, time and again. "Sometimes I feel that I am altogether broken-hearted; sometimes I feel as hardened as these stone walls. How will it end?"

"Yes. That I don't know," answered his wife. "This is certainly going to be the end of us."

And so their gaze of despair fell to rest upon the cold, hard floor.

FOURTH CHAPTER

Liberation

In the meantime, Mother Simple had received word as to how grave the matter had become concerning Adamsson and his family. Setting out at once, she found them in their desperate situation in prison.

"Oh, how are you all getting along here?" she asked.

"Well, as you can see, it really could not be worse," was the answer.

"Well, then – how long are you intending to remain here?"

"Remain here?"

"Well, precisely. For you must be aware that you could leave; I know that much about Lord Justus."

"No, no. My dear old girl – how could that ever be?" sighed Mr. Adamsson, while tears of despair streamed profusely down his cheeks.

"Well," replied the little old woman, "all that the Gracious Squire would need to do would be to simply submit a plea to Lord Justus, that he – out of his own free grace and mercy – might cancel the entire sum of the debt."

"Oh, you must not address me as 'Gracious Squire' any longer! I am a poor, lost prisoner. I have offended both Lord Justus, as well as you, yourself. My debt, he cannot possibly cancel. Early on, I asked him to defer payment on the principal and allow me to pay the interest. But even that he refused to do, and he continued issuing his dreadful threats. Then I asked him simply to decrease the debt only a little, but that prompted him to have me sent here, saying that I needed to pay everything immediately. And now, you suggest that I should go and request to be liberated from the *entire* debt – Oh! What could he possibly say to that? No, be serious, now. Tell me what I should do."

"Hmm, hmm! I see that the Squire is now in such a state of mind, that it is going to be very difficult to accomplish anything at all."

"Yes, but otherwise I will be forced to remain in prison forever!"

"Oh, no. Follow my advice, and the Squire will be set free for eternity."

"Oh, you have no idea the degree to which LORD JUSTUS despises me for my misconduct toward him."

"No. He loves the Squire."

"How is that possible? How could he love me?"

"Well – because he does. LORD JUSTUS is love itself, and love cannot help but love. It is for this reason that his son, IMMANUEL, has been sent to save the Squire."

"Love me? – me? What? I have never, never had any affection for him."

"But how would this prevent *him* from loving the Squire?!"

"Yes, if only he would, despite it all! Then I will do as you say. Oh, if only his grace now was as limitless as I have often heard you claim – though it used to annoy me so. If that were the case, then even I would have some hope for salvation."

"Do try," said Mother Simple, with a knowing smile. "Of this I am certain, ever since the moment Immanuel revealed to me the nature of his father's heart."

"My goodness, how happy and content you seem," sighed Adamsson. "But you have no idea how things are for me. If you did know, you would be in tears."

After this, Mother Simple excused herself, promising to return another day.

Now Adamsson, with much trepidation, made ready to write to Lord Justus by way of a man named Doubt, who had offered his services. But when Mother Simple returned, she found the squire in the same miserable condition.

"Now all hope is lost!" he exclaimed. "I have done just as you told me to do, but have been denied again."

"How did the Squire go about it?"

"Well, I sent my greeting to Lord Justus, carried by Doubt – you must know him, right? He is a very humble gentleman. Anyone can see that about him. He always hesitates in his speech and trembles in his boots. He never crosses the threshold, never presumes to just walk up and present himself. It was with him that I sent my message, that *if* Lord Justus would cancel my debt and liberate me, *then I would* forever be his humblest and most obedient servant."

"Well, well. Then it is no wonder that the Squire was denied."

"But, I did as you told me I should do!"

"No, the Squire did no such thing; I never told the Squire to propose some kind of an exchange, for Lord Justus is not in the practice of selling his grace – not for old services done in the past, nor for *promises* of Good Deeds to be produced in the future. And I certainly did not tell the Squire to send Mr.

Doubt. He is a lousy messenger. And particularly since Lord Justus has such a low opinion of him. Doubt once stated that Justus cannot really be taken at his word; and there are few things that displease him as much as shameful slander like this. Instead the Squire should send Bankrupt Faith, the husband of Mother Prodigal, and he can make a request for pure grace and mercy. Bankrupt Faith always receives what he requests. Whenever he knocks, the door is opened for him at once."

"Oh," sighed Adamsson, "Bankrupt Faith – well, if anyone was deserving of the nickname 'bankrupt' then it is surely poor old Faith. I have never known him, but I have heard people speak of him. Do you really believe I should send him? People have said that he is a bit presumptuous. He has been known to shake the hand of Lord Justus and even look him straight in the eyes. And that is going too far, you know? But – perhaps people are lying about him. I will do as you say."

Despite all this misery, Mother Simple could not keep from smiling when she heard these words. Instead of giving an answer, she read to Adamsson from the tale of the prodigal son. When she came to the line where the father "had compassion, and ran and fell on his neck and kissed him"[60] she pressed her index finger under every word and read the verse five times through. Upon the fifth reading, Bankrupt Faith peered in through the door of the cell, and Adamsson's heart was jolted by a beam of hope. When the errand had been explained to Faith, he began at once to prepare himself to set off on the assignment. Countless times before he had visited Lord Justus, and for this reason he knew the road quite well.

The little old woman dismissed herself and Bankrupt Faith set off. It was very dark. While on the way, he stumbled upon Doubt, who in his rage attacked Faith. For a time it looked as though Faith would yield, but at last he gained the upper hand. Nevertheless, for a long time afterward he walked along, shaking in his boots. Then he remembered a song, from which he had often found strength, and he began to sing!

Rock of Ages, cleft for me, let me hide myself in Thee…

His courage restored, he continued and hastened on his way through the deep darkness.

After a while the sun began to rise, signaling that the dire situation had passed.

With dread, Adamsson awaited his response. Even so, he did not have to wait long. It was IMMANUEL himself who came and liberated him from his shackles, assuring him that his debt had been forgotten and it would never again be demanded from him. Upon this, he began transporting Adamsson along a newly paved road called NEW BIRTH, through the so-called NARROW GATE,[61] and up on into the city EVANGELIUM.

This city, which has already been mentioned in this tale (and the history and constitution of which will expanded upon later), was built on the top and slopes of a mountain called GOLGOTHA.[62] There were just two sections to this city, which together were encircled by a thick and sturdy wall, which was well equipped with a corps of watchmen, especially at the gates. This was essential, for on all sides this city was surrounded by enemies, who plotted to bring about its destruction and its inhabitants to ruin. Foremost among these enemies was a mighty prince named BEELZEBUL, who was the arch-nemesis of IMMANUEL. This prince continuously encircled IMMANUEL's city with his hoards, lying in wait for the opportunity rush in and carry out his designs, in which he would dethrone IMMANUEL, wipe out his kingdom and assume governance of the city. He simply could not tolerate the fact that this free city had sprung up and managed to thrive under IMMANUEL's sceptre, right in the midst of his own territory. But all of BEELZEBUL's attempts had been in vain. IMMANUEL knew well how to defend his territory, so that his subjects, despite being threatened from every direction, could nevertheless live in peace. Yet it happened with some regularity that BEELZEBUL, due to the drowsiness of the watchmen, managed to find ways to convince one or another of the residents to leave EVANGELIUM. To do this, he employed every conceivable means, such as deception, enticement, persuasion, threats and so on. In particular he was quite savvy in taking advantage of the quarrels that could often arise among the residents – especially when these quarrels took place among the watchmen. For in these cases he could always be certain of carrying off his spoils. For this reason, IMMANUEL was diligent in his warnings to the residents, the watchmen in particular, to remain vigilant and on their guard against these threats. And as long as they obeyed this admonition, they would remain in safety. But, as mentioned, there were many people who failed to heed this warning and thereby fell victim to BEELZEBUL's plots, and often, oddly enough, without them even having the slightest idea that this had happened. For it was part of this shrewd enemy's strategy that, as soon as he had by one way or another lured someone out of the city, he allowed this person to walk about, idle and free, such that he could not sense any mischief or notice into whose clutches he had fallen, while at the same time he was being used in myriad ways to assail and harass the others.

In the meantime, the city of EVANGELIUM remained safe and secure, and even had been expanded and prospered under IMMANUEL's wise governance, like a blossoming sapling in the desert.[63] Right in the middle of this city there flowed a great and deep river, named RIVER OF BLOOD, which had its origin in HOLINESS, and also lapped at the foot of the mountain of GOLGOTHA. Its shores were garlanded by leafy palms with ample shade, and under these branches one could often see residents from the city gathering together in crowds of varying sizes, particularly at morning and evening, to join in resounding songs of praise to honor their King and Lord Protector IMMANUEL and JUSTUS ALL-POWERFUL.

It was to this fair city that Adamsson was brought by IMMANUEL, and it was here that he received a dwelling place assigned to him in one part of the city, a district which had an inscription over its gate that read: *Room for the Lost.* This district contained three subdivisions, namely an infirmary, dwelling rooms and a banquet hall for the inhabitants of the city, who all lived there at IMMANUEL's expense and patronage. At the entrance, Adamsson had asked IMMANUEL what this district was called, and received the answer that it was called THE FORGIVENESS OF SINS.

"Here is where you may live," added IMMANUEL, "*as long as you need;* and here you will be lacking for nothing that you need for your well-being."

"But," Adamsson chimed in, "you must remain here, too, of course, for otherwise, how can I really thrive here?"

"I do live in this city, although I often spend my time in a hidden room, which keeps me out of sight," answered IMMANUEL. "The residents here must diligently train themselves in the art of believing without seeing. Keep that in mind."

"Why, everything will be fine – that is, as long as you do not venture off."

"No, no. Rest assured that I will remain here with you all."[64]

"Well, can we count on you for that, then?"

"You of little faith,[65] I am with you every day, I have called you by name: you are mine,[66] and hereafter you will no longer be called Adamsson, but instead ABRAHAMSSON."[67]

With these words, they both crossed the threshold. And just think of the joy upon meeting MOTHER SIMPLE and MOTHER WOUNDED-HIP with her sisters! They were sitting there just then, feasting on GOD's LOVE at a richly set table, which they called THE BIBLE.[68] Now our former Squire and his wife were mighty glad to sit down and join their company and share this meal. And neither did these dear little old women restrain themselves as they wished our gentlefolk welcome. At the side of Mother Simple limped Mother Wounded-Hip, followed by the other two, to greet their friends and newcomers and embrace them; and their mutual joy found voice in moving songs of praise in honor of Immanuel. It was a moment that one might be able to experience, but which is impossible to describe. Abrahamsson felt as though he were a brother to these women. For now, he was their equal in poverty.

"Who would ever have believed," said Mother Wounded-Hip afterward, "that even the Squire himself would come here!"

"Well, I for one have believed that for many years," Mother Simple chimed in. "And now it has come to be so. May he always remain here in peace."

When Abrahamsson went to bed that first evening, he felt such an indescribable bliss, that he could not fall asleep until well into the night.

"What a wretched fool," he said to himself, "what a wretched fool I was, not to have understood this earlier. Oh, if only all of my friends would also decide to come here! First thing in the morning, I am going to write to them. There is no way that they would not come, once they hear how things really are here."

And so he reveled in this hope.

* * *

But in the city The World and on the estate of Industriousness a tremendous commotion had arisen when the squire had been taken into custody.

Mr. Admirer was completely beside himself. His wife had arranged a coffee hour, where everyone could have the opportunity to express their sympathy for this family that they had previously esteemed so highly. Everyone was able to tell some splendid story, some extraordinary aspect of the former lives of their dear squire and his wife. One person pointed out his generosity and self-sacrifice, another pointed out his uncommon zeal for everyone's spiritual and physical well-being, and yet another praised the institutions she had established, and this went on and on.

"And now all of this has regrettably come to an end!" burst out Mrs. Admirer, amidst her heavy sobbing, while the faces of all the others bore the mark of a deep sorrow and distress.

Never had there been such a display of sorrow there on the grounds of Self-Activity. Pastor Shepherd-for-Hire led a moment for devotions, which made a deep impression. Dismayed, they parted ways, and Mrs. Sensible felt that the one lesson that everyone could take away from this sorrowful event was to learn how essential it is to be cautious about taking things to extremes and to remain moderate in everything.

"If Adamsson," she added, "had remained in the city of The World, then he would have certainly still been doing just fine. But he wanted to be better than others. That is why he moved out of the city. For a while he was even able to shine like a star out on his estate, admired by all, but like a star that is on the verge of burning out. Now everyone can see the consequence of such striving; for a while this light can be dazzling, but in the end it will expire."

And all the ladies from The World agreed that Mrs. Sensible was correct in her assessment. Though Mrs. Admirer thought that it was somewhat one-sided.

It was in this way that Abrahamsson lost his former friends. Others defamed him and his reputation. His name was no longer printed in a large font in the reports of the mission society. He would not be re-elected to the board, and the following year he was excluded from the society, like someone who had fallen away.

During the initial part of his stay in EVANGELIUM, Abrahamsson managed to not be affected by all these darts that had been thrown his way. In his heart there was no room for worrying, for IMMANUEL remained within his sight all day long in one way or another. Abrahamsson took delight in his time there, unlike at any point in his previous life. And when IMMANUEL one day had spoken particularly loving and graceful words to him and his wife, they were both brought to their knees and exclaimed that they were unworthy of all this grace, unworthy to serve him. But yet they begged that, if it were possible, they should like to be allowed to go and perform some service for him on account of his mercy. This request was granted to them gladly, and so they were directed to the other side of the city, which was called SANCTIFICATION, and over the gate to which is inscribed the words *"Workshop for the Redeemed."* This district was made up exclusively of work stations and workshops. Unlike in THE FORGIVENESS OF SINS, in this district there were no sleeping quarters or dwelling places, and neither were there any meals served there. It was also in this part of town that MOTHER WOUNDED-HIP held the meetings for her work society. Mrs. Abrahamsson was now more than pleased to be able to be a part of this society, and her husband became a member in another mission society, comprised of several poor brothers.

FIFTH CHAPTER

The Gentlemen Bold, Dead-Sure and Self-Wise

Abrahamsson had, through his move to Evangelium, entered into a new era in his life. The past lay behind him, as though a dream. It was only now that he understood what he had previously never wanted to believe, that life outside of Evangelium, however nice it might be, is nevertheless an unhappy and sinful life without peace. He now found himself in that very city which he had always looked upon with suspicion, and about which he had always said terrible things. And yet, how entirely different everything had proven to be, compared with what he had expected! He had thought that Evangelium was a city where people went around trying to hide their spiritual laziness and incompetence by acting spiritual and using godly speech. He had expected that this would be a place where all joy and peace was banished, and that it was a city where people were forced to go around with hanging head and gloomy countenance, pressed down by an insufferable compulsion. And when he had heard Mother Simple say that people there lived completely at Immanuel's expense, he had always thought that this was a means of cushioning the burden.

"In truth," he had once said to Mr. Admirer, "the life people lead in Evangelium is a rather cushy life for slackers and ne'er-do-wells, and for this reason it is not surprising that all the broken-down and rejected wretches move there."

Now, when he looked back at his former life, what did he see? Nothing other than a life without peace, full of hardship.

What he previously regarded as happiness, joy and peace, he now saw as only unhappiness, sorrow and worry. Conversely, Evangelium now struck him as a true paradise, full of peace and joy. A remarkable thing, too, was his response to Mother Simple when she asked how he was doing nowadays.

"Oh," he said, "it would have been so great, if I had long ago been willing to understand how much happier it is to be poor in Evangelium than rich in The World!"

Another time, when he met her, he said, thinking of his relatives and friends in The World:

"There is plenty of room for them all here, and there is a joy that would cause their current joy to seem like mere sorrow. Here there is a happiness that exceeds anything that they might imagine, and anything that a human being can describe! But there they walk around, just as I did, in blindness, and suppose that they are happy enough. They do not know what kind of miserable life they are leading, and what a terrible end they will meet. Instead they feel pity for me, who has now finally been able to be rid of all the things that truly ought to be pitied."

Understandably enough, his experience in Evangelium had caused him to be filled with a burning love and desire to try to convince all of his friends – and yes, if possible everyone in The World – to move to Evangelium. Concerning this idea, he often asked the advice of Mother Simple and requested grace and wisdom from Immanuel. Time and again he wrote to his former friends, particularly to Mr. Admirer. With a burning zeal he encouraged them in his letters to reflect on these things, while there still was time. To this end, he described his own happiness and joy, as well as encouraged them to hurry up, so that they could come and take part in all of this.

"I feel," he wrote, "a peace that surpasses all understanding.[69] All my debts have been remitted, my sins and my previous life forgiven and forgotten. Immanuel has said to me that they will never more be considered, and that Justus All-Powerful has cancelled all of my promissory notes. What is more, he has assured me that he himself will sustain me with eternal grace, so that I will be lacking for nothing."

But his friends wrote back and said that despite the respect that they had for him, they nevertheless had no wish to follow him into his folly. Pastor Shepherd-for-Hire in particular wrote and expressed his pity for him.

"I have," he wrote, "over the many years that I have studied and worked as a priest, seen and learned various things. This gives me the authority to evaluate spiritual phenomena. And I can honestly say that I have never been as troubled about anything as I am about the errant path the Squire has taken, and to which he, to the astonishment of everyone, has allowed himself to become enthralled. I am certainly able to remain tolerant and calm when people swear, dance, gamble, drink and so on. But when I hear that someone has moved to Evangelium, then I am consumed by a fervent concern for the house of God."[70]

In the meantime, Abrahamsson had found real joy. And all the residents of Evangelium rejoiced with him, particularly Mother Simple. Still, he remained quite inexperienced. As much as he believed that he had truly come to know both himself and Evangelium, all the same there was much that he lacked in this regard. Yet everything was certainly well and good, as long as he simply lived on grace. Mother Simple also thought about it in this way: "Well now, Immanuel will take care of him. He is faithful. He has promised: 'neither shall anyone snatch them out of my hand.'"[71]

And because of this, she was at peace.

So the years passed by. Then Abrahamsson began to demonstrate several habits that caused Mother Simple concern. He continued to be a daily guest in The Forgiveness of Sins, of course, and was also diligent in spending time in

SANCTIFICATION. But it appeared that the *initial way that he had regarded his own humble station was on the verge of disappearing.* He had developed an air of authority and capability about him, or so MOTHER SIMPLE thought. Besides she had seen him a couple of times in the company of two gentlemen, BOLD and DEAD-SURE. And this troubled her. She was particularly saddened one time when she met him. She was not even able to speak a word. But the tear that ran down her cheek did not escape his notice. Yet, he said nothing about this. When they had parted company, he began to wonder.

"What could have come over that dear little old woman?" he asked himself. "She is always so cordial toward me and it hurts me that she would cry like that. It may be that she shed that tear for me, due to what I said. It is strange that she would not share in my joy, as she did before."

With thoughts like these he wandered on. But he did not have time to make it far, before he began to become all the more uneasy. He thus turned around in order to seek out MOTHER SIMPLE. After a little searching, he found her. She was on her way back from meeting with IMMANUEL. She had sought council with him on a few small matters of her own, as well as conversed with him about Abrahamsson, whom she beheld with a particular love and whose well-being was dear to her heart.

Immediately Abrahamsson began by asking her why she had been crying when they had last parted company, and why she wasn't instead rejoicing with him, and so on.

"Oh – well," she answered, "I am extremely happy that the Squire is here. I have coincidentally just now been with IMMANUEL in order to ask him to keep a watchful eye on the Squire, so that the Squire might not be allowed to wander any further off!"

"Me, wander off?" exclaimed Abrahamsson. "Why, and how,

would I do that? Oh, no. Oh, no! That would *never* happen. Never!"

"Well," answered MOTHER SIMPLE, "now the Squire knows the reason for my tears. The Squire has been rejoicing over his blessed condition. In that there is nothing wrong. However, I am reminded of the words of Old David, which sound like this:

Rejoice with trembling![72]

The Squire is by his nature an industrious, strong and enterprising man. These gifts have the potential to bring countless advantages and blessings for both the Squire and others. But I wish to warn the Squire, from the bottom of my heart, to no longer keep company with Mr. BOLD and Mr. DEAD-SURE, who have at various times, including today, been to visit the Squire."

Abrahamsson stood there, completely bewildered.

"What do you mean?" he asked. "I have never spoken with them. The men who came to visit me were named CONFIDENT and STRAIGHT-FORWARD, two dear gentlemen from THEOLOGY, who have been very helpful to me. Along with them, there also came a certain Mr. ENLIGHTENED, who had a particularly deep insight and experience in spiritual matters."

"Oh, be careful. Be careful," burst out MOTHER SIMPLE, "those are not their names! When they lived in EVANGELIUM, they did go by those names. But ever since they moved out of the city, their names are now BOLD and DEAD-SURE, although they would like people to still use their old names. And that Mr. ENLIGHTENED you mentioned is now called SELF-WISE, and he has caused a great deal of problems here. I can certainly imagine that they would like to have the Squire join them out there. But take caution!"

Completely bewildered, Abrahamsson departed from her. She had never acted this strangely before. And when he compared what she had just said with her earlier sentiments, she became altogether a mystery for him.

"What is this supposed to mean?" he said to himself. "She has of course spoken with such high esteem about Professor Conscientious in Theology and now she seemed so dismissive of that whole community. What is more, one time she expressed a wish that Schoolmaster Faithful would become a theologian. And now she gives me this warning, as though that were something dangerous! She is an odd person. Can Mother Simple really be this self-contradictory? Just think – I would never have believed this! Yet, I still want to believe the best. The little old woman is narrow-minded, that's just how things are. And one can of course expect nothing less."

While he walked along with his mind filled with these musings, he came across a friend, with whom he shared everything. This friend immediately understood what was the matter.

"Do not be surprised by this," he answered. "Mother Simple once got into an argument with Enlightened and his friends. Ever since then, she has not been able to deal with them very well, and instead warns people for them, as though they were dangerous people."

"That I would have never believed about Mother Simple," answered Abrahamsson, "but do tell me what this conflict was about."

"Well," this friend answered, "she had been spreading rather dangerous teachings among many of the residents here in the city, and Enlightened began to energetically speak out against her. She had said, namely, that it was not so dangerous to be lazy and indifferent about working, since after all, one was supposed to live on grace alone and not on one's own work."

"Well, shouldn't one live on grace, though?" asked Abrahamsson earnestly.

"Why, certainly, that is clear. Of course. But one should also be diligent and faithful in one's work."

"Then, has Mother Simple denied that?"

"Yes, that is exactly what is so dangerous, that she is spreading the sort of teachings that lead people to laziness. This was what Enlightened found objectionable. And that is not all. Since she herself is weak in her faith, she therefore wants others to be like her. She was of the opinion that it would be dangerous to be strong in faith and straight-forward. Besides, when she expressed this opinion that it was not so important to faithfully use the grace that Immanuel offered to everyone, it was then that she encountered the opposition of Confident and Straight-Forward. It was for this reason that she began using those nicknames, just like how she usually refers to Enlightened as Self-Wise."

"This is regrettable news," answered Abrahamsson, who now began to lose a great deal of the trust which he had for Mother Simple. He had always before taken a certain joy in her fellowship. She had, in his inexperience, served as a faithful teacher and had provided him with counsel, enlightenment, assurance, warnings and admonitions when she had deemed them necessary. Because of all this, the situation in which he now found himself was all the more painful, and he saw it as his duty to speak with Mother Simple in order to get to the bottom of this, as well as to find out how she was doing. Therefore he made his way to where she lived, but came across another acquaintance on the way, who asked where he was headed.

"To Mother Simple's," was the answer.

"Oh, you should really come with me to a devotional talk instead!"

Abrahamsson hesitated a moment. But soon he decided that as good as it would be to go and hear God's Word, it was nevertheless more urgent that he try to shed this ill-feeling and suspicion that he had begun to feel in his heart for Mother Simple. And so he continued on his way. Upon arrival, he asked her about everything openly.

That he would do so did not surprise her. "For," she said, "this is not the first time that I have been the object of such accusations. It will likely not be the last time, either."

"Well then, what are you thinking?"

"Me? The Squire certainly ought to know. I am thinking: Immanuel, *my all in all!*"

"Well, don't you think that Enlightened is thinking the same thing?"

"Oh, if only he would! But whenever he speaks of Immanuel, he always adds *'however'* afterward, as if his name was 'Our Gracious Lord Immanuel...*however'* and not just Immanuel. When Lord Justus says that his promises through Immanuel will stand *'forever and ever,'* then Self-Wise – for that is his name – says instead *'forever...however.'* But this is not acceptable. No, not for one minute."

"Dear mother," continued Abrahamsson, "I really don't understand what you are saying anymore."

"Well, you are welcome to have a seat here for a while, since I am happy to explain myself!"

Abrahamsson sat himself down, with his heart more at ease. Mother Simple continued:

"As the Squire knows, my husband was a cotter and served the Squire's father. We both served him with our whole hearts. And ever since, I have been referred to as 'the little old cotter-woman,' as the Squire knows me. Although people have now begun calling me 'that poor thing,' ever since I have become happier than everyone who calls me that. Since the time my husband was called away to HOLINESS for his day of reckoning, I began to consider moving to SELF-RIGHTEOUSNESS in order to serve LORD JUSTUS. But soon I found that I was too old and feeble to endure that type of slavery to the law. I would have been lost to my misery, if PASTOR EVANGELIST,[73] a preacher from EVANGELIUM, had not enlightened me about IMMANUEL's mercy and the peace of EVANGELIUM. That is why I moved here. Since then I have lived here on grace. During this time I have learned what people otherwise are not inclined to learn, namely that EVANGELIUM is a not a city like others, where one lives on the work of one's hands. Here one constantly lives solely on grace and at the expense and responsibility of IMMANUEL. And if it had not been so, I would have left long ago."

"But dear mother," interrupted Abrahamsson, "no one has denied, of course, that here one lives on grace alone."

"No, that is true," replied MOTHER SIMPLE, "no one says that in so many words. But there are many people who in their hearts have difficulty accepting this. Such is the case with SELF-WISE. He possesses something that he sometimes calls PHILOSOPHY, sometimes LOGIC. I do not know what it is made of. I once caught a quick glimpse of it in his workshop, which appeared to be quite a mess. It was full of very sharp tools, which he called 'subtle points.' I do not know how he performs his craft with these, as I am an uneducated woman. But this much I know, that with these tools he seduces people and brings them to their ruin."

"Well, dear mother," said Abrahamsson, "through using LOGIC, people learn how to think correctly."

"Yes, correctly according to *our* understanding, I would believe," interrupted MOTHER SIMPLE, "but IMMANUEL has his own way of thinking.[74] And if we are not going try to think like he does, then I would imagine that he wouldn't bother changing the way he thinks, just to align with SELF-WISE and the craft he practices."

Abrahamsson smiled at the dear little old woman's simplicity.

"However," he added, "it is odd that you say that there are many people who cannot accept the idea of living on grace alone. I, for one, have invested all of my happiness in this."

"Yes," answered the little old woman, "the Squire may think so now. But the Squire has not experienced much of this yet, and still knows himself quite poorly. So far, the Squire has been living in the initial joy of the honeymoon stage. Soon dark days will come, when the Squire will learn what he now does not believe to be the case. I was almost on the verge of perishing when I first started school here, and was supposed to learn how peculiar IMMANUEL was. It was the single most difficult lesson, as simple as it may sound for the Squire now. I had to repeat my lessons over and over, and was constantly worried that I would be expelled from the school on account of my ineptitude. And there were many who, on account of this lesson, not only left the school, but the city as well. But I wanted to finish what I had started."

"But first, tell me one thing," interrupted Abrahamsson. "Hasn't ENLIGHTENED attended this school?"

"Sort of," answered the little old woman. "He began attending, but when he had difficulty understanding the headmaster, whose name is FATHER EXPERIENCE, then he left for the great school in THEOLOGY. There he learned everything he knows from books. When he would later ask me and the others what the headmaster was teaching us, it seemed from his comments that, though he himself was rather familiar with all these secrets, it was just a dead knowledge in his head, which he had spoiled with that LOGIC of his. And he claimed that FATHER EXPERIENCE would never understand his LOGIC."

"Alright. But can it be certain that EXPERIENCE is right about everything?"

"Well Squire, more or less. Although this is how things are: FATHER EXPERIENCE is not the actual headmaster, but instead simply serves as his assistant."

"What is the name of the actual headmaster, then?"

"His name is THE SPIRIT OF TRUTH, and he is the author of the great book called GOD'S WORD, which is lying over there on the table. All FATHER EXPERIENCE does is to assist simple people in truly understanding it. When his teaching is understood in this way, then it is indeed correct."

"But," said Abrahamsson, "let us get back to what you said about living on grace alone."

"Well, now, the situation is like this: there is no one in this city who does not admit that he has been brought here by IMMANUEL's grace and mercy, instead of by his own actions. But with each and every person, in particular those who have not attended EXPERIENCE's classes very long, there seems to develop this kind of anxious mindset, in which one feels the need to contribute to one's own sustenance. For just as people *have come here* by grace alone, it is nonetheless difficult to *continue to live here* on grace alone, without trying to add one's own work into the mix. I have many times received stern correction at the hand of EXPERIENCE because I have had a difficult time learning this and have often resisted it. Yes, there are many people who, through long periods of bitter humiliation, have given up the thought of *being anything here and now,* but still dream of *being something in the future.* That is where they invest their hope. To depend on grace, live on grace, and dwell in and have one's existence in grace – pure and free and undeserved grace – in the long run that is no easy task, I'll have the Squire believe."

At this, Abrahamsson began to become uneasy. He had not expected to hear anything along these lines. It made him sad that dear MOTHER SIMPLE would espouse such dangerous views. He thus interrupted her again with this question:

"Dear mother, aren't you going a little too far, now?"

"No," she answered, "but I am well aware that many say that I am stubborn, one-sided and so on, because I think like this."

"Yes, but if one were to follow your advice, then one would certainly become lazy and indifferent and forget to work?"

"Well, that is exactly what MR. SELF-WISE says. I should think that he is viewing things through his LOGIC, of course."

"But you certainly have to concede," continued Abrahamsson, "that EVANGELIUM is not a city for laziness and inertia, but that here one must be diligent and work in SANCTIFICATION."

"Didn't I tell the Squire that he still does not really have a good sense of how things work here in EVANGELIUM?!"

"You are making me extremely uneasy with your talk, dear old girl. As enlightened and wise and experienced as you otherwise are, yet you strike me in this regard as somewhat of an extremist. I, for my part, thought that ENLIGHTENED had it absolutely right when he said that in order to come to EVANGELIUM nothing is required of us; but if we are to *remain,* then it is necessary for us to become co-workers with IMMANUEL in order to provide for our sustenance here. Otherwise it would be vain and false to take pride in his grace."

"All of this I knew before, but thanks to IMMANUEL, who has faithfully kept me in the school with FATHER EXPERIENCE, I have been able to learn something else!"

"In that case, what has he taught you, then?"

"Well, he has taught me two things in particular: the first is that the constitution of this city reads that *everything shall be by grace, that* IMMANUEL *might be our all in all and our only boast,* and the second being, *that* IMMANUEL *is such a man that he does not need any help from us.*"

"But nobody has denied this, of course."

"No, in our words we are all in agreement. But when it comes to putting this into practice in our lives, then there are indeed people who deny this."

"This is not possible. You must be misunderstanding them."

"Oh, no. Not at all!"

"But you must be. ENLIGHTENED shared this exact same sentiment with me, and had just just one essential qualification, that one also needed to strive and work if one wanted to be able to remain here in the long run. For, he said, coming here is free; but one may not just exist here for nothing. And I think this is correct."

"Yes, it is precisely with his unnecessary qualifications that he tears apart the foundation. That was what dear Old David once said about him."

"But, one must work and be diligent, right? You yourself are quite industrious."

"MR. MUST has never held citizenship in this city. For if he had, he would have long ago driven out both myself and MOTHER WOUNDED-HIP. Yes, MOTHER PRODIGAL and MOTHER PENNILESS would have probably also have been forced to follow us out. We are four of a kind."

"You are becoming all the more of a riddle to me, dear mother. I do not understand what you are getting at with all this talk."

"I am not surprised by this. FATHER EXPERIENCE would be able to teach you about it — if only the Squire would attend his school for a while. He knows all about this art, and if the Squire would just come to THE CLASS OF THE WRETCHED, then the Squire will be able to see this."

"What kind of a class is that?"

"Well, it is the class that meets behind that door that has the sign over it that reads: *Sold in Sin.* On the inside Old Paulus has written:

For what I am doing, I do not understand.
For what I will to do, that I do not practice;
but what I hate, that I do.[75]

Just ask SCHOOLMASTER FAITHFUL, who has sat there this whole term! I have sat there many times, and have certainly not sat there for the last time yet."

Abrahamsson gave a shudder, for he sensed something, but he could not put his finger on it. He could conclude that the little old woman was confident of what she was saying, of course, from the simplicity and certainty with which she spoke. At the same time, he felt a deep need to go to IMMANUEL and pour out his heart to him. For that was the remarkable thing about the residents of EVANGELIUM, that they always shared their joys as well as their worries together with IMMANUEL. Despite their various differences, they were yet alike in this one regard, that they could not do without IMMANUEL. They had a daily need to submit their prayers and supplications to him. To be specific, this was something that was always part of their new childlike mindset and was inseparable from it. Those who grew indifferent in this regard, would become fed up with the city and eventually move away, if they did not first encounter some difficult situation that forced them back to IMMANUEL.

Now Abrahamsson did not know what he should do. On the one hand, he needed to go to IMMANUEL, on the other hand, the little old woman's speech had so captivated him that he had a difficult time parting company with her. There was still so much that he wanted to hear and learn, so much that he wanted to ask. He had now begun to glimpse some of the riches that this dear little old woman possessed. But as soon as MOTHER SIMPLE noticed the conflict that was going on within him, she immediately stopped speaking.

"No – continue, continue!" exclaimed Abrahamsson. "I can go to IMMANUEL any time. But who knows the next time when I will be able to listen to you speak like this, in such peace."

"Dear Squire," answered the little old woman, "I would be guilty of a great wrong, if I said one more word that might keep the Squire from visiting IMMANUEL, when his heart was in need of it. The Squire will always learn more in a moment of personal prayer with him, than the Squire could ever learn from a long conversation with me or anyone else. For the Squire can be certain, and consider it an axiom, that even the most marvelous sermon could be a tremendous detriment to the Squire, if by this he were hindered from such an encounter when he was in need of it. For everything that might come in-between, whatever it might be, would only serve to make his heart sluggish and listless. Therefore, farewell for now! If IMMANUEL wills it, then we may meet again and continue. If not, then let his will be done! It will never cause the Squire harm. His will is better than our good intentions."

At this Abrahamsson departed, and what he shared in his conversation with IMMANUEL, the faithful soul will know better than can be described here. Calm and peace came over his soul when he left IMMANUEL, and he was glad that he had not stayed any longer with MOTHER SIMPLE. But after this, he began to be wary of BOLD and DEAD-SURE and SELF-WISE. Oh, if only he always retained this fear! Then so much suffering could have been avoided.

SIXTH CHAPTER

Sanctification – Mr. Listless – Mr. Weary

EVANGELIUM was a name that, as sweet as it was to the ears of the residents, was just as obnoxious for everyone else. It was a peculiar city. Anyone who had gotten the chance to take a peek inside and observe everything that went on in there had seen a sight they would not soon forget. The most unusual contradictions appeared there side by side. There was no one there who would not describe themselves as happy. But wherever one looked, one could still find lamenting and whimpering hearts. One person would be weighed down by one thing, the next person by something else. There were even those who felt sometimes as though their hearts were burning up like melted wax. During the day and even into the night, IMMANUEL's house was full of this sort of people, everyone having some kind of misery, some trouble, some sigh to confide with him. And yet, these miserable souls would still assert that they were so happy, that even if presented with all the joy that THE WORLD had to offer, they would not give up a single one of their most sorrowful days.

"We certainly have our share of distress and misery," many would admit. "But, oh, we also have IMMANUEL and THE FORGIVENESS OF SINS, and these things are all we need. We also have our share of days of indescribable happiness. Besides, we hold to the promise that there will come a day when every tear will be dried, and we will stand holy and pure before IMMANUEL's throne, full of praise and joy, without any pain or cause for complaint. We long for this hour."

IMMANUEL was the assurance of every sorrowing heart, and the joy of every jubilant heart. The degree to which they loved him was most evident in the fact that they could not live without him, and that for them there was nothing as terrible as the idea of sinning against him. When it therefore happened, and it often did, that they transgressed in some way, they would be inconsolable until they had confessed everything to him and begged for forgiveness. THE FORGIVENESS OF SINS was the place where they wished to live and spend all their time. It was here that they had made their camp. Here they could fully renew their strength with rich meals, which were offered to anyone who was hungry and tired. In SANCTIFICATION they worked with enthusiasm and joy. And among the most remarkable sights that those observers with attentive eyes would notice was that it was exactly those people who most lamented their weakness and inability, and therefore kept as close to IMMANUEL as possible, who were often the ones who accomplished the most, even if at first glance they appeared to be of no use. On the other hand, one could see others, mostly beginners, who burned with zeal and seriousness, and so they appeared to be quite outstanding. But the work of these beginners often ended up not amounting to anything. The difference lay in the fact that the former had learned more in FATHER EXPERIENCE's class about humility and patience; two things that one needed most of all in order to lead a peaceful and productive life in EVANGELIUM. But everyone had the same thing in common, that they were all still learning. Anyone who considered their education to be complete, or who wanted to become a master, had to leave the city. In these cases, some would move to SELF-RIGHTEOUSNESS, some to THEOLOGY, and some to still other places.

The direction and supervision of the work that was carried out in SANCTIFICATION was entrusted to OLD MRS. LOVE, and who was the daughter of BANKRUPT FAITH. Through the loving way in which she carried herself, her leniency and her tenderness, she held a powerful sway over everyone she worked closely with. And for all who lived in EVANGELIUM, her words and commands were received as a delightful charge, motivating them to give their utmost in service to IMMANUEL. Whenever she requested or invited them to do anything, she always began by pointing out what IMMANUEL had done for them, and seldom did this fail to produce the desired effect. For they deemed it unworthy of themselves to remain inactive, when they had time after time witnessed how IMMANUEL worked for their well-being. In this way, people were encouraged to be diligent and thorough in their work, such that the workshop was always a rich and beautiful spectacle of liveliness and movement. All the work was done according to several patterns that had been sent there by JUSTUS ALL-POWERFUL from HOLINESS, and these were commonly called *"the patterns of perfection."* Everyone was eager to trace them exactly. But, as their understanding of this work was minimal at best, and as they were also still unskilled, they never attained the ideal form despite all their striving. Their work was sometimes imperfect or marred with various flaws. Sometimes dirt found its way into them, such that they were always embarrassed to put them on display. This was a great disappointment to them, which brought much grief. Yes, it even happened that some people by their incompetence altogether destroyed the materials that came into their hands, and therefore were unable to create anything acceptable out of them. On occasion, this caused them to be afraid of losing the king's grace, and even of being driven out of EVANGELIUM. Yet there was consolation to be found, since IMMANUEL would always take the responsibility completely upon himself. That is to say, the madame supervisor would always deliver the work to him first.

Then he would cleanse them in the RIVER OF BLOOD before he sent them on to his father, who with great satisfaction accepted everything that came to him via this channel. But once, when a certain MISS BUSY sent, by way of MOSES, a lovely piece that she had completed, and which she considered so beautiful that it did not need washing, this was immediately returned to her along with the notification that it had rather displeased him. To be sure, this was to her benefit, as it brought her back down to earth so that she could once again live and work on grace. Otherwise she had been toying with the idea lately of moving to SELF-RIGHTEOUSNESS.

Despite the zeal with which many people worked, one had to admit that the products were rather few in proportion to the number of residents. Everyone readily admitted this, as well, that much more could have been accomplished. This was the result of the fact that many people were limited by a peculiarly weak, even sickly, condition, which caused them to be incapable of working. Concerning the cause of this weakness there was much speculation. Many, who had suffered from this longer, began to wonder if this was not a result of the monotonous, soft-textured food which they were regularly served in THE FORGIVENESS OF SINS. What had prompted this speculation was one newspaper in particular that was published in city SELF-RIGHTEOUSNESS.

"How can one expect anything else," the article said, "than that weakness would be the norm in EVANGELIUM, when day in and day out the people live on the bread of grace? This bread is sweet and, without doubt, is rather tasty at first. But eating it does not exactly put marrow in one's bones. Here things are different with us. Here the bakers place small pebbles in the dough, and this is solid fare. That's why we all are so strong and feel so good."

"Who knows?" many people said as they read articles like this one. "Who knows, if they are not right about this? We are constantly lacking something. There must be something wrong with the food."

But MOTHER SIMPLE, who knew a thing or two about medicine, asserted that their food contained the most essential nutrients, and that the weakness that some were experiencing was instead due to the fact that their eating habits had become sporadic and they were not eating proper meals, only occasionally taking a nibble here and there, which caused them to lose their appetite. This was very dangerous, she said, and rather common. In fact, there were many people whose death was speculated to have been a result of malnutrition of that sort. In the case of other people, she determined that the illness developed as a result of the fact that they rested too long after eating prior to resuming work, which she explained could also be rather unhealthy. If nothing else, everyone had to admit that she herself and many in her circle were particularly active, such that most people were embarrassed to be compared with them.

"And they, of course, are living on exactly the same food as everyone else," they would remark.

At first, Abrahamsson was among those most distinguished for zeal and seriousness. It was his desire to work. Everything he did was done quickly and methodically. There were also plenty of people who looked up to him with awe and admiration. Many were encouraged by him, many wished to be able to match his energy. But Mother Simple was worried about him, and wondered where all of this would lead in the end. She was certainly glad about the fact that he worked diligently. But his words had a self-aggrandizing tone to them:

"What I cannot understand is how it can be that some people work so little," he said. "That is not the case with me," he would think in his heart, although he never said it straight out.

Similarly, when others would praise his work and consider him exceptional, he had no problem accepting this. He would consider anyone who gave him these compliments to be a good judge of character, and so on. But if someone had a different opinion, it was indeed difficult for him to like them.

Mother Simple understood all of this, and it caused her much anxiety. Because of her love for him, she could not be content to keep her concerns to herself. And so, one day she went to visit him at his home. On the way, she ran across Mr. Listless, who, along with several other people, had a difficult time putting up with Abrahamsson. With these fellows it had reached the point where they, for their own part, had begun *to be satisfied* with being weak, comforting themselves with the idea that it was not everyone's lot to be strong. For this, they had received a stern, but well-deserved lecture by Abrahamsson, and now their relationship to him had grown cold. Whenever they found anything wrong with him, they did not hesitate to speak about it openly with many other people, but never with Abrahamsson himself, except in those cases when they were really indignant about something. For it could happen that they, in their fury and spitefulness, allowed their feelings to escape their lips. Otherwise, they usually spoke about this quietly and with a vow of secrecy, with one person on one occasion, with someone else on another. This was "not to hurt Abrahamsson," they would say, "but done out of love," so that they could all earnestly and faithfully pray for him. "For," they would say, "he is in a precarious place, and it is urgent that we, on the one hand, speak with Immanuel about him, as well as on the other hand, not express too much confidence in him; for if we did, he might become conceited."

It was just such an errand that had prompted Listless to go looking for Mother Simple, when he suddenly ran into her. He had just come from receiving yet another lecture from Abrahamsson. Since he knew that Mother Simple was a lenient woman, who was not harsh in her judgments, he had decided that he would go and discuss everything with her now, hoping to find assurance and affirmation. When he suddenly found her out walking, he quickly asked her where she was headed.

"To Abrahamsson's!" was her cheerful response.

"What are you going to do there?"

"I want to speak with him."

"About what, then?"

"I really don't have time, nor do I really wish to discuss that now."

"Well," exclaimed Listless, "things have been rather strange with that man lately! Haven't you heard anything about all that? Though, I probably shouldn't be mentioning this. But since I know that he's a close friend of yours, and since you hold considerable influence over him, then you can hear about this – as long as you promise not to share it with anyone else. Well, you see, it happened this morning that…"

"Stop right there!" interrupted Mother Simple with a serious tone. "Have you told all this to Immanuel?"

"No, not yet. But I intend to do that this evening, before bed."

"Have you discussed this with Abrahamsson, then?"

"No, but I'll do that, of course, whenever I get the right chance. He will certainly hear the truth eventually. Of that he can be certain."

"Then in that case, I don't want to hear about it. For now I can see that you are harboring spite and bitterness in your heart. For this reason, I would advise you to search yourself, and find out how things are standing with you, especially since it has been several days since I saw you in either The Forgiveness of Sins or Sanctification. It will never do for you to walk around town idly like this."

At this she left him, without giving him the chance to respond.

Furious, he went along on his way, without a clue as to what he should think. Then on the road he ran into Mr. Weary, who was in a similar mood when it came to Abrahamsson. So he immediately struck up a conversation with him.

"Things are really getting out of hand here in this town," he said. "Can you believe that Mother Simple, who has always been so lovely, can now be so changed? Before, she was always so gentle and ready to console; now she has become stern and quick to make harsh judgments, such that I wonder what Immanuel will say about all this."

"Dear friend, what are you saying?" answered Mr. Weary. "Oh, that poor soul. She has been completely harmed by her association with Abrahamsson. Believe me – a stuck-up personality like that can easily cause weaker people to stumble, if one doesn't have the grace to be on guard against it. It is certainly good that you and I and a few others have eyes to see how things really stand for that fellow. But most people have blinders on and don't see a thing. And among them is certainly Mother Simple. I have been sensing this lately, although I have been hesitant to say anything about my fears – except to Mrs. Back-Stabber the day before yesterday. But she gave me her word that she would not let this slip for anyone other than Mrs. Gossiper."

"Yes," said Listless, "because Mother Simple is so blind to the truth about Abrahamsson, she will not tolerate hearing that anyone has a complaint against him. May Immanuel quickly come to the rescue! Otherwise, I just don't know how all this will go."

"Yes, my brother," said Mr. Weary, "we understand one another, you and I. Oh, how good it is to be of like mind and bonded in brotherly love!"

Upon this, they embraced one another, and went their respective ways. But neither of them went to Immanuel.

All this time, Mother Simple was on her way to Abrahamsson's residence. But since her conversation with Listless had so troubled her, she had first turned off at a street corner and went to Immanuel in order to ask for forgiveness for her hard-heartedness. For she knew that she could not properly love him like this. In addition she asked for grace and for a speedy intervention for Listless, so that he would get back on track and not go astray. At last, she got to talking about the errand that had prompted her to set out to Abrahamsson's in the first place, requesting the grace to be wise and loving.

Immanuel answered succinctly: "Go in peace!" and Mother Simple left with her heart set at ease.

When she entered Abrahamsson's workshop, he was busy writing. As soon as he noticed her entry, he rose from his desk.

"Well, it is good that you have come! That slacker, Listless, has just now left, and you must have run into him."

"Yes, that I have."

"And what did he say?"

Mother Simple did not at first know how she should answer. For a second, she felt tempted to point out his shortcomings, but caught herself, and after a moment said:

"We were discussing matters concerning our eternal well-being."

"Yes, that is the sort of thing he needs, and I was actually in the middle of telling him a thing or two just now."

At this he took the paper in his hand, saying:

"Would you like to hear? Lately, I have been writing a book on spiritual idleness."

And after having read a section, he asked:

"Doesn't this describe Listless word for word? What do you think?"

"Uh…well," answered the little old woman. "I do believe that with IMMANUEL's help, things will go better for LISTLESS; but I am more concerned about the Squire, and I would advise the Squire to put an end to this writing project. The Squire is too inexperienced to start writing; and if the book were to be published now, it would not be a good thing for him."

"What are you saying?" interrupted Abrahamsson. "Doesn't it ring true, what I just wrote about LISTLESS?"

"In some ways – but, at any rate…"

"Are you saying that I should be prevented from presenting the honest truth?"

"Wait, until the Squire has calmed himself down!"

"But my zealous efforts are only a result of my desire to bring glory to EVANGELIUM."

"If that were indeed the case, then I wouldn't have much to say; but as it stands with the Squire right now, this is an unwise zeal, mixed with bitterness toward a person."

"How can you make a claim like that?"

"Well, now I see then. The Squire has ingested a dangerous poison from the gentlemen BOLD and DEAD-SURE, such that the Squire has started to resemble them; and the Squire will most definitely remember the warning I gave him about those fellows, when we last were talking about them."

"Yes, but since you are being so frank with me, then I would like to point out a shortcoming of yours, if you would allow me to do so."

"Allow it? Oh, I wish nothing less than that everyone would be so loving toward me, that they would do just that."

At these words, Abrahamsson was taken aback, and fell into deep reflections.

"Loving?" he thought to himself. "Loving enough to point out shortcomings! What is this? – Can something like that be done in love? Well, she must be right; but I am lacking this kind of love. I was furious over the fact that she had criticized my book, and my gut reaction was to lash out at her. But now she speaks about 'being loving enough' to give such reprimand."

With these thoughts he was reminded of the conversation he had had with Listless that morning.

"That was not loving," he thought. "But Listless himself was certainly also full of bitterness..." he added under his breath, which Mother Simple could still hear. And so, she interrupted him:

"And the Squire supposes that Listless has committed a sin, then?"

"Yes, of course," answered Abrahamsson, "he violated the commandment *'Thou shalt not kill'!*"

"And which commandment did the Squire break, when he was bitter in return?"

This question, accompanied by the little old woman's tender, but serious and unrelenting gaze, was more than Abrahamsson could stand.

"Against the same commandment!" he sighed heavily, and trembling as he threw his paper into the tiled stove, he began to cry. "Against the same commandment!" he repeated, as he sat himself down again. "Whatever shall I do?"

Abrahamsson sat there now, as though he were a convict sentenced to life. The power of the little old woman's words had taken him captive, with bands that he did not have the power to cut. He now believed that the little old woman's devotion and love toward him would be lost for all time. He considered himself as having forfeited any expectation of earning the respect of any honorable person. He wanted to run away, for he could not stand to remain here in his state of wretchedness, sitting beside someone whose very presence seemed to imply an immutable judgment of everything he stood for. He felt as though he wanted to shout at her: "Leave me, for I am a sinful person."

But MOTHER SIMPLE slyly noticed how his hand was quivering, and whispered:

"Doesn't the Squire think that we both ought to be on our way to IMMANUEL to speak about our troubles with him? He can certainly offer help."

Abrahamsson shot up, terrified. "IMMANUEL!" he cried, "To IMMANUEL? – now? – in this condition? – he would drive me away!"

"No," answered MOTHER SIMPLE, "Never. Not if he intends to keep his word, like when he once said:

'The one who comes to me, I will by no means cast out!'"[76]

"But I am completely lost; those words would certainly not apply to me?"

"And yet he says himself that it was precisely for those who were lost that he came!"[77]

"But you must understand that..."

"I am uneducated and I understand nothing more than that IMMANUEL will keep his word."

It was in this way that she finally managed to bring him with her to IMMANUEL. And she truly reveled in this. She felt that she had managed to save him from the brink of ruin. Once they arrived at IMMANUEL's, everything was put right again. He did not reproach Abrahamsson at all, but instead allowed his grace to flow and cover all of his sins. A blessed sense of peace was poured out over Abrahamsson's soul. He felt fortunate beyond words and indescribably small.

When Mother Simple and her friend left Immanuel, they set out to find Listless. Abrahamsson had, namely, an irresistible need to ask him for forgiveness, as well. But when they had only gotten a little bit down the road, they ran into him. He came running at full speed.

"What shall I do?" he cried to Mother Simple. "I am doomed to be thrown into prison!"

"Not to worry," answered Mother Simple, "grace and help are still to be found."

"No, no. Justus All-Powerful has said this himself, and Moses is out to get me in order to have me arrested!"

"Oh, you wounded soul!" answered the little old woman, "come with me, and Moses will not touch you!"

This terrified Abrahamsson to see the torment and anxiety, from which this poor man suffered. But Mother Simple remained calm. She had seen this kind of thing many times before; and what strengthened her now was the feeling of certainty, that all of this was simply an answer to a request that she had submitted to the heart of Immanuel when she had been on her way to Abrahamsson earlier. Therefore she said, frankly:

"Come with us to Immanuel!"

"To Immanuel, who was the very person who ordered that I should be taken to Gehenna?"

"No, you can be certain about this, that he will surely help you! Come! Hurry up and come!"

All the while, Mother Simple was quickly realizing that her efforts here would be in vain. Therefore she did not waste any time, but left Abrahamsson with this suffering man and hastened on her way back to IMMANUEL. Due to her persistent appeals, he came and carried LISTLESS into THE FORGIVENESS OF SINS. This was a place where MOSES was not allowed entry, and thus he remained outside. After a while, IMMANUEL came out and presented him with proof that he had canceled LISTLESS's sins. Upon seeing this, MOSES was satisfied and departed in order to discuss the matter with Mr. JUSTUS.

But in THE FORGIVENESS OF SINS a precious sight unfolded. Since LISTLESS had received IMMANUEL's assurance of grace, he turned to Abrahamsson to confess his sin and receive forgiveness. And together they acknowledged that they were mutually guilty and worthy of punishment. Afterward, LISTLESS turned to MOTHER SIMPLE and confided a conversation that he had had with MR. WEARY

"We had made up our minds," he said, "both of us, to move to LOOSE LIVING, and WEARY has already departed. But when I myself was about to go home and pack up my things, it was then that I met MOSES. Now I am glad of it, for I have been rescued."

And all three of them rejoiced greatly over this great grace, which had proven to be so sufficient. While IMMANUEL sat himself down at a great pipe organ and played a magnificent postlude in his father's honor.

SEVENTH CHAPTER

Abrahamsson in the Class of the Wretched

The visible appearances that Immanuel made to Abrahamsson had begun to become both more rare and brief. This became rather troubling, and Abrahamsson was afraid that Immanuel intended to abandon him. Of this he could not bear the thought. Rather often he thought that he did not have any true love for him, and that pained him grievously. But all the same, he could not live without him. Mother Simple explained that this was the true kind of love. But Abrahamsson did not believe that she really understood him and gave him too much credit, more than he deserved. He wanted to constantly remain in *those initial euphoric emotions,* and when he did not have them, then he thought that he had lost this first love. Once, when he complained about this matter to Mother Simple, she responded like this:

"My dear Squire, those euphoric emotions you mention are like burning straw. It might certainly cast a bright light, but it does not give the same good, even warmth that the coals of a birch wood fire will give. They do not flicker at all."

Abrahamsson shook his head at these words and wondered how this could be.

But let us return to the tale.

The previously happy Abrahamsson had begun to be in low spirits and complained often about his weakness. Of course, he had heard the others do similarly, but he could never bring himself to believe that they could be as wretched as he was. When he heard them complain, he always thought:

"Oh, to be as humble as you! Oh, if I only could have such a deep conviction of my sins!"

All the while, the thing that was sustaining the spirits of the weak was the inscription over the door inside the house, where one could read the following:

No resident here shall say: I am weak;
for all who live here shall have the forgiveness of sins.

If not for these words Abrahamsson would have surely been lost to despair. Now, however, they somewhat managed to keep his spirits up. Yet, it was often difficult. He was now attending the school of Father Experience and the basic section of the Class of the Wretched. There he was supposed to learn what Mother Simple had so many times spoken to him about. Often his worries were so severe that he did not know how it would go for him in the end.

"I will not last here in the long run!" one could hear him often exclaim. "I cannot manage to learn a single thing, but instead I am becoming decidedly worse and more ignorant day by day."

However, one evening in particular he came to Mother Simple, altogether exhausted and lost. It was namely the case with him that he was beginning to *really* despair.

"Oh, my dear Squire," said Mother Simple, upon his entrance, "how are things going now? I can see that all is not well."

"No, it is precisely as you say, for now things have become altogether lamentable."

"Oh, it cannot be all that lamentable, I should think. The Squire just has to learn how things work in Evangelium, and how great grace is."

"But I am not learning anything, and am instead becoming more wretched day by day."

"Well, the Squire does not understand that he is now studying the most difficult subject to learn. But this art is the most important of all, the art of living on grace alone."

"Yes, I remember, that we spoke about this once before, and that you promised to continue when the time was right."

"We can do that now, if the Squire has a moment."

"Yes, I would really appreciate that, for I need it now as much as ever."

"Then I would first like to say, that *EVANGELIUM is the kind of city where one never needs to despair.* For IMMANUEL's grace is altogether unchangeable and independent of us and all of our doing and being."

"But how should one behave, then, when one cannot do anything? For instance when even IMMANUEL himself has said that one must be diligent and faithful?"

"One should diligently practice being..."

"Yes, one should do that," interrupted Abrahamsson, "and I have been devoting all of my strength to it, but it does not work. It only becomes worse."

"The Squire needs to hear the rest of what I was going to say! I did not say that one should be diligent in work; for even the greatest diligence in work and attempts at moral improvement can never be able to right a wrong that has already been done. Besides, it is not possible to diligently continue to work during those times, when one has neither the courage nor the strength for it."

"But that can certainly not be helped; one can always make the exertions of despair?"

"Oh, my dear Squire, one will not get very far with those; and furthermore, those types of efforts do not please IMMANUEL in the least. His desire is that everything would be done out of a willing and confident heart, and not out of despair."

"In that case, what kind of a practice are you suggesting?"

"Well, I mean that when we find ourselves in a situation like that, where the Squire now finds himself, then we should diligently practice *believing in the unchangeable nature of IMMANUEL's grace.*"

"But he must have made the condition of his grace dependent upon some requirements."

"Yes, on the condition that we remain in this city."

"...and that we work diligently," added Abrahamsson.

"What does the Squire mean by that?"

"Well, I mean that we must still be faithful in practicing all of the works that one does in SANCTIFICATION, such as earnestness, the fear of God, prayer, and so on."

"In that case, why doesn't the Squire do that then?"

"You see, of course, that I do not have the strength or ability to do anything."

"What will the Squire do about that then?"

"This is exactly the problem, to which I do not know the answer. This is the cause of my despair."

"But the Squire knew what he needed to do just a moment ago."

"Knew what?"

"Well, that the Squire needs to begin practicing humility, the fear of God, and so on. This is, of course, what the Squire himself just said he needed to do. And now he says that he does not know what he needs to do?"

"But I am lacking the ability and strength to do any of that."

"And where will the Squire find the strength then?"

"Yes, tell me! From where?"

"Without a doubt, from IMMANUEL."

"But we have no grounds on which to expect his grace. He has most certainly forsaken me, and the worst thing is that I have earned this myself."

"Yes, is the Squire thinking of picking up and moving someplace else?"

"Dear friend, where would I go? My soul would be lost in misery, if I were forced to leave EVANGELIUM."

"But, in that case, what is the Squire about to do, then?"

Poor Abrahamsson became silent, for he knew that he had been ensnared by the little old woman's questions.

"Yes," he exclaimed after a moment of silence. "I do not even understand myself. Sometimes I think that I must despair and move to THE WORLD. But then when I begin to set out, I cannot even do that. Can you tell me, what is going on? Have you ever heard of such an odd person before?"

MOTHER SIMPLE smiled. She thought, with a certain triumph in her heart:

"I would be curious to see how far MR. SELF-WISE would get in solving this with his LOGIC."

But after a moment, Abrahamsson said, with a calmer tone:

"I see now that there must be some secret here that I do not properly understand."

"Yes, the secret is great," answered the little old woman, "and it is called living on free grace. One does not really learn how to do this until one has started to attend the Class of the Wretched."

"But if one is sinning, though, as I am?"

"Then one should believe in grace."

"But if this sin has its basis in the fact that one is not faithfully using the grace that Immanuel provides?"

"Then one should believe in grace."

"But if one is lacking enough faith to even do that?"

"Then one should believe that there is grace, even for that."

"But if one is not really aware, is not remorseful or does not pray for one's sins, and instead is sluggish and listless?"

"Then one should believe in grace."

"But if one *cannot* believe in grace, then?"

"Then grace will remain the same, even then."

"Yes, this must certainly be an assurance to every honest soul. But you do not know how it is with me. I am false and a hypocrite; I see that now. What shall I do about this?"

"Just believe in grace."

"Oh, you precious soul…if you only knew…yes. You see, I am shuddering as I say this. But listen, this morning as I lay in bed it came to me: 'I ought to be up by now and at work.' But then it occurred to me: 'Oh, it is not so urgent either; here one does not live on the work of one's hands, and there is certainly enough grace to go around.' Now you must be able to see that I have reached the point where I cannot be helped."

"No, there is nothing to do but believe in grace."

Abrahamsson hid his head in his hands and trembled.

"Listen," he said at last, "listen to my confession! The day before yesterday I was tempted by an appalling sin, and the temptation had such a hold on me, that I even thought: 'This is not so dangerous, since this experience can teach me more about sin.' Is that not a sin against grace? I fell, and now I must..."

"Believe in grace," interrupted MOTHER SIMPLE hastily, when Abrahamsson's speech trailed off into sniffling.

"Believe in grace," repeated Abrahamsson. "Believe in grace! Yes, I would do that, if it had only been that one time that this had happened to me. But this has regrettably happened to me many times now, and so..."

"The Squire must believe in grace."

Abrahamsson sank into deep contemplation. He did not know what he should do.

"Oh," he thought, "may I believe in grace, even now? Me – me? Is this possible? Oh, how blessed it would be if I could do just that!"

But while he sat there like that and thought, MOTHER SIMPLE began puttering around and lit some lamps, as it had already gotten dark. Then she opened up that great book that lay on the table and read, with a clear voice:

Though your sins be as scarlet, they shall be as white as snow; though they be red like crimson, they shall be as wool.[78]

These words rushed through Abrahamsson's soul like a stream of living water, and he felt himself assured by them.

"See," said the little old woman, as she went over to him, "these words stand more secure than all the mountains, for it says in another place:

For the mountains shall depart and the hills be removed;
but my grace shall not depart from thee,
neither shall the covenant of my peace be removed.[79]

"And in another place:

And even to your old age I will bear you,
and even when you turn grey will I carry you:
I will lift up and carry, and deliver you.[80]

"And again:

As birds flying, so will I protect the Holy City with my wings;
defending also I will deliver it; and passing over I will rescue it.[81]

"See, with words like these one can feel security, no matter what the distress. For IMMANUEL would sooner prove to be a liar, than that words like these should prove to be false. As he has said himself:

Heaven and earth shall pass away, but my words shall not pass away.[82]

MR. SELF-WISE and his friends judge me as being exaggerated and stubborn because I have these views. For, they say, constantly believing in a grace like this, one which covers over all of our sins, that this is a concept that easily leads people to idleness and sin and disbelief in grace. But if one has really begun to be distressed, then that is when one first realizes out how difficult this art can be. They judge it as being a loose teaching and a heresy. But we shall see whether their strong teachings will come to their aid. Does the Squire find it at all easy to believe in this grace?"

"No," answered Abrahamsson, "I have never studied anything more difficult. But now that I can believe, I feel an indescribable assurance."

"And has the Squire now, because of this assurance, become weighed down in idleness or developed a lesser desire for goodness than before? Or has this belief in free grace caused the Squire to feel that it is dangerous to share his doubts with IMMANUEL, since he will certainly forgive anything at all, yes, even such disbelief?"

"Oh, no," answered Abrahamsson enthusiastically, "quite the opposite. Through this assurance I now feel twice as much love for IMMANUEL and a truly urgent desire, yes, even a deep need to serve him, since he wishes to make use of my meager service."

"Yes, so it is. And this is how it usually is, when the heart finds the true kind of assurance. Sacrifices like this also are pleasing to IMMANUEL. It is insanity for one to argue that it is easier to believe in a free grace than in being righteous and diligent in the production of GOOD DEEDS. Instead, if the heart can just find true assurance in IMMANUEL and his mercy, which goes over all boundaries, then it will become *a joy* to produce GOOD DEEDS. The most difficult commandment that one could receive would be if IMMANUEL said that one was not allowed to do him any service. Such a prohibition would quite simply rob the heart of all courage. Therefore, when life is lacking, when the heart becomes heavy and listless and, because of sin, falls into anxiety and distress, then one should get out of SANCTIFICATION, then one should get rid of any thought of DEEDS, until one has once again found peace and assurance though diligently spending time with IMMANUEL and meditating on his grace. A sick person should not torment himself with working. A sick person should lie still. A sick person *has the right* to lie still."

While these words full of grace were flowing through the lips of the little old woman, in Abrahamsson's heart, joy was beginning to mix with fear. He drank in these words of indescribable, heavenly assurance, as a thirsting deer drinks when he has found a spring. But at the same time he felt deep within as though he had the impulse to add something, or to give some objection, that would set some limit on this boundless freedom that the dear little old woman had heralded with such enthusiasm and warmth. Yet he could not bring himself to say anything about it. His heart was too full. For the moment, he had received more from this little old woman than he had room to store in his narrow little heart. When he left, he stretched out his hand to MOTHER SIMPLE and said:

"Thanks be to God for this indescribable gift!"

"Yes," answered the little old woman, "through the life of the one who believes will flow rivers of living water."[83]

EIGHTH CHAPTER

The Freeness of Grace

When Abrahamsson departed from Mother Simple, he felt deliriously full, as though drunk on the bounty of God's table. His heart played and sang for the Lord the whole way home. This joy even lasted for several days. Occasionally, the question arose for him if the little old woman had not been too exaggerated and, if in his own heart, he had not been caught up in a bit of fanaticism. One day, in order to clear up this matter for himself, he hurried to her house once again. She received him cheerfully, and then asked how he was feeling.

"Well," he said, "I have felt an indescribable happiness since I was here last. I have been walking in idyllic sunshine. But now and then, there have been storm clouds that have passed through. Is it true, that one may receive grace as freely as you said?"

The little old woman observed him for a moment. Then she asked:

"Has the Squire been keeping company with Mr. Doubt?"

"No," answered Abrahamsson, "I do not want to have anything more to do with him. But it occurred to me that you may have gone too far. So, tell me, are you *really certain* that grace is as immeasurably vast as you make it out to be?"

"Well, yes. Yes, of course!" exclaimed the little old woman succinctly, but emphatically. "For here," she added, as she took hold of the great book, "here in EVANGELIUM it is never to be a matter of living on one's own work. IMMANUEL has taken upon himself the responsibility of providing for us, and he is opposed to the idea that we would try to meddle with it in any way.

I have a little story to tell. The Squire was still young when my husband and I moved to INDUSTRIOUSNESS. But the Squire probably can still remember well how things used to be for us. It was namely the case that we had been cast out by our previous lord, even though my husband was in such poor health that he could not endure any strenuous labor. There we stood, down on our luck. But the Squire's father took us in. Back then, we had not yet heard about EVANGELIUM. That was how it came to be that time, that without any of our own doing, we received a refuge with the Squire's father. He also came to our assistance when my husband fell ill. But at any case we had the additional requirement that if we were to remain there, it would be on the condition that we continued to be diligent and faithful in contributing to our own subsistence. This is exactly the same way that MR. SELF-WISE would like for things to be run here. And that is certainly how things would go, if he were allowed to run EVANGELIUM according to his LOGIC. What he cannot accept is that the residents of EVANGELIUM are not IMMANUEL's cotters, but instead are his true brethren and, as he is in the habit of calling them, his 'bride,' and who have full claim to all of his property."

"What are you saying?" Abrahamsson interjected. "Is this possible? Or don't you mean that it is presumptuous to believe that?"

"It would be terribly presumptuous," answered the little old woman calmly, "if he had not said this himself. But since he has said it, then it would be just as presumptuous if we were to start contradicting his own words, as though we did not believe that they were completely true."

"But can one take these words to such a literal extreme, down to the last letter?"

"Yes, entirely. And nothing less. For IMMANUEL's heart overflows with a steady stream of pure grace and mercy; and there is no power that can hinder this stream or stop up the veins that feed it. It would be detrimental for someone to imagine that grace was something that we could snatch up for ourselves, bit by bit, with our efforts and our work; for grace can exist for no other reason than that we have a gracious and merciful master, who wants the best for us and who does not ever experience a change of heart regarding us."

"Do our deeds, then, and our behavior have no meaning?"

"No, *in this regard,* none. For just as we are unable to increase IMMANUEL's grace through our good deeds, we are equally incapable of changing who he is based on bad ones; and he is grace and goodness itself, once and for always. It is not in my power, nor in the Squire's, to take away or add anything to this. This is why he has allowed dear Old Paulus to give assurance to all those who sit in the CLASS OF THE WRETCHED, by writing there on the walls these words:

Where sin abounded, grace abounded much more.[84]

And so it is. The one who cannot accept that IMMANUEL is such a person, he has full freedom to depart from the city and place himself under the power and governance of another master. Here in EVANGELIUM, it is 'grace alone.' The law of the city is grace, and by that law every resident is bound."

It seemed during her speech as though the fire in the little old woman's heart steadily flamed stronger and stronger. Her eyes radiated with joy, and her entire being was one of unwavering triumph in the knowledge and experience of the blessed nature of this grace, about which she was speaking. Abrahamsson's heart was strained, as though he were trying to stretch its walls.

But it remained too cramped in there to be able accommodate the fullness of the riches of grace. And although he experienced the great power of the little old woman's speech, his natural sensibilities rose up in opposition. He once again felt that the little old woman had gone too far. Still, out of his awareness of his own inexperience, he did not dare to oppose her, but simply asked:

"But do you not see any way that such unqualified talk about grace could become rather harmful?"

With the fire of rapture in her eyes the little old woman retorted by asking:

"Does the Squire think that it could be damaging to speak well of IMMANUEL? Can one say too many good things about him? No. Think of every good thing that can be found in a father's, or a mother's or a bridegroom's heart. Paint a picture of all this. It will be beautiful. But certainly the picture of IMMANUEL would be even better, yes, to the extent that the sun is better than this little lamp, which is burning before us."

"Well, yes. But you would still do well to rein in your speech a bit, for otherwise it could lead to the result that many people might become less cautious about sin and think that it was not all that dangerous."

"Well, then. Now that the Squire has experienced the power of this teaching, he could certainly go out and try to sin at any time!"

Abrahamsson was taken aback. "What?" he said. "Should I go out and sin? No – no! Far from it!"

"Why not?" answered MOTHER SIMPLE. "For I can assure you that it in no way would alter IMMANUEL's grace."

"But dear mother, *should I* go and sin?"

"Sure, why not?"

"No, I cannot do that – I, who have grace and the forgiveness of sins. How could I want to sin again?"

"Yes, that was exactly the answer that I was waiting for. I wanted to demonstrate for the Squire that it is precisely in this free grace that there is the power *against* sin. This is what Old Paulus also once said:

How shall we who died to sin live any longer in it?[85]

Even Mr. Self-Wise tries to find assurance for his heart by speaking about Immanuel's grace. But since he does not understand that it is exactly in this *assurance* that its *power* lies, so he thinks that he can guard against *sin* with the addition of 'however,' which he has derived from Logic, I expect. By doing this, what happens is that with all of his 'howevers' he destroys all *assurance* and thus diminishes its *power*. In this way, he opens the windows and the doors to sin. And he claims that this is a true explanation of Sanctification. I get so vexed by his Philosophy or Logic, or whatever he wants to call that arithmetic with which he does his spells. No, it is only after one has realized that grace is independent of all of our doing and being, it is first then that one can stand up to sin, it is first then that any real work can be done. And I know examples of just this type of person, who precisely because of the fact that they have not discovered this secret, have grown weary of Evangelium and moved away from here."

"However, there are of course also examples of people who because of this teaching have become lazy and indifferent," answered Abrahamsson.

"No, not one," interjected the little old woman, enthusiastically.

"All the same, this is what Mr. Enlightened has told me."

"Yes, that is probably what is written in his Logic. For he is in the habit of weighing down this *teaching* with all sorts of conditions that are dependent on *people*. But, let us say that someone, as a result of *his own falseness* – because he only gave assent to this idea in his head, but in his heart did not have any experience of it – were to allow himself freely to go about sinning in grace. Then this would not be the fault of the teaching, but his own. This is what takes place in the city of LOOSE LIVING. But here in EVANGELIUM a different *spirit* prevails. For we here are of a different *mindset,* in such a way that one would not *want* to sin, even if given permission. Or how would the Squire answer if IMMANUEL were to say to the Squire: 'Now you may live however you want for a while; I will not restrict you in any way, nor hold it against you, no matter how you live'?"

"Oh," answered Abrahamsson hastily, "I would be overjoyed by a promise like that, and would make good use of it that whole time."

"And, in that case, what would the Squire do?" asked the little old woman.

"Well, you can certainly guess; for that entire time, I would be so holy and perfect, that no sin would come near me. If only I *could* just live as I *wanted,* oh, then I would not be sitting here sharing my troubles with you!"

"And why wouldn't the Squire sin, then?"

"You already know the answer: the one who has the freedom to be healthy and happy, does not willingly cast himself into suffering and grief."

"But what suffering and grief would there be, if IMMANUEL is not holding any sins against the Squire?"

"Oh, it is not having these things *held against me* that is the cause of my suffering, but it is *sin itself.*"

"And how can this cause suffering if there is no accountability?"

"Well, I do not know why, but I still sense that it is so."

"Yes, this comes from the new mindset. Once I wanted the very same things as the Squire. But if such permission had been granted to me while I lived in SELF-RIGHTEOUSNESS, then I would have thought: Oh! It would be good for me to catch my breath for a moment!"

At this the two friends became silent and sank into self-contemplation. A fear of self-deception came over them. But after a while, Abrahamsson opened his mouth.

"MR. ENLIGHTENED ..."

"His name is not ENLIGHTENED, but SELF-WISE," interrupted MOTHER SIMPLE.

"Well, yes," continued Abrahamsson. "He told me once that he had heard you spreading the teaching: 'Believe in grace alone and then live as you will.' Tell me, honestly: can this be your opinion?"

"I do not recall," answered the little old woman, "ever saying that, exactly. But *if* I had done so, I am not at all concerned."

"But this certainly cannot be right?"

"Yes, but it is so. In this there lies a glorious truth, which at the same time causes a profound *trial of the heart.* For if someone *believes* in grace without having received a new mindset, which makes him *willing* to live a holy and righteous life, then he remains a hypocrite. He is not helped by other people setting these two things *against* one another: *believe in grace* and *live holy.* It is altogether as if they have missed the fact that the one thing is essentially tied to the other. And SELF-RIGHTEOUSNESS is full of these kinds of hypocrites. Yet it does not surprise me that MR. SELF-WISE considers this teaching to be dangerous. He knows that if he himself were to *live* however he *wanted,* then he would break out into all manner of sins. This is how all hypocrites are, and why Mr. Self-Wise seeks to assist them with his 'howevers,' which he is so quick to do."

Abrahamsson, who many times during this conversation had felt offended by the fact that the little old woman had so often dragged Self-Wise in front of her judge's bench and accused him for everything, finally could not restrain himself, but said:

"Pardon me, if I interrupt this conversation with something that really does not belong here. It strikes me as perplexing that you would keep on speaking ill of Self-Wise, when you never do the same about others, but instead maintain that one should overlook the faults of others and always see them in the best light, but never expose them."

"It is good that the Squire noticed that. But this is the situation. There was a time when Mr. Self-Wise lived happily in Evangelium. But soon he began to show signs of various bad habits. I went to him to caution him to be on his guard. This offended him. Then I went to Immanuel to seek his advice. He asked me to take Pastor Evangelist and Mother Wounded-Hip and go back. This I did, and we went. On the way we stopped in with Immanuel to request from him the grace to be wise in our conduct. He added Old Mrs. Love to our company. Then we gladly went on our way. However, then Self-Wise became so furious that he moved to Theology and began to publically defame me, as well as spread erroneous and seductive teachings. Then I went with my concerns to Immanuel and interceded for Self-Wise, asking what I should do. At this Immanuel answered that I should warn everyone about him. And if there was any one particular sin that he had committed, then I should not say one word about that. But now it is another matter, when he is intentionally promoting a teaching like this, whereby he is *clearly leading people to their ruin.* Then I simply cannot keep silent. Old Paulus was a man of peace, that is certain, but when he saw people like this who, by means of Philosophy and Proud Delusions or with teachings about works, going around confusing simple folks so that they fell away from grace, then there was no longer any mercy in his speech. No, in those cases his words burned like a brushfire. There are many different opinions that hold sway here in this city, the Squire is well aware of this. This is something one has to tolerate. For we all understand in part; and we all in one way or another make our mistakes. But everything will go well, as long as everyone is *standing on the foundation.* But those who tear away at the foundation, those people are not to be tolerated."

While Mother Simple was speaking about all this, a tear appeared in her clear eyes. Abrahamsson, who could plainly see the compassion that she felt for Self-Wise and these other souls, found himself set at peace by her explanation. Therefore, he decided it was time to return to the topic of the recently interrupted conversation.

"You spoke," he said, "about believing in grace, and then living as you will. Tell me then, is it not also necessary to place emphasis on Good Deeds?"

"Why, certainly," answered the little old woman, "as long as it happens in the right place and right time. If our flesh were wholly overcome, then we would not have any more need of admonitions than Immanuel does. But since the old nature is still always battling against the new person in us, and seeks to suppress this new person, it is thus essential that we diligently keep watch, and faithfully and constantly struggle against the flesh. Here is where patience is tested, and it is often a heated campaign. But if the new person is knocked down and the heart is trembling and terrified and even begins to lose its foothold in free grace, then that is not the place for admonitions, but instead, then one has to set himself in ardent opposition to all talk about Good Deeds and only emphasize grace. For all admonitions – yes, even the most compassionate ones – bring *no power whatsoever* to the new person, but instead only act as a spur in the side. And then a person will only be able to come as far as the assurance of grace gives her the strength to do so, but no further. If she has lost her foothold, then the spurs will not help her any more than they can help a horse, who out of exhaustion has collapsed into the dust. She will only suffer because of this, and perhaps meet her end if help does not intercede. In contrast, if she has peace and assurance, then the spurs will not cause pain, but she will simply become enlivened by them to run on in the race. And, just watch, that is when she will be able to get somewhere; then she will have the strength, *not because of the spurs, but because of grace."*

"But, then tell me, how shall I be able to always keep this new person not only awake, but even lively and full of strength?"

"Only by steadily observing and believing grace, as well as faithfully using the strength that IMMANUEL gives for each occasion. For here our faithfulness matters a great deal. The more faithful one is toward grace, the more strength one will receive from it, the more steady the journey will become, and the healthier life will be."

"However," interjected Abrahamsson, once again somewhat distressed by a sense of his own unfaithfulness, "what if *I* should have the misfortune of not being that faithful to grace, but instead start sinning dreadfully in this regard?"

"Then the Squire shall believe grace!" exclaimed the little old woman, triumphantly, "for grace is not only supposed to be the first step, but also the last."

At this unexpected reply, it was as though Abrahamsson felt faint.

"You always have grace close at hand," he said.

"Yes, grace, Squire. Grace. She is like a rock that will not give way, especially not just because some broken-down wretch has set himself on it."

"But aren't you making light of this matter, and thereby dulling the point of all admonitions?"

"About this we will certainly have the opportunity to speak another time, for now it is already late. So, I would like to only say a few more words. There are many, who because of their disposition in the flesh, distort this priceless teaching, to their own downfall and ruin. And the entire city of Loose Living is built on this foundation. But it is *not the fault* of the teaching; *she* must be all the more set free to bring assurance and rejuvenation to the miserable. No hypocrite will ever be helped by her being hidden away. And if the Squire would only practice this faithfully in his life, then the Squire would still see how difficult this art is. The Squire would also come to experience how this same teaching will be all the more able to break sin, and add just the right amount of sharpness to all admonitions. And now, to briefly repeat and summarize what we have spoken about, I would like to add this: *When the Squire has sinned, then believe grace! And when the Squire believes grace, then in earnestness see to it that the Squire lives holy and righteously!*"

Upon this Mother Simple read a passage in the great book called God's Word, and Abrahamsson listened attentively to this. It was for him just then as if every line in that precious book was being illuminated by a new light. Then both of these friends went on their way to Immanuel, whom they praised for his great grace, and urgently requested that he protect them in everything ahead. He replied, compassionately: "Remain in my love!"[86]

NINTH CHAPTER

Mother Simple's Crisis of Temptation[87]

It was already late in the evening. Abrahamsson had bid the dear little old woman a tender and heartfelt, "good night," as she was even dearer to him now than before. He was well on his peaceful way to his own home.

"Oh," he thought to himself, "that was such a delightful conversation! How sweet it was to have been able to clear up that matter! But it is unfathomable to me how people can portray MOTHER SIMPLE as having taught anything that would lead people to laziness and sin. It is *their understanding* that is skewed, but they say that it is *her teaching* that is lopsided. And there is no one here who would dare suggest that she herself has become lazy or indifferent. For who could ever match her in being energetic, capable, and useful? She is of course humble and self-sufficient to such a degree that it seems to be a delight for her to make sacrifices for others. On grace she lives, and in grace she works. 'If I am able to accomplish anything,' she once told me, 'then it is a result of the fact that I have been freed from the heavy burden of working for a day-wage, or for that matter, of having to worry about earning my room and board. Since IMMANUEL is living for me, then *that* is certainly reason enough for me to live for him.' Oh, what a dear friend she is to me! *Her* life must be a delightful existence, every day! What freedom, what peace! She is able to avoid experiencing the troubles that I have – I, who am full of all kinds of misery. Oh, that the time would soon come, when I might be able to arrive at such a happy state, when neither doubts nor disbelief would cause me to be anxious and wear on my poor heart! However, I will never, never forget these lessons that I have received from her today."

Filled with these thoughts, Abrahamsson wandered ahead slowly and at ease. He felt a particular peace and security in his heart. This dear man had, as of yet, not experienced much. And he thought he would never forget the little old woman's lessons! He did not yet understand, that it was *just as difficult to keep them, as it was to accept them in the first place.* He had no idea that he would soon find himself in even more desperate straits than he found himself in that evening when he visited the little old woman. He thought that he understood the little old woman's words completely, but he could not anticipate the painful times that were to come. Neither did he know that he would come to experience far more difficult moments of temptation than he had already. Therefore, he imagined that the little old woman's life was so easy, and he longed for the day when he too would be able to have such an easy life. He shared this with everyone he encountered in the next few days.

But while he occupied himself contentedly with these illusions about the little old woman's life, constructing bright hopes and future visions for himself, we ought to take a look into the home of MOTHER SIMPLE to see if it really was *always* so bright in there. Certainly she was a happy little old woman, that cannot be denied. But you can be sure that even she had her tumultuous times, times when her heart seemed to melt like wax, when her temptations were so difficult, that she was brought to almost complete despair. Those who had not experienced much even might even believe that she was out of her mind.

* * *

It had not been more than a few weeks, and what a change we see in her! Of that halo of light that Abrahamsson's imagination had painted around his picture of her, we can now hardly see a trace. For about a week now it has been very dark for her, and it has gotten worse day by day. As we enter unnoticed, she is lying on her bed. That courageous spirit with which we heard her proclaim the truths of grace, that is now gone, and that peace and joy, which beamed from her eyes, has now vanished. She wriggles and writhes like a worm in the mud, and waters her bed with bitter tears of sorrow.[88] Heavily and slowly, deep sighs rise up out of her dejected heart. What she herself had so often said to the assurance of Abrahamsson and the others, she now has forgotten when it comes to her own situation. For everyone else there is grace, she thinks – just not for her.

"Oh," she sighed, "such an old creature as I am, who ought to be filled with nothing but humility and love. But I am hard as a stone. I presume to teach other people, but have learned nothing myself! Where will all this end? Oh, if only IMMANUEL would have mercy on me and quickly come to my aid!"

At this she began to recollect her past life. The memories flashed before her soul, and brought drops of anxious perspiration to her brow.

"I," she continued, "I have spoken about and praised the power of free grace. But how much of this do I even have myself?"

Now the storms of doubt and blasphemous thoughts raged through her soul, which tormented her all the more.

"What shall I do? With my sins I bring both myself and others to ruin."

At this thought, she shuddered. She did not know where she should turn. Doubt, as to how she could dare claim grace for herself, was in the process of stealing her sanity. Yes, at times she felt a sense of loathing at the very thought of EVANGELIUM. In despair, she sat up and cried out with a horrible and hollow voice:

"Well, so be it! If IMMANUEL will not help me, then he can go ahead and do just that! Then I will forever be a witness to the fact that he has deceived me!"

She got up at once, intending to end her miserable life, but collapsed and fell down to the floor. She sank into a trance-like sleep. The exertions of her soul and her despair had overwhelmed her weak body. During her slumber, her whining and lamentations continued. After a while, she awoke.

"Where am I?" she cried out, "where am I, you insane woman? What have I gained by my despair? Blasphemy, blasphemy!" she moaned, and a deathly shudder coursed through her limbs. "It is over for me…over…for me. And my lot…woe is me!"

She did not have the strength to say anything more, but instead sank back into her trance. During this episode, she envisioned spirits of torment gathering around her, and weighing her down with heavy chains. These spirits pulled her down into a horrible deep, as they snickered contemptuously at her torment. As she fell, she reached out her feeble hand in order to grasp a rope, which seemed to her to be being lowered by someone far up in the heights. But the rope snapped, her fall accelerated, the spirits of torment rejoiced, she saw fires and flames beneath her, and heard terrifying wailing rising up out of the deep. Now it seemed to her that serpents had wrapped themselves around her and were injecting their burning venom into her limbs. She sank deeper and deeper. With the spirits of torment screaming their satanic jubilations, she plunged down into the flames. Suddenly she let out a wail, which jolted her back to consciousness.[89]

The perspiration beaded up and dropped from her brow, her whole body shivered, and she did not know where she should turn. She once again fell into a trance-like state, and now she saw her own body, bound and being carried out before the judgment seat of JUSTUS ALL-POWERFUL. With a glance that flashed like fire, he tossed her to the ground, and brought forth a great book, in which her sins were recorded. This register he placed before her eyes and with a thundering voice, he pronounced his judgment, saying that she must be removed from his sight for all eternity. In her unconscious state, she rocked herself back and forth on the floor, wrung her hands and poured out her blasphemies against JUSTUS ALL-POWERFUL, IMMANUEL and EVANGELIUM. As she did this, she woke herself up once again.

"So, I am to be condemned!" she exclaimed, at the same time being reduced to convulsive sobbing. Though her heart was somewhat eased by her being able to release all of this through her tears, and she regained her composure enough that she could get up and leave her room. When she emerged, everything was still and calm. The entire city was resting in a deep and peaceful sleep. This bothered her even more, for it seemed as though everyone but her was living in idyllic peace. It was only she who was without peace, and was forced to bear within her this depth of suffering. Exhausted, she was forced to sit down. She hid her face in her hands and sobbed loudly. When she managed to get up again, she wandered slowly forward with a quaking heart through the empty streets of this peace-filled city.

"There is no one here, who knows or understands my distress and lamentations," she sighed, "no one who can show mercy to me, and speak a word of peace to me. Even so, what good would it do me to hear a word of peace? It would not be true for me."

Nevertheless, she directed her path toward IMMANUEL's dwelling.

"If I am going to leave EVANGELIUM and be cast out," she thought, "then I at least want to be able to see him first, the one person who for so many years has been my heart's only assurance and joy. I want to speak with him, in the chance that I might receive a friendly word or at least a compassionate glance from him. I just want to glimpse his face one last time."

Filled with such hopes, she was walking along with blinders on to everything around her, when all of the sudden she felt a heavy hand on her shoulder. A shudder rushed through her. She turned herself around and sank to the earth.

"Where are you headed?" asked the cross voice of this newcomer. "You imagine that IMMANUEL, whom you have so deeply offended and blasphemed so loudly – so loudly that I could hear it through my window – you imagine that he still will receive you? No. Depart from here, before he releases his wrath on you. For you, all grace has run out."

"But where can I go?"

"Go wherever you will!" answered CONSCIENCE, even more indignant, "but know that, wherever you are, even there the hand of the one whose grace you have so often enjoyed, but have now blasphemed, will find you and bring you before the judgment seat of vengeance!"

"But I want to first speak with IMMANUEL."

"From him you will be separated for all time, for you have committed that one sin, which cannot be forgiven."

A deathly darkness shrouded the little old woman's whimpering soul as CONSCIENCE pronounced these final words. And here she would have been lost – had not BANKRUPT FAITH in that same moment walked by. As soon as he realized her distress, he rushed over and whispered in her ear:

"The one who comes to me I will by no means cast out."[90]

He did not have time to say anything more, before he was chased away by CONSCIENCE, who boxed him rather violently. Yet, MOTHER SIMPLE rose up and said to CONSCIENCE:

"Oh, Immanuel may say to me whatever he will. But before I leave the city, I want to see *him* once more. I know that there can be no more grace for me. But I want to *see* him; I *must* see him, even if my sentence will be increased by it."

At this, she left, even though Conscience tried to stop her by continuing to paint a picture of the judgment that awaited her with Immanuel. When she arrived at Immanuel's door, she found it locked. She pounded frantically on it, with all the strength that she had. But everything remained silent. Only the harsh voice of Conscience interrupted the horrible stillness.

"Now, you can very well see," he said, "that Immanuel has abandoned you, and that you do not have the right to come near him. Accept your judgment in submission, for it is well deserved; accept that, and depart from here!"

There are not words to describe the little old woman's anguish. She was in despair and did not know where she would find any relief for her anguish.

"Turn back!" she thought. "Turn back – be driven out of Evangelium, and become the prey of Beelzebul! – And without even being allowed to see Immanuel's face!"

At this she sat herself down in order to at least cry one last time at Immanuel's door. But she had no more tears left.

"Oh, poor me," she moaned. "How have I been able to become so hardened? Before I could at least cry. Now even that has gone."

With her seated like this, she heard a voice in the distance calling: "He has come to seek and to save that which was lost!"[91]

It was Bankrupt Faith who was calling out these words to her. From this she gained a little more courage.

She pounded once more on the door, praying:

"Lord, my Savior, I have cried day and night before thee, let my prayer come before thee and incline thine ear unto my cry! For my soul is full of troubles and my life draweth nigh unto hell!"[92]

Again she listened, in order to perceive some answer from within. But all was silent as death. She cried out once again:

"Lord, I am counted with them that go down to the pit. I am as a poor woman that has no help. I lie forsaken among the dead, like the slain that lie in the grave, whom thou rememberest no more, and who are cut off from thy hand. I am shut up and cannot come forth. My face mourneth by reason of affliction; Lord, I have stretched out my hands unto thee. Lord, why castest thou off my soul and why hidest thou thy face from me? I am afflicted and ready to die for I am so forsaken; I suffer thy terrors so that I am distraught."[93]

But it seemed as though the poor little old woman's cries fell on deaf ears. When no answer was perceived, CONSCIENCE said, once again:

"Now, you must understand that it is over for you. IMMANUEL does not wish to speak with you, nor see you."

And now the little old woman turned around and went back. Along the way, she often looked over her shoulder, in order to imprint the picture of IMMANUEL's dwelling on her memory, since she was prevented from seeing him. In the midst of this deepest darkness, her heart still clung tightly to IMMANUEL with bonds that could not be broken. But she did not understand this herself.

She could see only darkness.

With heavy steps she wandered like this through the familiar streets of the city.

"Now I will – I must – leave you, you holy city, for I have blasphemed your lord," she exclaimed anxiously.

All hope was already gone; she thought she could already see the satisfaction of Beelzebul and his minions celebrating her downfall; she imagined the suffering that he had in store for her. Her eyes were becoming glazed over in a trance, and letting out a primal scream she collapsed to the ground. At that moment, a window opened nearby.

"Is that you, Mother Simple?" called out Mother Wounded-Hip, who had been awoken by the little old woman's cry. "What is the matter with you?"

Mother Simple neither heard her, nor could she have answered if she had. Terrified, her friend woke up Mother Prodigal, and the two of them came outside.

"What is the matter with you?" they asked anxiously.

"Oh, it is over for me!" sighed Mother Simple heavily, twisting this way and that.

"No," cried Mother Wounded-Hip, "come with us to Immanuel, and all will be well again!"

"Oh, oh!" moaned the little old woman, without opening her eyes or looking at them.

These dear friends used every means to try to bring her back to her senses. When they had managed to do this, they tried to convince her to come with them to Immanuel.

"No, no," she exclaimed, "I have been there just now. But he did not allow me to enter, nor did he answer me. He has altogether rejected me."

In the meantime, Bankrupt Faith returned. He was very pale and weak.

"Come to me, all you who labor and are heavy laden!"[94] he whispered in the little old woman's ear.

These words shot through her soul like a flash of lightening, though briefly. But soon the thick darkness enfolded her once again. Yet she had gained enough courage and strength from these words that she, supported by the arms of her friends, was once again able to take up the journey to IMMANUEL's dwelling. When they arrived and found the door closed, MOTHER PRODIGAL began pounding on it. The door opened. MOTHER PRODIGAL was the first to walk inside, followed by MOTHER WOUNDED-HIP; but when MOTHER SIMPLE attempted to follow them, the door was closed once again. When CONSCIENCE, who had kept himself at a distance, saw her alone again, he walked up to her. But MOTHER SIMPLE cried out in her distress:

"Lord, enter not into judgment with thy maidservant: for in thy sight shall no one living be justified."[95]

"Stop this!" interrupted CONSCIENCE. "Stop your hypocrisy! Do you mean to suggest that you are the maidservant of IMMANUEL? No, you were once, but now that has ended."

Yes, now it was over for her. It would be good for us to spare our ears for a moment from her lamentations.

When both of MOTHER SIMPLE's friends entered IMMANUEL's dwelling, they threw themselves down before his feet and called upon him to quickly come to her help. For otherwise they did not know of any other option than that the little old woman would have to perish. But IMMANUEL answered calmly:

"I know very well the thoughts that I have regarding her.[96] Go and carry her home! She will not die, but live."[97]

At this they set out on their way, carrying their friend home again, assured by the truth of IMMANUEL's words.

"Yes, she will live."

As they did this, morning dawned. MOTHER SIMPLE had, despite all of her efforts, not found any peace. News of her condition soon reached Abrahamsson's ears. He hurried on his way to her, but upon seeing her torment, he nearly fainted. He had never before witnessed anything like this. Here she lay before him, full of the anguish of despair, she who had so recently been teaching him about the unchanging nature of IMMANUEL's grace with so much confidence. Here she lay, a victim of unbelievable suffering, the one person he had imagined was living a life of happiness he could only dream of. Unable to bear this sight, he rushed outside and ran off to IMMANUEL. Anyone he happened to meet along the way he brought with him, and very quickly IMMANUEL was engulfed by a great crowd of people, all of whom were begging for help for MOTHER SIMPLE.

"She is worthy of your help!" Abrahamsson exclaimed, who apparently had already forgotten what the little old woman had so recently tried to imprint on him, namely that everything should come by grace and not of one's own worthiness or merits.

"Lord, have mercy on her!" begged the aforementioned LISTLESS, who now had become tenderly devoted to MOTHER SIMPLE. "Hurry to her rescue. What will become of us, if she perishes?"

When IMMANUEL had listened to these and other intercessions for a moment, he answered:

"I hid my face from her for a moment, but with everlasting grace I will again have mercy on her."[98]

Rejoicing, they returned home to MOTHER SIMPLE to relay his response to her. But she remained deaf to any and all words of assurance.

"It is over for me!" was practically the only response she would give.

Over time, the news of this horrifying event even reached MR. SELF-WISE. Without being the slightest bit moved by the little old woman's distress, he responded in a cold tone:

"Of course, I certainly expected that one day she would taste the fruit of her own seductive opinions, and by doing so, would serve as a warning to the others, that they should avoid following her path."

He could not help but feel just a little bit glad about what was happening, although he had enough sense not to share this with anyone.

At Mother Simple's bedside there now gathered a large crowd of her friends. And although they watched her with deep compassion and observed her heart-wrenching anguish, her weakness, her heart-broken eyes, in which only a silent despair could be seen, they nevertheless took comfort in the hope of the imminent help that Immanuel would soon be bringing. But one hour after the next passed, and no one came. It was already getting on towards evening, and Immanuel was nowhere to be seen. Terrified, Abrahamsson hurried back to Immanuel's dwelling, but was not granted entry.

"What does this mean?" he asked, in an anxiety that bordered on despair. "Has Immanuel forgotten to be gracious?"

"No," cried a voice behind him; it was Bankrupt Faith , who had just now come from his home, a little house called Prayer-Closet, which lay in the district, The Forgiveness of Sins.[99] There he had eaten until he was satisfied at the table of grace and been resting for a while, so that he felt strong and in good spirits again. "Do not be uneasy," he added. "Wait upon his word and depend on it! Heaven and earth will pass away, but Immanuel's words will not pass away. What he has promised, he will certainly keep."

Strengthened by this answer, Abrahamsson returned. But neither he nor the rest of them could yet free themselves from their fears and anxieties, particularly when he heard the little old woman's constant cries:

"It is over for me! Oh, woe is me, woe is me!"

Night had already fallen when IMMANUEL sent for his servant EVANGELIST:

"You have heard," he said upon entering, "that I have made up my mind to send this period of anxiety on MOTHER SIMPLE. I have allowed BEELZEBUL to torment her.[100] She is to me a priceless instrument, and as such I must see to it that she is refined in the furnace of affliction. She was on the verge of becoming pleased with herself for her deep insights regarding the secrets of grace. Therefore, I feared for her and needed to allow her to once again experience what she amounts to on her own. Now she believes that I have completely abandoned her, but she does not know how my heart is breaking with mercifulness. Go now to her and say to her on my behalf that I will be gracious to her and will never consider her sins. I hope that she will remember this lesson for a long time to come.

Rejoicing with this task of grace, the faithful servant raced to the suffering old woman.

"Dear mother," he said as he reached her bed, "you have sinned greatly, but in the name of IMMANUEL and on his behalf I say to you, that he is still gracious and will never consider your misdeeds. The mountains shall depart and the hills be removed; but his grace shall not depart from thee, neither shall the covenant of his peace be removed.[101] He himself has sent me with this message for you."

The little old woman, who had been lying with her eyes shut as though dead, looked up as he said this. It seemed as though her despair began to depart. She said nothing. But a strange calm began to spread over her whole being. In this same instant, her eyes fell upon the door, which now was opened. All of the sudden the little old woman turned around, hid her face and began to weep loudly. The new arrival, who was IMMANUEL, walked up to her and spoke to her in the most tender way.

And what followed was the most precious conversation, for which even the most vivid description would be unsatisfactory, especially for those who have experienced something like this themselves. Therefore we ought to leave her alone as she apologizes for her unbelief, confesses her sins and everything else, as well as receives in response IMMANUEL's wondrous answers and repeated assurances of grace. Everyone present felt moved by a sense of holy reverence, and none of them went from that place with a dry eye.

TENTH CHAPTER

Abrahamsson's visits to Loose Living and The World

Throughout EVANGELIUM the days and months passed by under a sky of alternating darkness and light, sorrows and joys. It was a blessed city, and IMMANUEL was the source of everyone's heath and assurance. To be sure, people did have a difficult time understanding his peculiar style of governance, but this was something they had come to accept about their situation and so they held their peace. On the other hand, Abrahamsson, with his strong temperament, continued to be troubled by this. However, his interaction with MOTHER SIMPLE seemed to be an endless source of blessing for him. Time after time he felt the need to go and speak with her, just in order to hear her explain one more time how it was that a person in EVANGELIUM was supposed to live on grace alone, for he had so often forgotten it. And if it hadn't been for MOTHER SIMPLE, then he would certainly have become fed up with FATHER EXPERIENCE and long ago left EVANGELIUM.

"I haven't got a clue," he said one time to MOTHER SIMPLE, "what this fellow FATHER EXPERIENCE is trying to say. I asked him yesterday to help me to learn what true strength is, and he promised that he would. But then he brought me into the CLASS OF THE WRETCHED, and there he took away all my strength, so that I was about to drown in weakness."

"Ah, yes…that sounds like his usual method," answered MOTHER SIMPLE, smiling, "and there is no other way to learn, that the greatest source of strength should be from IMMANUEL through grace, which is the true and free kind of grace."

So Abrahamsson attempted to live his life according to this advice and enjoyed some relatively calm days for a while. He seemed to begin all the more to understand this holy city. In The Forgiveness of Sins, he thrived well enough, and in Sanctification he kept himself busy every day. With faithfulness and propriety he attended to his work and made a great impression on many.

In this way, as we have mentioned, things progressed for a rather long period. That is, except for one morning. All of the sudden, Abrahamsson burst out from his room and darted into another room, which had a door that led to the courtyard. Almost deathly pale, he banged against this outer door. It was locked. Mother Simple, who just at that moment came onto the scene, positioned herself in his way and asked just where he intended to run off to.

"Out of the way, out of the way! Open the door, at once!" was his anxiety-ridden answer.

"Does this mean that the Squire does not need to remain here any longer?"

"Oh, but of course I *need* it. But I simply *may* not."

"Doesn't the Squire remember that Immanuel said he brought him here with the idea that the he would be welcome to stay as long as he needed?"

"Well yes. But what he meant was: as long as I was like all of *you*."

"What exactly are *we* like, in that case?"

"You know that well enough yourself. But I am miserable beyond all description."

"Yes, God help me, that is how I am as well."

"Yet, you're never as bad as I am: open that door at once!" But Mother Simple had a hold on the door, and she refused to open. Instead, she saw to it that the door was firmly bolted and removed the key.

"The Squire must not allow himself to lose his mind," she announced. "Has the Squire already forgotten what we spoke about concerning grace, this very grace, about which Old Paulus said: 'Where sin abounded, grace abounded much more'?"[102]

"Yes, grace – GRACE – it is always this grace that you prattle on about, as if there were altogether nothing else to speak about. But you ought instead to speak more about *strength*. With that you would have a greater gain."

"Hmm. Yes, strength – that is a part of grace, the free kind of grace, the grace that soars to the heavens, about which David sings:

For as the heaven is high above the earth,
so great is his grace toward them that fear him.
As far as the east is from the west,
so far hath he removed our transgressions from us.
His grace stretches as wide as the heavens."[103]

But Abrahamsson's ears would not tolerate a lecture like this.

"I have got to get out of this place!" he cried.

He had hardly gotten these last words out of his mouth when the door was opened by someone entering from the outside. Abrahamsson rushed out blindly, but collided with the one who was entering, who took him in his arms and bore him unconscious inside again. After a moment, he dared to open his eyes, but was struck dumb in a sort of joyful embarrassment when he realized that it was Immanuel who was holding him up. He then heard his assuring voice whisper:

"Take heart, your sins are forgiven!"[104]

Now he candidly admitted everything. The matter was namely as follows. His son VIGILANT had on several occasions demonstrated himself to be a good and dependable young man. Because of this, Abrahamsson had *increasingly come to trust him,* and began depending on him more and more. But at breakfast earlier that day, while all those at the table were eating and chatting about vain things, DROWSY had managed to slip some sleeping drops onto VIGILANT's plate, upon which he dozed off. HATEFUL made a surprise ambush on his father and knocked him to the floor.

Poor little CONSCIENCE-PEACE, a lovely girl that his wife had borne him in EVANGELIUM, was startled with fright, and hopped out the window and disappeared. This scare had badly shaken his confidence. But when IMMANUEL had set things right, CONSCIENCE-PEACE returned to her former seat. At any rate, Abrahamsson had, from all of this disturbing behavior, come to realize that his son VIGILANT was not as dependable as he had once believed.

"At last I am beginning to believe," he said, "that, pure and simple, there is no one else to depend on other than IMMANUEL. There is nothing as reliable to hold on to as grace."

Abrahamsson would have done well to remember this lesson, bought at such a high price, but unfortunately he would not. A bitter experience would once again have to teach him this lesson again, as illustrated by the following sorrowful events.

The house where Abrahamsson lived was situated in such a way that it enjoyed a sweeping view out over a great plain, called EMPTINESS, beyond which was visible the great city of LOOSE LIVING, beautifully situated in the distance.[105] This city was different in many respects from the city of EVANGELIUM, even though they were not all that far apart. To begin with, there were neither city walls nor watchmen, but instead the city was completely free and open. The people appeared to be prosperous, each face communicated peace and ease of mind. There was also abundant joy to be found here. Particularly delightful were the short day trips and pleasure excursions that were arranged by the residents so that they could visit the city THE WORLD[106] situated a few miles away. The purpose of these visits was to attend the various shows enjoyed by that city's inhabitants, which were referred to as "innocent pastimes." To be clear, they themselves did not participate, but simply remained in the audience.

Leading into the city of LOOSE LIVING there was a gate, called CARNALITY, but it was seldom that anyone entered by this gate, for inscribed over it were the frightening words: *Go not astray! God does not allow himself to be mocked, for whatever a man sows, that will he also reap!*[107] For this reason, people tended to make use of another backroad, and went through a gate called FREEDOM, which was much less intimidating. The inhabitants of the city thought of themselves as "liberally-minded," though they were not all that particular in terms of ideology or lifestyle.[108] What they actually placed value on was not really peace with IMMANUEL, but rather *mutual* peace, love and harmony. They were also famous for a number of good characteristics. This drew many people to their fold who had begun to be suspicious of the inhabitants of EVANGELIUM because of the fact that the people in that city could at times be embroiled in arguments with one another over various matters. It was also rather remarkable the testimonies that would be given by these people, who had previously regarded the city with suspicion, but later allowed themselves to decide to move there. Many of them said that they had never before, prior to their move, been able to find any stable and lasting peace or certainty in their minds, but instead were always tempted by fear and anxiety.

"There is no true freedom in EVANGELIUM," they asserted, "for that reason, neither can there be any lasting peace."

Others stated, in a comforting tone, that since they had moved to Loose Living, they had never been plagued by sin or by Beelzebul to the same degree as they had been before their move. Yes, there were even some who asserted that here they had been altogether free from any temptations.

"All of that whining, which people suffer from in Evangelium, is simply nowhere to be found here," they said.

There were two other noteworthy men who also had their dwellings in Loose Living. The one was called Have-Enough and the other one's name was Need-Nothing. They claimed to be the half brothers of Bankrupt Faith, and they were quick to praise their city.

"Look at us," they said, "and the luxurious, contented, and good lives we lead. Compare us with Bankrupt Faith. It should be plain to see which city is the more healthy one to live in."

All of this Abrahamsson had often heard already, yet he always felt a certain suspicion each time. But the longer this went on, the more he began to become anxious by this talk, in particular since Immanuel had behaved so peculiarly during his recent visits with Abrahamsson, which were becoming both rare and brief. Sometimes Immanuel said nothing at all when he came, and sometimes he only responded to their questions with short replies. It seemed as though it did not interest him to find out how they were doing. Sometimes his replies were so indefinite and unclear, even ambiguous, that they left Abrahamsson in a tortuous anxiety and uncertainty. Now, with this last visit, when Abrahamsson had complained about his bitter distress, Immanuel had altogether nothing to say, but simply shook his head and walked away, acting in a way that made it seem like he was upset. This pained Abrahamsson more than anything else, for he could not *fathom* such strange behavior on the part of Immanuel. He tried hard at first to be patient and to suffer through it, as well as to avert his eyes from all the distracting enticements around him.

"Grace, grace," he mumbled to himself. "I think I will indeed continue to rely on that grace which is free, as high as heaven and which covers every sin."[109]

But when it just never seemed to get better and IMMANUEL kept him guessing regarding what he thought about him and would not answer to the constant stream of messages that were sent to him, then Abrahamsson became all the more anxious. When it finally came to the point where he repeatedly was denied entry to IMMANUEL's residence on several occasions when he tried calling on him, Abrahamsson grew rather weary of these apparently pointless errands. Day after day, he went about with hanging head and a sorrowful countenance. All of MOTHER SIMPLE's words and attempts at assurance were fruitless, and she wondered where all of this was going to lead for her friend. Abrahamsson acted as though he was trying to avoid her company and did not wish to speak with her, with whom he had previously been so close. In the midst of these worries, this endearing little old woman knew of no other recourse than to dutifully go to IMMANUEL to speak with him. But he answered so vaguely and ambiguously, that she did not really understand what he meant. Yet, she did not let herself be frightened away by this, but instead became all the more resolute and waited in stillness for whatever might come.

It was to be expected that Abrahamsson would not be able to work while he felt like this. The whole of his existence bore the mark of powerlessness and weakness. This was worsened all the more by the constant reminders brought to him by his bookkeeper, CONSCIENCE, of the need for him to remain diligent and faithful. In particular, he felt ill whenever he saw the inscription above the gate that led into SANCTIFICATION, which read: *Without sanctification, no one shall see the Lord.*[110] There arose in his heart thoughts of resentment toward JUSTUS ALL-POWERFUL. He felt that he was not free. When anyone suggested to him that all was not well with him, he became bitter, and when he would hear others singing their songs of praise with delight and joy while they were carrying on with their work, this bitterness grew all the more. In this way, his condition was worsened by the day.

"Around here people are under the yoke of slavery," he said to Mother Simple one day.

"People? Which people?" she asked in return.

"Well, all of us," Abrahamsson answered. "I read just today something that Old Paulus had written. He says: 'Be not entangled with the yoke of bondage. It is to freedom have you been called.'[111] And then I thought 'that's precisely it!' He has figured it out. What we are lacking is the true freedom."

"Alright. But didn't the Squire read the words that Paulus wrote directly after that?"

"No. My heart had gained enough from those words that I didn't need to read any more."

"That's too bad, then. Otherwise, the rest of Paulus' words are: 'You have been called unto freedom; only do not allow freedom to be an opportunity for the flesh.'[112] I have seen over the past several days how the Squire has become ensnared in a kind of slavery that is quite distressing. Evangelium is not to blame for that."

"Of course, slavery and freedom – those are words that you constantly have on your lips. But what do those words mean? What is it to be a slave?"

"Hmm, well, I mean, in my uneducated way," responded Mother Simple, "that a person is a slave if he is under a law that commands and forces him to do something that he himself does not want."

"That's a strange answer!" exclaimed Abrahamsson. "But tell me this: who then is free? Can you also tell me that, in your simple way?"

"Free…yes, the one who is free is the one who, from the bottom of his heart, wants the same thing that the law requires, and because of this, fulfills his own will when he follows what the law commands. The Squire knows this quite well. There have been times when the Squire felt that he was free, and even fortunate and happy, under the very same commandments that now seem heavy to him. Back then, it was the case that what the Squire himself loved and wanted was the same as what was required by the law. The Squire does not have the same willing spirit as he did before, and for this reason feels that he is not free."

This felt like a stab in the heart to Abrahamsson when he heard these words. It made him very anxious. But he did not allow himself to be humbled. Lately he had allowed his spirit to become obstinate. The reasons for this were many. But contributing to this was, in particular, the careless way in which some of his friends behaved when they spoke with him. Instead of speaking with him lovingly and with encouragement, they were harsh in their words. Some of them even went so far as to tease him. Thus he began all the more to feel that his situation was unbearable. And yet certainty remained elusive for him.

"Oh," he sighed once, when he was standing by his window one evening, looking out toward the neighboring city of Loose Living, which was all lit up beautifully. "Who knows if they aren't right, after all! I suffer so often from suspicion, anxiety, fear and uncertainty, and it truly is confining to sit here like this, penned up within these walls, and being watched from all sides, as though I were a slave. On that point, they all are right. And anybody who has lived in both places and is familiar with both situations must have a good idea which city is the better one to live in. It would be wise for me to follow their advice. Oh, I wish I could be certain what it is I should do! Perhaps this is what the words of Paulus are referring to when he speaks of slaves to the law?"

While Abrahamsson was immersed in these and similar reflections, he heard footsteps in the distance. This walking sounded like it was continuing to grow nearer, and when he peered out through the window, Abrahamsson recognized his dear old friend, Admirer.

"Good evening, dear brother Adamsson," was the greeting of this newly arrived friend. "It has been a while since I saw you last."

"I go by Abrahamsson nowadays, not Adamsson," he interrupted.

"Dear brother," answered Admirer, as he with a serious look lifted up his index finger, "be on guard against presumptuousness!"

"But it was Immanuel himself who gave me that name."

"Yes, yes, that can be so; I have heard about that. But let's not speak any more about that. You go ahead and keep your new name. But how are you doing?"

"How am I doing? Oh, well…." Abrahamsson hemmed and hawed and had difficulty articulating himself.

"It does not seem to be all that good," interrupted Admirer. "And how can it be good in that city where you live? The air around there is altogether too heavy and stuffy, which is hard on the heart and the lungs. Many who used to live in Evangelium, but now live in Loose Living, have confided with me that when they lived in Evangelium it was quite often that they felt they had difficulty breathing, particularly in the district Sanctification. Occasionally they even suffered from heart trouble. Now, by contrast, they feel much better and quite healthy in the lighter air that is typically found in Loose Living."

Abrahmsson's spirits sank with these words. Admirer, noticing this, stopped in the middle of his story.

"Well, well," he said, "excuse me if I am hurting you. You know that I always just have to say what is on my mind. But we shouldn't talk any longer about this matter; come and follow me!"

"Where to?"

"Home to my house, of course, because I have invited some friends from The World to come for a visit! You have nothing to be afraid of, for despite the fact that they are people of The World, they are quite principled and serious people. And, in their own way, they too are quite pious. Besides, if you don't have a good time in our company, you can always come back here whenever you like."

Abrahamsson felt indecisive and uneasy.

"But Immanuel, though – what would he say about something like this?"

"Immanuel!" answered Admirer. "Do you honestly think that we don't also serve Immanuel, just because we don't go around moaning and groaning like all of you people do here in Evangelium, just because we feel so free and happy? You could see this for yourself, if you came to our church. But hurry along now, the day is wasting. The friends from The World will be gathering in a couple of hours. I have a quick horse and a comfortable surrey hitched outside. We can be over in our town in no time flat. Come, now, let's get a move on!"

"But hold on," said Abrahamsson, after pondering this for a moment as he sat quietly. "What prompted you to move to Loose Living and leave behind that beautiful estate of yours, Self-Activity?"

"Ah, it happened because of the simple fact that the estate burned down. Since it was not insured for fire, I found myself homeless. Then I had the choice of whether to move to Evangelium or try to build up my fortune again, since I did still have a few resources left. But just as I was in the middle of these plans, I ran into my old friend Weather Cock. He talked me out of pursuing any kind of plans to rebuild, and also discouraged me from moving to Evangelium. He said that at one point he had lived there himself for a couple of years. But when he found it difficult to live there, then he had ended up moving to Loose Living. And there, he assured me, he had discovered that it was the easiest place he had ever lived. Since I myself had no way of judging the matter, I was thankful to get advice from a man who had some experience. It seemed to me to be a God-send, that he would come my way at just that moment. I am glad, too, that I followed his advice. Though Self-Activity had its charms to be sure, there was also a great deal of toil and hardship involved in living there, especially taking care of the estate and keeping up its ancient prestige."

Abrahamsson became all the more anxious. Finally he asked: "Why did Weather Cock find it hard to live in Evangelium?"

"Well," he said, "among other things, because the only joy that people had there was to get to see and meet Immanuel. But he reveals himself so seldomly that people are often left in fear and uncertainty. Besides he described what the air is like there, as I just told you. He was the first person who I heard that from. Since then, there have been many who have confirmed that what he said was true. And I would expect that you have probably felt the same thing, even you, if you were to be honest about it."

"Yes," sighed Abrahamsson. "I have not seen Immanuel now for a long while." He thought about continuing to share what was on his mind, but Admirer cut him off.

"Let us not waste time with discussion of all that! There is something else that I might mention to set you more at ease. I can tell you that Dean Orthodox, the generally respected man, who lives in our city, has accepted my invitation and promised to come this evening."

"But one shouldn't keep company with the people of THE WORLD. It is always dangerous, and I in no way wish to go back to THE WORLD again."

"There is no danger in it. But for safety's sake, take VIGILANT with you!"

"But he is not really dependable. To place oneself in harm's way, relying only on VIGILANT, that would be a risk for sure. I am apprehensive about this whole get together."

"You nut!" exclaimed ADMIRER, laughing. "Do you, at your age, still not have enough character and experience that you can keep company with a few respectable children of THE WORLD without being scarred by that? At this point, you ought to be advanced enough! Or is this one more example of how all of you in EVANGELIUM are not learning anything and have stopped growing? Can you all be so stunted in your development?"

With these words, ADMIRER touched on a rather sensitive point. For Abrahamsson was certainly always willing to admit his weaknesses and inexperience to himself, but he did not tolerate it well whenever anyone else criticized him. So, now he *fortified* himself, donned his coat, took VIGILANT by the hand, and walked out through the back entrance to ADMIRER, who heartily embraced him. When they were seated in the surrey, VIGILANT remarked:

"But what will IMMANUEL say about this?"

Abrahamsson was caught off guard, but answered:

"I hope that he will not say anything."

VIGILANT withdrew to silence, and fell asleep in the back seat of the surrey. And then it took off with breakneck speed.

"This is an excellent road," said ADMIRER. "It is uphill when one travels from LOOSE LIVING to EVANGELIUM. But when one travels the other way, it is all downhill, so it is an enjoyable ride."

A diverse and lively conversation arose between these two friends as they started on their way, since they had not seen one another for a long time. But what Abrahamsson really wished was to get to the bottom of why ADMIRER had made the move to LOOSE LIVING. For this reason he decided to once again ask the question, and ADMIRER was not in the least bit unwilling to tell about his "conversion," as he called it.

"As I already mentioned," he said, "it was the fire that devoured my property. You also know about the advice that I received from WEATHER COCK. Because of his encouragement to make the move, that's what I did. Yet, I was still uncertain where I was headed, because I kept thinking about all your well-meaning but simple-minded letters from EVANGELIUM. Forgive me for saying what is on my mind. So, I set out on the road OWN BOOTSTRAPS. I had taken with me all my money in a cash box, and had also packed up the GOOD DEEDS that I had been saving, and which had been left over after I had paid my debts. After a few days' journey, I caught sight of SINAI. As I made my approach, there came a band of ten men who attempted to attack me and make off with all of my possessions. Their aim was to have me thrown in prison. I was instantly terrified, and would have certainly fallen victim to their violence if it had not been for MR. FALSE ASSURANCE, who, by God's grace, had been sent to my aid. He now rushed to me, and cried out with JUSTUS ALL-POWERFUL's own words: *'It is to freedom have you been called!'*[113] and then, thankfully, transported me past this most unpleasant prison. In this state of happiness I traveled on and, after a journey of several days, arrived at THE ROCK OF OFFENSE[114] where, as you know, there is a fork in the road. It was there that I encountered the TEACHERS OF SCRIPTURE from THE WORLD, of whom Paulus speaks so contemptuously.[115] They were for the most part balding and nearsighted old men with long, moth-eaten robes with pompous collars. They appeared like a lot of deep thinkers indeed. Out from their mouths poured a great deal of hot air. They were hard at work trying to excavate that great rocky outcropping and carry the debris away so that people could travel on this route more easily. Some of them were busy trying to blast it all away, bit by bit. But since it didn't seem to be working out very well, there were others who tried to use a large crane, which they called ENLIGHTENMENT. Now it was their idea that as the lifting motion of this crane slowly raised the whole rock (or as they phrased it, 'as everything progressed according to ENLIGHTENMENT'), then THE ROCK OF OFFENSE would simply topple over and roll away."

"I could not make up my mind as to which course I should take. Then I met Mr. GOOD NATURED, who happened to walk by SINAI as well, as luck would have it. This man had previously found shelter at a wayside inn, which was called BROKEN HEARTEDNESS, situated at the base of the mountain. Here he said he had spent some time, and that now, like me, he was in the same state of bewilderment. As we stood there and weighed our options, we received some advice from a missionary, who was said to be from EVANGELIUM. He told us that the road that went directly over the mountain was called NEW BIRTH and led to EVANGELIUM. The road which veered off to the right, he said, was called MORAL IMPROVEMENT and led to SELF-RIGHTEOUSNESS. The third road this simple-minded creature called HYPOCRISY; this went off to the left of THE ROCK OF OFFENSE and led to LOOSE LIVING. At that point, I would have just as well desired to travel to EVANGELIUM. However, the rock was so steep and difficult, that I am sure that even if I thought I might have been able to make it up and over it by making a concerted effort, it still would have been impossible to bring along my bundle of belongings and my cashbox. It was at that point that I decided to take WEATHER COCK's advice, and so I followed the road that led off to the left. After a pleasant journey, I arrived at LOOSE LIVING. GOOD NATURED, who was afraid of ruining his fine clothes by climbing over the mountain, took off to the right toward SELF-RIGHTEOUSNESS.

And he is apparently doing well there, according to what he has told me in a letter that I recently received from him. He seems to be oblivious to how good I have it here, since he also tried in his letter to encourage me to move there, among other recommendations."

After ADMIRER finished this story, he continued to praise the virtues of the city, speaking about how people there "don't bother so much about one's shortcomings, since a person could never become perfect, of course, no matter how much one exerted oneself," and on and on.

In the meantime, they were nearing their destination. Abrahamsson felt a little bit sick after listening to this speech ADMIRER had given. He had really wanted to give ADMIRER a word of warning about all of this. "But now is not the time for that," he thought. Thus he decided to wait until a more appropriate occasion. When the surrey stopped outside the entrance to ADMIRER's fashionable and magnificently illuminated home, Abrahamsson simply said to his friend something that he thought was more important at that moment:

"Now you ought to present me as Mr. Adamsson, for it will serve no purpose for people from THE WORLD to know my name, not least since they would almost definitely just make fun of it."

"But of course," answered MR. ADMIRER, "for in everything we should see to it that we act wisely, and don't irritate people unnecessarily. What is more," he added, "have a look around. Here everything is up-to-date. We are not as old fashioned as all of you tend to be in EVANGELIUM."

This was the kind of thing they discussed as they entered ADMIRER's home. Everything was very fashionable. Many people were gathered there. Soon they were caught up in a lively conversation about everything imaginable; about politics, the year's crops, fashion magazines, the faults of their neighbors, and so on. All of these mouths worked and ground away like so many windmills grinding away at anything and everything at hand, but without any of it being the grain that gives nourishment. Abrahamsson quickly found himself in high spirits. VIGILANT would, of course, give him an elbow in the side now and then, trying to keep him on his guard. But Abrahamsson simply answered:

"Oh, this is not so dangerous."

When VIGILANT saw how easily he was dismissed and since he was getting so tired, he simply fell asleep again, completely unnoticed. Abrahamsson had gotten caught up in an interesting conversation about the church and its affairs with a certain Mr. PRIMITIVE PIETY, with whom he soon began to confide openly. In this way, several hours passed by in a most respectable manner. That evening, DEAN ORTHODOX held a Bible exposition, which Abrahamsson enjoyed very much. Afterwards, they ate the evening meal, during which the conversation continued, touching on all kinds of topics. The dean himself even came up with several entertaining stories to share, which prompted uproarious laughter. Then they arranged an evening devotion service with hymn singing. The evening concluded with a jovial exchange of farewells as they bid one another good night. Although all this had been a far cry from how things were done in EVANGELIUM, still Abrahamsson thought that this was downright enjoyable and did not see anything harmful in it.

The following day was a Sunday. Abrahamsson gladly followed along with his friend and his family to church. There things proceeded in a completely different way than he had seen before. The dean's sermon was full of amusing anecdotes, to which the audience could not help but respond with laughter. All throughout, he made use of an impressive vocabulary, which inspired general admiration. After the sermon, they sang spiritual songs set to dance melodies from THE WORLD. In the evening, a party was thrown at the church, with solo performances, applause, laughter, and shouts for encores.

When Admirer and Abrahamsson left the church, Admirer said:

"It is unbelievably lively in our church. Everyone who previously has lived in Evangelium and now lives here says that during the services in Evangelium it is so stiff and monotonous that people quite simply fall asleep."

Abrahamsson was at a loss for words. He felt ill, but figured it was probably because of the fact that he had grown accustomed to the narrow-minded way people did things in Evangelium, which had by now become ingrained in him.

"And our beautiful church, as well!" continued Admirer. "The money to build it was raised through a special lottery. Tickets were bought by many of our friends, both from The World and Evangelium, and the whole enterprise was managed splendidly. Dean Orthodox, who knows human nature well, came up with the idea, and it was true what he said: 'Whenever people's willingness to make sacrifices runs out, then it is good to play on their love for entertainment in order to make up the difference.'"

Primitive Piety stayed at Admirer's house for a few days and the friendship between him and Abrahamsson continued to grow. But when on the last evening of his stay they were about to part company, Primitive Piety asked if 'Adamsson' had any desire to follow along and make a visit to the city The World. Vigilant was sleeping and heard none of this. Abrahamsson accepted the invitation and followed along.

"For," he thought, "Primitive Piety is, after all, a pleasant and endearing person, even though he lives in The World. And I can talk with him about a great many important matters, although not about Immanuel. Yes, maybe I will even have the chance to share with him a serious word of awakening."

Little VIGILANT, who was assumed to be resting well and who was supposed to be gaining his strength from this healthy sleep, was not wakened, but instead was left behind to sleep at the house of MR. ADMIRER. Thus, Abrahamsson got under way with his new friend. They boarded a train, and Abrahamsson marveled that there could be such a rapid and comfortable form of transportation, and that one could travel to THE WORLD in such a short time, despite the fact that the distance was so great. The official name for the railway was INDOLENCE, but people usually referred to it as CONVENIENCE. And now we shall leave Abrahamsson for a moment.

ELEVENTH CHAPTER

The Five Cities – The meeting between Abrahamsson and Watchman

At this point in our story it seems timely to give an account of these five cities and the histories of their founding. So, we will take our leave from Abrahamsson and the others for a moment in order to familiarize ourselves with some of these new environments and the people who live there, which we have not yet had time to describe.

What first catches our attention is the city of HOLINESS. This was a great and magnificent city, filled with splendor and glory, and surrounded by walls that shone like pearls and precious stones. The city was divided into two halves by a broad stream, which was called the RIVER OF LIFE. It was here that JUSTUS ALL-POWERFUL held court, surrounded by hosts of servants who sang his praises, called ANGELS. Everything in this city was sheer joy and blessedness. There was no sin, no sighing, and no weeping to be found here. At one point in the city's history, however, there was one person, LUCIFER, who broke ranks with JUSTUS ALL-POWERFUL. As a consequence, he was expelled from the city, though not before taking a large following with him. After assuming the name BEELZEBUL, he established a wide-reaching and powerful kingdom, called the KINGDOM OF DARKNESS, in which he ruled as king over the other fallen ANGELS. This kingdom was in every respect the exact opposite of HOLINESS.

After this schism in HOLINESS had taken place, LORD JUSTUS decided to found another city, which would also be full of his glory. After he had established and organized it according to his wisdom, he populated it with people who were to be a reflection of him, with the idea that it would be these people themselves who would be responsible for the ownership and governance of the city. This city was called PARADISE. In the early days, the people here were thriving, and counted themselves fortunate to live under his love and be obedient. They were righteous and holy without any sin. But from the moment BEELZEBUL laid eyes on the city, he was overcome by the lust to conquer it. This was in part because he harbored an overwhelming hatred for LORD JUSTUS, and also because he could not stand the fact that there were people living such happy lives. Because of this, he made stealthy visits into the city and, with great cunning, lured people away to a life of unfaithfulness and disobedience against LORD JUSTUS. As a result, these people were expelled from PARADISE.

These people would then go on to establish another city, called THE WORLD. This city was under the authority of BEELZEBUL, but was directly governed by a burgomaster whose name was SELF, a very mature gentleman, who had as his assistant another very decisive person, who was called WILL. In all practical matters, it was this latter gentleman who held council and wrote laws. In his assistance was also a lackey by the name of SHALL, who was both hard and heartless, as well as a rather arbitrary man.[116]

Indignant about this course of events, LORD JUSTUS was of the mind that the city ought to be destroyed. Yet, when he considered these poor people, whom he created to be his own children – when he looked at them and saw their fallen and lost state, his heart was broken with mercy, and he made up his mind to save them. At that moment he turned to his son IMMANUEL and said:

"You see, I love them and will not suffer them to be lost to their misery; no, I must help them, and it is you, my son, who will carry out this work for me."[117]

This greatly pleased IMMANUEL, and so he was sent off to THE WORLD. Enraged over this, BEELZEBUL incited the burgomaster of the city and the rest of the population to rise up against IMMANUEL. In response, IMMANUEL summoned all of the forces he could (though they were a desperate band) and made his advance against BEELZEBUL, with the climax of the campaign taking place on the mountain of GOLGOTHA. In this bloody, pitched battle, it was IMMANUEL who emerged with the victory. LORD JUSTUS rejoiced over this and appointed his son to govern a great city that was to be established on the slopes of the mountain GOLGOTHA and along the RIVER OF BLOOD; this would be called EVANGELIUM. In this city, it would be IMMANUEL himself who would be king and lord, and this was to be a refuge for all miserable souls who wished to be liberated from BEELZEBUL's insufferable tyranny. It was for this reason that IMMANUEL saw to it that the SPIRIT OF TRUTH composed a great book, which provided thorough instructions regarding the city's constitution, construction and the glorious benefits of living there. This book was sent to the city THE WORLD. In addition to this, there were teachers who were sent as well, who were to give a more direct explanation of his will, as well as extend an invitation to the residents to move to EVANGELIUM.

But BEELZEBUL would not rest. When he saw that every storm that was sent against EVANGELIUM amounted to nothing, then he decided to dedicate his energies instead to arranging everything so that the people in THE WORLD would enjoy themselves. In this way he sought, and made much progress, toward causing them to forget that it was *him* who was actually their lord. This was also why he allowed the burgomaster SELF and the councilman WILL to be the ones who gave the city its three constitutional laws, which delighted the inhabitants most of all. These laws were: the DESIRES OF THE EYE, the DESIRES OF THE FLESH, and PRIDEFUL LIVING. With these laws he extended to the inhabitants an almost unlimited degree of freedom. For the most part, he achieved his aim. For when the missionaries came and offered them freedom in Evangelium, then the inhabitants of The World answered that they had plenty of freedom and could not possibly have it any better than they already did.

But Beelzebul did not stop there. In response, he sent out his own teachers to say to the people that neither he himself nor Justus nor Immanuel ever really existed, and that the great book only contained a bunch of fables. These teachers he called Freethinkers. But in reality their name was Thoughtlesslings. Whenever he now and then was not able to seduce and lull to sleep as many people as he would like, then he had some other teachers to rely on. These people warned the residents against the Freethinkers, but had their own unique message in which they placed such an emphasis on Justus All-Powerful's mercy and indulgence, that they claimed there was no danger at all in living in The World, as long as people lived sufficiently respectable lives.

One could almost conclude that this was the most powerful method of seduction. For these teachers, after all, did warn people against the wiles of Beelzebul and his preachers, the Freethinkers. And they always expressed their great respect for the words of Justus All-Powerful, highly praising his love, and even quoting him whenever they made references to it.

In the meantime, Justus All-Powerful had sent his servant Moses with his law to The World in order to expose to its residents their true predicament and the terrible end that awaited them all. He told them namely that a judgment of wrath would be passed over the whole city, at which time all of them who lived there would be thrown into prison and serve an eternal sentence in Gehenna, which had originally been prepared for Beelzebul and his servants. His intention was that this law would inspire the inhabitants to abandon the city and move to Evangelium. This vexed Beelzebul, but he did everything he could to counteract this, secretly spurring his preachers to remain diligent in their work. As part of this effort, he devised a plan to send to THE WORLD a preacher named LIBERALLY-MINDED, who tried as hard as he could to demonstrate that the threats of MOSES were thought up by none other than the shrewd enemy BEELZEBUL, so that by this strategy he could capture people in his claws. Since he made frequent use of JUSTUS ALL-POWERFUL's own words, this had a tremendous effect, which was particularly pleasing to BEELZEBUL.

Whenever these measures failed to catch as many people in his snares as he might have wished, he called his servants to council, so that they could evaluate their options. In these meetings, many proposals were laid out by those who attended. But there was one in particular that caught his attention and praise. This proposal was made by someone who stood among his inner circle.

"You are aware," this man said, "that EVANGELIUM has been built with the goal to serve as a refuge for anyone and everyone who has grown weary of THE WORLD. Now you have certainly been preaching to the inhabitants of THE WORLD that they have a great deal of freedom to enjoy. But this freedom is of an entirely different nature than the freedom which IMMANUEL has preached for those who have settled in EVANGELIUM. For this reason, my advice to you is that you should also build another refuge on roughly these same principles. In THE WORLD, the inhabitants can claim a physical sort of freedom, whereas in EVANGELIUM the freedom is more of a spiritual nature, built on the law: *grace for everything*. Now you can certainly build a city like that, where people can retain their *physical* freedoms, but at the same time have a law, which also points to a *spiritual* freedom: for example, the law could sound something like this: 'There is no danger from sin, for IMMANUEL has access to a bottomless well of grace.' This," he continued, "will without a doubt deceive many."

Quite pleased with this, BEELZEBUL announced that construction should begin immediately according to this plan. This was how the city of LOOSE LIVING was founded. He also saw to it that a convenient highway was built that could serve as an easy means of traveling between the new city and THE WORLD. Then he eagerly sent out a host of preachers to the various parts of THE WORLD. With burning zeal these preachers proclaimed to everyone that, while there was still time, they should flee from this unfortunate city and set out for LOOSE LIVING. The impact that these preachers had on people was great indeed, particularly for those who had already begun to become anxious about their situation. Great crowds were assembled, and in a short time the new city was populated.

However, even this plot of BEELZEBUL's soon met with a rather formidable obstacle. Namely, there was a missionary who started preaching zealously against LOOSE LIVING. He made the case that it should make no difference where people lived, so long as their old carnal spirit remained.

This caught BEELZEBUL's attention. So he now decided to found the city SELF-RIGHTEOUSNESS, to which he created a long, winding and difficult highway. Soon he had even managed to have this city populated. Among those who distinguished themselves in advising numerous people to move there was burgomaster SELF. BEELZEBUL sent out a company of preachers, whose mission was to prove that SELF-RIGHTEOUSNESS was the only safe refuge for lost sinners.

That all of this would mislead many people was to be expected, for now there were three sorts of preachers, who all had one thing in common; they all encouraged people to abandon the city of THE WORLD, but to three different destinations. In order to make this scheme even more complex, BEELZEBUL incited these preachers to engage in bitter debates with one another. This caused many people to be hopelessly confused. Some began to doubt JUSTUS ALL-POWERFUL's words, since they could be interpreted in multiple ways. Most people, however, were fortified in their convictions in these battles, and preferred to listen to those people who asserted that it was best to remain in The World and avoid getting bogged down in such heavy contemplation.

"For," they said, "such brooding can cause a person to go insane."

All the same, there was a modest number who heeded the missionaries of Immanuel and were thus saved from their ruin. Among these missionaries there was one in particular who distinguished himself, not only in diligence and faithfulness, but also through his great talents. His name was Watchman.[118] Day after day, he wandered about, from one house to the next, sincerely begging and exhorting each and every person to carefully consider how they might escape the judgment that would soon be pronounced over the entire city. If all of the missionaries had carried out their work like he did, then this enterprise would have borne more fruit. But many missionaries were rather easy-going, and there were even a few who had become somewhat enamored with life in The World, such that they lost their salt and were next to useless. People liked listening to their sermons, to be sure. But afterward everything floated away, like so much hot air.

However, there were some who took after the example of Watchman. There were crowds who were even moved by their sermons, although in most places these preachers encountered a great resistance. Some in these audiences explained that their life was good enough as it was. Others could not believe that Immanuel, as mild as he was, was capable of following through with the type of grave judgment that Watchman described. Instead they expected that Immanuel would certainly look upon them with his grace, even though they were not as perfect as Watchman expected them to be. At the very least, they explained that just as they were now, they were already better than many other people. Some voiced the opinion that everyone ought to respect the conviction of everyone else regarding these matters. But when it came to the missionary WATCHMAN, they managed to forget their own principle, and did all they could to mock this poor missionary's convictions, even though all he had done was testify to what he himself had witnessed and heard in EVANGELIUM, as well as what IMMANUEL had commanded him to preach. When WATCHMAN thus would begin to explain to them that *their* conviction was false and would bring them to eternal ruin, they denounced him as intolerant and arrogant, explaining that in this enlightened age a person was just not allowed to be so bigoted. Freedom of thought, they said, was one of the most sacred rights of humankind, and anyone who made an attack on this principle should not only be considered sacrilegious, but even regarded as the spirit of darkness, since he was attempting to stop the spreading of light and all spiritual development. With the exception of the missionary WATCHMAN, everyone else's convictions ought to be considered unimpeachable.

One can easily see how this might leave a deep wound on the poor missionary. But he did not allow his courage to fail, but instead continued his indefatigable preaching, and was glad whenever a single soul embraced his message and started the move.

But not everyone was intolerant and cruel toward him. Many there were who thought that he was in fact correct, and these people daily defended his teaching. However, they themselves never seriously considered moving. Others were glad to hear the invitation, even to the degree that they were moved to tears. They sent with WATCHMAN their best wishes and thanks to be relayed to his master, saying that they would *soon* be coming. But just not right now, since they were currently too busy. Well, there were even some people who did set out for EVANGELIUM, but upon looking behind them, turned back.[119]

The days passed by like this in a constant labor. But one day, WATCHMAN suffered a setback that was worse than usual. This occurred as he was going about his work, weighed down by heavy reflections, walking through the streets of the city, and grieving over its miserable condition. All of the sudden he looked up to see a great crowd of people file into a house.

"I ought to follow them," he thought, "for there must be some kind of gathering taking place in there."

He went in and found a seat. After a moment of silence, in came a dignified older man who took his place behind the lectern. Warmly and earnestly, and with a flourish of eloquence, he made a speech to the great amusement of all those present, in which he sought to prove that the story of IMMANUEL was nothing more than a saga from days of old. In those days, it can certainly have been expected to serve the worthwhile purpose of keeping people in line. But nowadays, a saga like this one had become highly dangerous, since it hindered the free progress of enlightenment, and prevented people from giving scientific inquiry and its results the allegiance that it deserved. The audience appeared to be very pleased, and clapped their applause. Close to where WATCHMAN was sitting there was a man, who elbowed his neighbor in the side, and asked loudly, so that WATCHMAN could hear:

"Do you have any idea, which scientific results he is referring to?"

"No, but this professor certainly knows what he is talking about; for he is really sharp."

"Yes, of course. You are probably right about that."

And then the hands burst into applause again. The missionary WATCHMAN became painfully self-conscious.

"Is this man crazy?" he thought. "I know IMMANUEL personally, but this man asserts that he is nothing more than a saga hero. He can't seriously believe that."

However, WATCHMAN became deeply troubled by the whole business. Afterwards, when he had come out of that poisonous air, he asked who this man was. He was informed that this man's name was WORLDLY WISE and that he was a teacher in a field of study called PROUD DELUSIONS, but was commonly referred to as PHILOSOPHY.

Thus weighed down, WATCHMAN went to the place where he himself was supposed to preach. The audience members came in good numbers. He spoke with great power about the necessity of leaving THE WORLD, but there were few there who actually took this message to heart. After the sermon had concluded, he met MRS. WORLD ENAMORED who was elegantly dressed in silk, pearls, gold and things of that sort. With this woman he struck up a conversation, which quickly turned personal. When he had finished explaining to her the danger in which she stood, she answered:

"Oh, you know it is not all as bad as you say. Abrahamsson himself, who is a man from EVANGELIUM, has certainly managed to live here in THE WORLD. I even saw him yesterday having a lively conversation with MISS IMMODEST."

As though struck by a bolt of lightning, WATCHMAN stood silent for a moment.

"Oh," he exclaimed finally, "now EVANGELIUM is suffering abuse on account of its inhabitants! Before it was the other way around, that they had to suffer for the sake of EVANGELIUM."[120]

Now as he scurries off to look for Abrahamsson, we will also rush ahead of him, to find out what Abrahamsson is up to.

As we come into the room, we find him pacing back and forth across the floor with an expression of satisfaction on his face. He has recently come home, and we hear him say to himself:

"Oh, what a sermon! What precious and powerful words!"

At the same moment, in comes Watchman. Abrahamsson rushes to meet him with an embrace, exclaiming:

"Thank you, thank you, dear brother, for that sermon! Think of the effect that had on all of them!"

"Who do you mean by 'them'?" interrupted Watchman crossly.

"The children of The World, who were gathered there in the audience!"

"Well then, what about yourself, who is also presently living in The World?"

"Me? What about you? You're also here, aren't you?"

"I am here on the instructions of my lord, Immanuel. But who has sent *you* here?"

"Um, me…well…"

He did not have time to say anything more, as Vigilant entered at that moment. Shortly after that, even the bookkeeper Conscience burst in, out of breath and announced that Immanuel was not far behind. Terrified, Abrahamsson rushed out and fled into the woods. There he was attacked by a band of ten thieves, who robbed him of everything he had and gave him a thrashing which left him lying there, half dead. All the while, Immanuel had been riding after him, mounted on a small, lean but nevertheless strong steed, named Promise. He had been informed by Mother Simple that Abrahamsson had traveled to Loose Living, and her persistent prayers had begged him to go out and find him. This dear little old woman had been quite beside herself with sorrow, not allowing herself a moment's peace, until she received from Immanuel this promise:

"I will seek that which was lost, and bring back that which was driven away."[121]

When IMMANUEL had arrived at the place where Abrahamsson lay, he asked Abrahamsson once again in a gentle tone:

"What do you want me to do for you?"[122]

"Oh," sighed the poor man, who was lying there, bloody and out of his senses, without any idea where he should go. "Oh – do with me according to your will!"

Then IMMANUEL, with compassion, picked him up, bound up his wounds, treated them with oil and wine, and lifted him up onto his steed in order to carry him back to EVANGELIUM.[123] But along the way Abrahamsson encountered a terrible mishap. Due to his exertion and the loss of blood, he had become so weak and exhausted that he did not have the strength to hold onto the horse, and fell off into a deep mud puddle, landing in such a way that he broke his neck rather seriously. In this weakened state, IMMANUEL had to place him in front of him on the horse and hold on tight, so that he would not fall again. Riding like this, they made their way. At last IMMANUEL got him settled once again in the previously mentioned *Room for the Lost.*

Among the first to come out to greet this poor man was MOTHER SIMPLE, of course. As much as she had grieved over the fact that he had left, she now rejoiced just as much over his return; and just as earnestly as she had prayed for him during her time of sorrow, she now just as earnestly praised and thanked IMMANUEL for the unfathomable grace which he had shown. And the remarkable thing was what she said to MOTHER WOUNDED-HIP one day, shortly after all this took place:

"I believe," she said, "that IMMANUEL's grace is becoming greater with each passing day; at least it appears to *me* that it is."

To Justus All-Powerful the message was sent from Immanuel that Abrahamsson had been saved. At the news of this, Lord Justus let out a shout of joy, which could be heard throughout the city. And all the angels joined him in this joy.

It would be impossible to describe the state of mind of this recently lost but now recovered man Abrahamsson. He grieved and rejoiced all at once. With embarrassment, he burrowed his head into his pillow and out of shame didn't dare speak. But the tears which flooded down his cheeks spoke more than any words could have expressed. He certainly had lost the desire to visit the city, Loose Living. As a miserable pauper he was now content and glad to be able to live in The Forgiveness of Sins. Everyone else also shared his happiness.

Several days afterward, Immanuel received the orders from his father that he was to transport Mother Wounded-Hip to Holiness. And so he went to her. She had by this time become extremely frail and had been bedridden for quite some time. This news she received with joy. But Mother Simple and Mother Prodigal felt a terrible loss. When Abrahamsson received the news about her journey home, he sighed deep in his heart:

"Oh, to have been able to follow along!"

TWELFTH CHAPTER

The Hidden District

In Evangelium, life was proceeding along as it usually does. Sometimes people had their troubles, sometimes life was blissful. Here one could sometimes hear resounding songs of praise, while at other times one could make out the sound of heavy sighing, weeping and grief. If you were to ask the joyful people: "Why are you so glad?" one might receive the answer: "How could I not rejoice, when Immanuel is so good?" followed by an exhilarating account of what he had done. If you were to ask one of those who were grieving: "Why do you weep?" then the answer might be some confession of sin. At this point, we will now jump ahead a little bit in time, as a way of demonstrating that Immanuel remained constant. At times, he revealed himself in the full light of grace and its mighty accomplishment; at times he concealed himself and was not seen for long periods. Each day there were new people who arrived, looking for a refuge with him in Evangelium, where they could live and escape the great corruption that prevailed everywhere else outside of the holy city.

Life was proceeding as it usually does. But one day, something happened that caused a great deal of commotion and would become the subject of much confusion and speculation. Namely, there came to Evangelium three poor creatures from The World, who were admitted to the great hospital. They were called Miserable, Depraved, and Fallen. Anyone who looked on them in their wretched state, bodies emaciated and suffering extremely, could not help but shudder. Even Mother

Simple had started to believe that such wretches as these had never been brought to the holy city before. But a serious discussion with Conscience soon managed to convince her that she did not have any reason to boast about herself in front of them.

In order to find out a little more about the history of these new arrivals, we need to go back to The World and take another look at the activity that the missionary Watchman had been carrying on out there.

When Watchman had first arrived in The World, he went around observing the streets of the city in order to become familiar with the miserable conditions that prevailed there. What first caught his attention was a district which was called the Fear of God.

"What kind of a place can this be?" he thought, as he went in, believing that he would be warmly greeted here. And this did happen. It was a Sunday, and the people were dressed in their best. The inhabitants in the first house he visited were a distinguished couple, getting ready to leave at that moment.

"The pastor wouldn't like to join us, would he?" asked Mr. Primitive Piety.

"Where are you headed?" asked Watchman.

At this, Primitive Piety took him by the arm and led him toward the window.

"There," he said, as he pointed toward a great building, "there the pastor can see a great factory, which we call The Church where we gather on Sundays to produce Devotion and Worship under the leadership of the reverend Doctor Godly."

Stunned by this, Watchman replied that he did indeed wish to follow along, but wondered how it was possible that things like Devotion and Worship could exist anywhere other than in EVANGELIUM.

However, when the people had been gathered, he soon witnessed what he had not dared to believe about respectable people, such as this host and wife most certainly were. The people here were now really getting to work with great seriousness, and all this activity truly became quite the chore. DOCTOR GODLY, dressed in velvet robes with gold embroidery, went before the whole congregation. In the beginning everyone worked with passion and satisfaction. But when the reverend doctor began to go on a little too long, one by one people started to grow a bit tired. Many people began looking at their watches, wondering if this wasn't soon going to be over, so they could get out of here. Some people were starting to think about the nice dinners that were waiting for them. Others had a few chores to take care of at home. In the evening there was also going to be an "innocent pastime" at the home of the good doctor. Yet there were also many who made the valiant effort to try and finish strong.

During this entire time, WATCHMAN observed all this in anxious astonishment, and without any idea of what he should do. When he left with his host, he was asked what he thought about everything that had taken place.

"Where is the good doctor from?" asked WATCHMAN, who really wished to avoid making a direct answer to PRIMITIVE PIETY's question.

"He comes from here in the city itself, but is a highly educated man with a great deal of experience. He has studied at the college in THEOLOGY where he was supported by our good burgomaster, MR. SELF. But tell me, what did the pastor think about his officiating abilities?"

WATCHMAN simply gave a sigh. This only caused PRIMITIVE PIETY to become even more curious, and so he repeated his question.

"Oh," the missionary finally answered, "I would truly have wished to see DEVOTION and WORSHIP. But all I saw were PRETENSIONS."

Indignant about this reply, PRIMITIVE PIETY said an abrupt goodbye and turned his back on him. Otherwise, he had been thinking of inviting WATCHMAN to dinner.

WATCHMAN now went wandering along, quite disappointed. "If this is the best district in the city, what are the others going to be like?" he exclaimed.

And so he wandered past the districts of ADULTERY, FORNICATION, IMPURITY, IDOLATRY, WITCHCRAFT, ENMITY, QUARRELING, ZEAL, WRATH, STRIFE, DISCORD, PARTISANSHIP, JEALOUSY, MURDER, DRUNKENNESS, GLUTTONY, VANITY, GREED and several others, all of which made him want to immediately give up and flee this city.[124] But a renewed order from IMMANUEL forced him to remain where he was. And his work was not altogether fruitless, either, as he had initially expected it would be. One could even say that the most fruit was born in the worst districts.

Well, he had been working here for a long time, when he discovered a district in this city that had no name.[125] He asked many people what its name was, but everyone said they did not know. But when he asked what kind of people it was who lived here, he received the response that it was usually young people, both men and women, from every class, and even the upper crust of society. This became an unsolvable riddle for WATCHMAN. And his puzzlement only increased when he observed the outward appearance of these residents. It was the case that those who lived there were of a weak nature, typified by pale complexion, tired eyes, lack of energy and sluggishness in their whole being, experienced exhaustion and lack of inspiration in their work, a dejected and irritable spirit, and were not seldom depressed with life.

To resolve these deep questions of his, he went into one of the better houses.

Upon entering, he was greeted by a young woman, who was very welcoming.

"Please, enlighten me, what is the name of this district?" he implored.

The young woman's beautiful cheeks suddenly blushed with embarrassment, and she closed her eyes evasively.

"What the name of this district is?" she repeated his question. "That I cannot say, for its residents have come to agreement among themselves that this is to be kept hidden."

"Why is that?" asked WATCHMAN.

"Well, we have good reasons for that; and this matter is so secret, that we do not even let our parents know about it."

"You all aren't up to something wicked, are you now?" continued WATCHMAN.

This only provoked a renewed blushing in the face of the young woman. But in a sharp tone she answered:

"I hope that the pastor has not discovered some personal fault of mine that is driving this interrogation."

WATCHMAN thus continued on his way without receiving the information he was after. The young woman had revealed an obvious indignation by this unprompted insinuation. However, WATCHMAN asked another one of the residents that he passed by if he knew the name of the district.

"No," he answered, "throughout the whole city, it is only known as THE HIDDEN DISTRICT."

Yet, finally the day came when WATCHMAN figured out what the truth was. After one of his sermons concluded, a man by the name of MISERABLE came up to him and asked if he could have a word with him. WATCHMAN was happy to oblige, and so this man began to explain what the true name of the district was, as well as confess the secret, wicked activities that people were involved in there.

"After hearing your sermons," he continued, "on the terrible judgment to come, as well as on the glorious freedom in EVANGELIUM and IMMANUEL's grace toward the lost, I would like to ask you, if it is possible, that even someone like me might be able to take refuge in that holy city?"

WATCHMAN had been taken aback by this poor man's story and did not have any idea how he should answer him.

"How long have you lived in this awful district?"

"One and a half years."

"But if you intend to come to EVANGELIUM, then you will have to first be done with this wickedness."

"Dear sir, that is not possible. I have been trying to quit for a long time. But every time I have tried, I have fallen even worse back into the bonds of this wickedness. I would have long ago made this confession about everything that is going on in our district, if I hadn't heard the pastor so often speak about how one had to first be done with sin. That is what I have been trying to do, but it has not worked. And so I decided to keep quiet, for I found that it just did not serve any purpose to go through the pain of confessing. But yesterday, when the pastor spoke about how grace was free and was sufficient for all sins, and that *'Where sin abounded, grace abounded much more,'*[126] then I started thinking: 'Maybe this grace can be sufficient, even for me.' And that is why I have come here."

"Yes, yes, this is most certainly true," answered WATCHMAN, "but only once you have abandoned your sin."

"That was exactly what I should have expected!" exclaimed MISERABLE, bursting into heavy sobs. "I heard the pastor say in his sermon that in EVANGELIUM there is a river, that cleanses from all sins and from all uncleanliness. When the pastor spoke about that, my heart nearly leapt out of my chest, and I began to imagine that I might actually be allowed to come there, just as I am. But now I realize that I have misunderstood the sermon. First I will have to make myself pure, which is what I myself always believed, and that is probably true. But I have no strength to be able to accomplish this."

In this way, poor MISERABLE departed from there, without any assurance from the missionary, who believed that if a person were truly sincere in his efforts, then he should certainly be able to resist and even be done with *outbreaks* of this type of wickedness.

"Oh, what was I trying to accomplish there?" sniffled MISERABLE, when he came out on to the street. "I certainly ought to have understood, that there was not any real grace for a sinner such as me."

But when MISERABLE had gone, WATCHMAN was overcome by an indescribable anguish. In his anxiety, he sat down and wrote a letter to IMMANUEL, in which he described the whole course of events. It was not long before CONSCIENCE returned, carrying with him IMMANUEL's reply. In this letter, IMMANUEL said to WATCHMAN that when he sent him to THE WORLD, he never gave any such order to discriminate between people in this way, but instead to announce to all people, without exception, that they were free to move to the holy city. The letter concluded thusly:

"You received my words to carry with you, that '*Where sin abounded, grace abounded much more.*' This you should *take seriously* and use, precisely in all those places where sin is abundant; and furthermore, what do you have to boast about?

Haven't you, too, received everything by grace alone?"

Now WATCHMAN felt duty-bound to go out and search for MISERABLE. When he caught up with him, he said to him that grace did exist even for him after all, and pleaded with him to come home to discuss this further. As soon as MISERABLE had heard this, he raced around to his other friends in order to relay this same news to them so that they could accompany him on his journey. But, it was terribly difficult to convince them. They simply shook their heads.

"We have of course heard that sermon, as well," they said. "But it is impossible to take that literally. Then even the worst of people could become saved, and that simply cannot be."

However, finally there were two of them who decided to follow along.

"It certainly couldn't do any harm," said MISERABLE. "Just think if there was grace, even for us! And if there is not, then things will just continue as they were before. But then at least we would have tried."

A little while after WATCHMAN had arrived at home, in walked MISERABLE, no longer by himself, but bringing along with him DEPRAVED and FALLEN. Wondering what kind of people these two were, WATCHMAN asked them:

"Are you also from that same awful district?"

"Yes," answered both of them, fighting back tears.

"How long have you lived there?"

"Fifteen years," answered DEPRAVED.

When FALLEN saw how WATCHMAN was startled by this answer, he did not dare to open his mouth, until at last WATCHMAN asked once again.

"Twenty-some years," FALLEN sighed heavily at last.

WATCHMAN shuddered at these words. But since he had this letter from IMMANUEL, in which it stated "all," "each and every person," "without exception," he simply gathered up his courage and boldly extended them this permission to move to the holy city.

"And," he added more candidly, "In EVANGELIUM, you will *soon* be free from all your wretchedness. You will soon be completely healed, through the tender care provided at the hospital, as well as your own diligent bathing in the RIVER OF BLOOD. Journey in peace!"

As WATCHMAN pronounced these parting words to the poor creatures, they just stood trembling before him. They did not know if they should believe their own ears, and they asked him several times if this was *really* true. He answered time and again, "yes." With this information, they set out. But when they had gone a ways down the street, they ran into DOUBT, who shook his head at them. So they stopped in their tracks, and looked at one another. After they had exchanged a few anxious words with one another, they turned around and went back to WATCHMAN, who was very surprised.

"What is it now?" he asked.

"Well, you see," answered FALLEN "you see – can this be completely true? We just have to ask you about this one more time. Has the pastor thought this through properly? If he is misleading us, then…"

For an instant, WATCHMAN became anxious. But he took out the letter again and read it once more for them. He read the word 'all.' He read it forwards. He read it backwards. And it remained all, and nothing less.[127]

"Travel with this word!" he said. "It will last you on your journey."

And so they set out, and after entering the holy city were brought into The Forgiveness of Sins. The city was in a commotion, the news traveling from mouth to mouth. They themselves were rejoicing over grace and expecting that their misery would finally come to an end. After a while, a couple more people arrived from the same place, Vile and Wretched. A short time later, still more arrived. They too were vocal in their praise of the mercy which had been shown to them. They thought, in those first overwhelming emotions of grace, that they were altogether liberated from their misery.

Many of them, furthermore, would later go on to be immediately healed. Though for others, by contrast, the sickness began to reappear after a little time had passed. They lived in The Forgiveness of Sins, were attended to in the hospital, they bathed in the river – but nothing seemed to help. Of course there were certain times when they did get better. But then the attacks would break out again, to their own horror and that of the others. Earnestly they prayed to Immanuel and begged for his presence, but it seemed as though he did not want to help them. They began to doubt themselves, as well as Evangelium and Immanuel. Among the other residents, there was no one who was able to give any advice or was able to inspire renewed courage, except for one person. This was Mother Simple. Faithfully sitting by their bedsides, she encouraged them to *have patience and wait, as well as to remain diligent in believing in grace;* "for," she would say, "there is nothing else, after all, which can help."

"But Watchman said that we would soon be healthy again!" they objected, one after the other.

And so this progressed over a long period, and watching these poor people in their mourning and grieving was heart-wrenching. They paced about their rooms, tossed and turned, they sighed and they screamed. But when the attacks came, they lost their senses, and the storm winds bore them away.

Yet, after a year there began to be a slight change that appeared. MISERABLE became entirely healthy. This caused many to rejoice. "This comes as proof," they said, "that grace is powerful." But this caused the others who were sick to become even more disappointed. They had already been aware that many people, upon arriving in EVANGELIUM, had become healthy; now they saw that even MISERABLE after his long struggle had become completely free from his sickness. Therefore they had made up their minds that it was all over for *them,* since *they* had not received this kind of healing. And Abrahamsson, along with many others, also began to be convinced that things had never actually been right with them. If things continued to go this way for them, then eventually they would need to be on their way and leave EVANGELIUM, he thought.

"This cannot be good in the long run," he told them, once again.

But in a situation like this, no chastisement would help. This only increased their suffering. Heavy sighs and anxious lamentations were the only response that he got from them. Deeply saddened and without a clue as to what he should do, he sought counsel with some of the others. They came to the conclusion that people should earnestly pray for these people and try to surround them with love. But all efforts seemed to be in vain. Sometimes it would appear promising, as mentioned before, and everyone would rejoice. But then the attacks would come again. Then people would agree that someone ought to tell them, in no uncertain terms, that they should not go around making claims of having received grace, as long as they remained in such a condition. On this point even MISERABLE agreed. People explained that giving them these admonitions would prompt increased seriousness and greater efforts. This message was communicated to them one evening, and the result that it had could already be seen the following morning. Namely, during the night, DEPRAVED and VILE, who could not stand any more of this, had both set out from the city, the former on his way to THE WORLD and the latter on his way to

Loose Living. What had been keeping them in Evangelium thus far and had maintained their spirits were the words of assurance that Mother Simple had been so earnestly speaking to them. Now they found themselves instead under a terrifying judgment, and this was something they already had plenty of experience with from before. When they were not allowed to depend on Immanuel's grace, then they just could not endure any more of this. As soon as word reached Abrahamsson's ears, he rushed off to tell Mother Simple.

"Oh!" he exclaimed, "what are we supposed to believe about these people, who have been lying here like this for three years without becoming healed?"

"Well," answered Mother Simple calmly, "if you ask me, it is high time that the Squire ought to start thinking about himself, and let Immanuel take care of those who are sick."

"But their wretchedness is in stark opposition to grace!"

"And why is that?"

"Because it is so horrible and so foul!"

"And when is sin so beautiful, that it is not in opposition to grace?"

This question Abrahamsson was not prepared to answer. But scrambling for words and avoiding a direct answer, he shot right back:

"Are you trying to defend sin?"

"No, that is the last thing that I would ever do! But I do wish to defend grace."

Abrahamsson was completely bewildered. "Defend grace?" he asked, "What do you mean? Defend it against whom?"

"Against the Squire and other people of the same mind,"

answered MOTHER SIMPLE hastily. "All of you simply will not allow grace to be as high as the heaven is over the earth.[128] You do not allow it to overflow and cover every sin."

"Is that so? Then I imagine you are indifferent as to whether people sin or not, and would like to rush to the defense of each and every person who is living in sin. That is quite a remarkable doctrine!"

"I wish that the Squire would go and think about this matter, and then come back when his senses have returned. Or what is it exactly that the Squire himself thinks he can boast about? Go ask CONSCIENCE, he will surely tell the Squire. And when the Squire yesterday, like so many other times, became irate with SCHOOLMASTER FAITHFUL, what was that other than a form of murder? And can't that also be considered a sin?"

"That was nothing more than a moment of rashness, and now everything is fine again."

At these words, MOTHER SIMPLE recoiled.

"Has it gotten to the point now with the Squire, that he has started to excuse and try to diminish his own sin? Oh, then the Squire is already in a much more dangerous place than these poor people, for whom he has so much concern. For know this – that even the sin that seems most innocent can be fatal, if one tries in some way to excuse or make light of it, in such a way that it seems to be far better than the sins of another person. This is the sort of thing that directly challenges grace. But when the sinner sticks to judging himself for his sins and begs for grace, no one shall ever be able to rob him of grace or drive him out from THE FORGIVENESS OF SINS, even though there will still come times when he is caught off guard by recurring moments of wretchedness. In these cases, one must return to the words of the old apostle: 'If a man is overtaken by any sin, you who are spiritual, restore such a one in a spirit of meekness.'[129] The kind of spirituality that is hard on the weak – which breaks the bruised reeds and extinguishes the smoking wick[130] – this is an immature spirituality. The proper spirituality is to have mercy on them and help them. I would much rather be weak than to be a bully to the weak."

"Is that so? You think that every conceivable form of wretchedness can stand alongside grace?"

"No, of course not; but on the basis of the word of truth, I do believe, more firmly than I ever have, that even the worst form of wretchedness can indeed stand *under* grace, just as I believe that nothing, not even the most innocent of sins, can stand *alongside* grace."

"You are impossible; one never gets anywhere talking with you."

"The Squire shouldn't get upset. I am nothing more than a frail little old woman, who can easily be knocked down. But there is one thing which I am very stubborn about, and that is that one should never let go of grace."

"Well, you must admit that these wretches ought to, at some point, be made well."

"Dear Squire, do not start talking about 'wretches.' That can have a negative effect. We have not yet seen the end. Of course, I agree that they ought to be made well; and I have never seen anything that has caused me so much confusion as all of this. Even Bankrupt Faith is also bewildered. But what does that matter? There is no other advice to follow than to try to support them with grace."

"But remember, you yourself said, that the sin that is in opposition to grace, is the one that one tries to diminish?"

"Yes, of course, for when one tries to excuse or diminish sin, then one tries to defend its place alongside grace, and that is a falsehood."

"Now, how do you know that DEPRAVED and VILE aren't exactly this sort of people?"

MOTHER SIMPLE became uneasy, for she sensed something, but she could not put her finger on it.

"Tell me," she asked anxiously, "what exactly is the Squire getting at? Has something happened?"

"Well, they would not tolerate a healthy word of instruction and a serious word of warning."

The little old woman became even more anxious, for now she understood that Abrahamsson had done something terrible. Therefore, she asked him once more if something had happened to DEPRAVED and VILE.

"Yes," answered Abrahamsson, "haven't you heard that sometime last night they left EVANGELIUM? They made clear that it was because I, following the mutual agreement of several of us who have no tolerance for the flesh, finally told them the honest truth. That is what they could not endure."

At these words MOTHER SIMPLE burst into a flood of tears.

"May IMMANUEL forgive the Squire for what he has done!" she gasped. And upon this she made haste to the hospital, without waiting for Abrahamsson's answer. When she arrived there, it was confirmed that DEPRAVED and VILE had gone, and what pained her even more was to hear the mourning of both of the others. The judgment had also hit them hard, and WRETCHED himself was just getting ready to move out of the holy city. For not only had he begun to lose confidence in IMMANUEL's grace, he had also that morning received a letter from an acquaintance, who was suffering from the same sickness, but who had moved to the city SELF-RIGHTEOUSNESS, where he said he had become completely healthy. Poor old FALLEN. He did not know what he was going to do. His despair exceeded everything imaginable.

"If I may not believe in grace," he exclaimed, in the midst of bitter sobs, "if I may not believe in grace, then I am lost. Tell me, MOTHER SIMPLE, can I believe in grace?"

"Yes!" exclaimed MISERABLE, who at that moment came in and heard these last few words. "There is nothing preventing you from believing in grace. But in the condition in which you now find yourself, there is no room for grace, and thus you can have no benefit from it..."

Engulfed in a blaze of zeal, MOTHER SIMPLE swung around, and the dead-serious look in her fiery face reduced MISERABLE to silence.

"Who has given you the right to drive people out of EVANGELIUM?"

With that she made her way to the beds of the sick and now, sparing no pains, gave them words of assurance regarding IMMANUEL's unchanging grace, which was wholly independent of all their being or doing. In this way, she managed to finally restore them both to a posture of patience. She then read to them from a letter of Paulus, where it was written:

> *For we know that the law is spiritual, but I am carnal, sold under sin. For what I am doing, I do not understand. For what I will to do, that I do not practice; but what I hate, that I do. If, then, I do what I will not to do, I consent to the law that the law is good.*
>
> *But now, it is no longer I who do it, but sin that dwells in me. For I know that in me (that is, in my flesh,) nothing good dwells; for to will is present with me, but how to perform what is good I do not find.*
>
> *For the good that I will to do, I do not do; but the evil I will not to do, that I practice. Now if I do what I will not to do, it is no longer I who do it, but sin that dwells in me. I find then a law, that evil is present with me, the one who wills to do good.*

> *For I delight in the law of God according to the inward man. But I see another law in my members, warring against the law of my spirit, and bringing me into captivity to the law of sin which is in my members. O wretched man that I am! Who will deliver me from this body of death? I thank God, through Jesus Christ our Lord. So then, with the spirit I myself serve the law of God, but with the flesh the law of sin.*[131]

These words sank in like a healing balm in the wounds of these wretches. The pain subsided, and they were able to rest.

But MISERABLE, who had overheard the words of assurance that MOTHER SIMPLE had just communicated to them, exclaimed, indignantly:

"No. Here, in this home of LOOSE LIVING, I cannot remain any longer!"

That moment he began packing, and he moved that very day to SELF-RIGHTEOUSNESS. This turn of events rattled Abrahamsson so much that he was finally able to return to his senses, recognized and confessed his sin and presumptuousness, and through grace returned to humility.

But time passed by, and in the end it became apparent that WRETCHED's condition had changed. After so many years of sickness, he finally became well, which made MOTHER SIMPLE very happy, as well as many others. They thought that what had taken place could be seen as renewed proof that this free grace and its assurances were the only sure means by which they could help a depraved creature mend his ways, even if progress might be slow. "Think," said MOTHER SIMPLE, "about what might have become of him, if we had driven him away from here? No, let us persevere in grace."

On this point the others agreed. And together they took up a song of praise.

But for as much as these developments for WRETCHED brought much joy, and as he heartily praised IMMANUEL for his return to health, it brought nothing but anxiety for poor FALLEN. His courage was about to fail him altogether, when he saw that even WRETCHED had become well.

"Why can't I also get well?" he sighed. "IMMANUEL is not concerned about me. He has withheld his mercy out of wrath."

But besides MOTHER SIMPLE, he had now also found a mighty comforter in WRETCHED who, from his own experiences, understood the awful tortures that were involved in this sickness. It was also a tremendous solace for FALLEN to be able to pour out his concerns to this prized friend, the only one who truly and fully understood him. Neither did WRETCHED pass up the opportunity to paint a picture for his friend who was still sick, a vivid and colorful picture of IMMANUEL's mercy which "knew no bounds."

It goes without saying that in EVANGELIUM there were many people who remained quite confused in regard to FALLEN, and who also thought that MOTHER SIMPLE was not all that wise. She ought to restrain herself when it came to all of these unqualified assurances of grace, they reasoned. Of course they had no desire to pass judgment on poor FALLEN – they did not really dare – but to emphatically assert that he was covered by grace, this they thought was going too far. Because of this, one of them came to speak with MOTHER SIMPLE one day, none other than COUNCILMAN CAUTIOUS. CAUTIOUS was an upstanding man, whom MOTHER SIMPLE greatly esteemed. He had previously lived in SELF-RIGHTEOUSNESS, where he still had brothers living. After having moved to EVANGELIUM, he had done quite a lot of good, and thus his advice was usually weighed heavy. Yet it happened from time to time, that a sort of peculiar spell came over him, which caused him to become dizzy and even to fall down. One time because of this dizziness he fell right at the feet of BANKRUPT FAITH. FAITH was in such a hurry that he was running with all his strength. It was an awful spectacle to see him trip over Councilman Cautious and be launched into a couple of somersaults, so that he was left with his head spinning. When Bankrupt Faith stood up, he did not get his bearings for quite a while, and couldn't tell in which direction he should keep running.

This peculiar illness had infected Cautious as a result of the large amount of leaven that he had eaten during the time when he lived in Self-Righteousness.[132] This illness could even be contagious, and even Mother Simple had caught this bug a couple of times. One could tell that she was coming down with one of these spells, whenever she tilted her head and looked askance as she began reading God's Word. Yet, she had always been able to snap out of this by administering a certain kind of bitter drops, which Immanuel had sent to her by way of Father Experience. Now, as mentioned before, Cautious had come to speak with Mother Simple and Fallen. After he had first greeted them and emphasized his heartfelt appreciation for all of her care for these wretches, he added:

"But don't you think that one ought to be a little more careful about presenting grace to Fallen as freely as you have? I believe that we, in this peculiar case, must keep our personal opinions to ourselves and leave him to the mercy of Justus All-Powerful."

"What is the Councilman saying?" objected Mother Simple with astonishment. "Oh, if I did not allow myself to be left to the mercy of Justus All-Powerful, then I would be lost."

"Don't misunderstand me," interrupted Cautious, "I did not mean that. It is clear that we all need to throw ourselves before the mercy of Justus All-Powerful. But what I meant was that we shouldn't try to make any particular evaluation regarding Fallen, nor relate this to him. We ought not judge him, but neither should we try to make any assurances to him regarding grace. We should leave him to the mercy of Justus All-Powerful."

"It is impossible," answered Mother Simple, "for me to understand what the Councilman is really trying to say here. Does the Councilman mean that I may not tell him for certain that Immanuel's blood was shed for all of his sins?"

"Well, that is clear; what has been done, that has been done and may freely be preached. But one needs to be careful about saying this to a man in his condition, as if this applies to him and that he has some claim to this word."

"Oh," exclaimed Mother Simple, "Is that what you meant? Then the Councilman wants us to not give this poor man *any firm word of grace to* cling to, but instead means that he should be abandoned to *doubt and uncertainty!* And the Councilman explains this as 'leaving him to the mercy of Justus All-Powerful'!"

The good councilman became rather troubled by this exchange. He did not know for sure how he should get himself out of this. For he must have realized deep down that this plan he had articulated – of leaving Fallen to the mercy of Justus All-Powerful – would in reality be the same thing as leaving him to uncertainty and doubt. And that this was a bad example of pastoral care, he could not deny. Yet, he had soon collected himself and retorted:

"But look at Wretched; he has certainly become healthy, while Fallen is still lying in bed."

"Yes, I can see that well enough," answered Mother Simple. "But was it through doubt and uncertainty that he was healed? No, most certainly not! I know that much, I being the one who watched as it all happened. But if now Wretched has been healed solely as a result of these certain and confident assertions of grace, why should we then try to heal Fallen through uncertainty about grace and by withholding grace? And this method of healing him will not be made any more effective by calling it 'leaving him to the mercy of Justus All-Powerful'?"

Now the councilman was stuck once again and did not know how he should answer. After a moment of silence, he said:

"But you must understand that if these kind of ideas of yours start to spread, then some people might find cause to live freely in sin and rest on the assurance of grace. Think how terrible that would be!"

"Well, if hypocrites misuse grace to their own ruin, then that would not be the fault of grace. If anyone reads the story of the thief on the cross and thinks: 'Oh, I think I would like to be a thief, and then in the last moments before death become converted,' then that is his own business. No one can blame the thief for that, nor should they tear out his story from the Bible.[133] For this story has been a source of salvation for a countless number of souls. And there remain countless souls who still need to hear it. There were many people who drowned in the flood that saved Noah."

Now there was again a moment of silence. Then Mother Simple continued:

"The Councilman is now on the verge of having one of his old spells again, and needs to go and receive treatment."

These words startled Cautious, and he answered:

"But you know you have an obligation to admit, that it is grace that is necessary to treat sin?"

"Yes," answered Mother Simple, "that is exactly what I am doing, and if the Councilman himself were to admit this, then he would be acting the same way I am."

"What?" exclaimed CAUTIOUS, "aren't I admitting that? That is what I have been trying to do."

"In words, yes," answered MOTHER SIMPLE, "but when the Councilman attempts to heal FALLEN by *withholding grace,* then he is demonstrating the opposite. Whatever people might now be saying about FALLEN, what is certain is that *if we take away* grace, then that cannot possibly cure him."

CAUTIOUS began to ponder this, and MOTHER SIMPLE kept quiet for a moment. After a while, she began to speak again, saying:

"Listen now, Mr. Councilman, may I ask a question?"

"Yes, absolutely," answered CAUTIOUS, although he did not absolutely look like he wanted another question. He of course knew by now that MOTHER SIMPLE's questions were quite difficult for him, particularly as he was now in the midst of one of his spells.

"Well then," said MOTHER SIMPLE, "we mentioned WRETCHED just now. Does the Councilman believe that he was a true resident of EVANGELIUM, before he was completely healed?"

"Certainly," answered CAUTIOUS, "that one can see clearly by the fact that he was healed."

"But if he had departed this life before that day, when he became fully healed, would he then have been thrown into GEHENNA?"

"That is a question that we will have to leave to JUSTUS ALL-POWERFUL," answered CAUTIOUS, though overcome by indecision.

"No," interrupted MOTHER SIMPLE, "*it is we* who need to know your answer to this question. For if anyone, despite being a true resident in EVANGELIUM, can still be thrown into GEHENNA, then we are all lost. Then we have no hope. Or has the Councilman by now conquered all his sins, such that he can never fall for any of them anymore?"

"No, God knows I have not," answered CAUTIOUS.

"And despite this, the Councilman expects that he will still be counted among the righteous, even if he were to depart this life today?" MOTHER SIMPLE chimed in.

"Yes, through IMMANUEL's grace."

"Well then," continued MOTHER SIMPLE, "then that would mean that the Councilman was allowed to be counted as one of the righteous, despite the fact that he has not yet conquered all of his sins? Tell me, do these qualifications for righteousness only apply to the Councilman, or may other people also be judged by these standards?"

"Of course," answered MR. SELF-WISE, who had just then entered and heard these last words: "Of course, other people may. But for someone like FALLEN, who is openly living a life in the flesh, this simply does not apply."

These words threw MOTHER SIMPLE into a fury. With a flash in her eyes, she answered: "Yes, I see that you, who lives his life in the flesh in secret, has made this sport of trampling on the wretched part of his own path to righteousness. But," she added, now turned to CAUTIOUS, as SELF-WISE angrily left the room, "I have witnessed enough to be able to conclude this: however it might be regarding FALLEN's life, this one thing is certain: he is not *living* a life in the flesh. No, I have seen him *fall* into, but never *live* in sin. If he has fallen, it has been as though into fire or water. He has never been able to remain lying there. And know this, Councilman – I believe that there is more hope for the one who is drawn up out of a deep pit, than for the one who remains lying in a pit that appears to our eyes to be shallow. It was this kind of pit that Petrus was in, when he sat at table with the Lord and said: 'Yet, will I not deny you.'[134] This pit was more dangerous than the one that he would fall into later that night, when he actually did deny the Lord."[135]

"God be gracious to me a sinner!"[136] exclaimed CAUTIOUS, and he departed from there, fully animated. But MOTHER SIMPLE hurried off to FALLEN in order to tell him that it was indeed for certain that his sins were forgiven. And that is what she considered "leaving him to the mercy of JUSTUS ALL-POWERFUL."

After about a year had passed, still FALLEN had not yet been healed from his wretchedness, and over and over again this surprised and defeated him. And then an event occurred that quickly sent a wave of alarm throughout EVANGELIUM. FALLEN was called to HOLINESS. The summons had to be obeyed, and so FALLEN set out. Hardly anyone could escape feeling some emotion of dread at this news. Everyone was forced to wonder how his case had gone for him. Well, even MOTHER SIMPLE now began to doubt, for she had nevertheless always hoped that he would become healthy eventually. Neither did WRETCHED have any idea what he should believe about all this. In his distress, he went to IMMANUEL in order to ask him about it, but he only received the response: "See to it that you yourself shall endure to the end."[137] Thus, one had to simply come to peace with this. MOTHER SIMPLE and WRETCHED hoped for the best for their departed friend, particularly when BANKRUPT FAITH pointed out to them the passage in GOD'S WORD where it says: "But to him who does not rely on works but believes on him who justifies the ungodly, his faith is accounted as righteousness."[138]

And when they compared these words with what IMMANUEL once had said, "Whoever believes in me shall never die,"[139] then they became almost certain that all had gone well for FALLEN.

THIRTEENTH CHAPTER

Disputation – Abrahamsson becomes a Preacher

But now we return to Abrahamsson. When we last encountered him, he was on the verge of acting recklessly, and because of this had entered into an important conversation with Mother Simple. We had earlier recounted how he had been called back to his senses, and was thus pulled back from the brink of his own destruction as a result of his arrogance. When Fallen had been called away to Holiness, Abrahamsson was among those who doubted that it could possibly have gone well for that poor man. Yet in the end, he allowed Mother Simple to reason with him, and was now at a point where he at least no longer tried to express his opinions on matters that were none of his business. What is more, the other people in Evangelium had soon forgotten all about Fallen, not to mention Wretched, who after living out the rest of his short life of alternating sorrows and joys in Evangelium was finally able to follow his friend home.

Everything in the city had returned to being calm and peaceful once again. Whenever anyone happened to mention either Fallen's sorrowful departure or Wretched's jubilant farewell from Evangelium, it was as though these were memories from long ago, which were on the verge of being lost in the fog of time. Abrahamsson's life continued to flow on as before, as he continued to navigate between sin and grace. But even now, he had not yet learned everything that he was to learn. He had a fiery disposition and found it difficult to remain still and patient. Whenever he took on a new enterprise, he usually did so with great zeal and seriousness. But if these projects did not go well, then his courage and energies were quickly exhausted. To live in this constant grace, as well as to be patient with having this same grace serve as the basis for his work – this was rather difficult for him to come to terms with. Whenever it happened – and this was rather frequently – that he made a mistake now and then, or he began to become tired and lazy, then he would forget the free grace on which he was supposed to live. Instead, he would begin trying to get himself out of these situations by increasing his efforts, which only resulted in ever more sluggishness and depression. Sometimes, his perspective on grace was as though he began to think that it was no matter if he didn't visit SANCTIFICATION *every single* day. We have already seen in the past how MOTHER SIMPLE helped bring him back to his senses, when he was in danger of forgetting grace. This was her constant way of dealing with him in each one of these recurring cases. But, as we have already said, it unfortunately also could happen that Abrahamsson sometimes interpreted her advice to mean that he didn't need to bother with producing GOOD DEEDS. And this was how things had been going for a while, when the events we are about to explain took place.

In EVANGELIUM, a decree had been issued from IMMANUEL, which gave his subjects certain instructions. This decree was read closely and earnestly by all. But there were also several sayings included in it that were rather hard to understand, and on these points people soon developed many different opinions. SCHOOLMASTER FAITHFUL wrote a good, detailed exposition on these points.[140] There were many people who read it with great satisfaction and thought that he had most certainly solved these problems of interpretation. But Abrahamsson did not agree. Through his own negligence in both the practice of faith, as well as GOOD DEEDS, his heart had begun to suffer from a great feeling of emptiness. It needed to be filled in some way. This prompted him to hungrily seize the opportunity to write a dissertation of his own, in which he tried to refute several of the points in SCHOOLMASTER FAITHFUL's book that he could not entirely accept. His fervor and argumentative spirit grew all the more. Many other people also joined in this debate, each publishing their own dissertations. At the same time as the combatants themselves seemed to be enjoying this battle, this caused others to be alarmed. Though they too wished to arrive at come clarity, they were concerned that this battle was only bringing even greater confusion. Finally Abrahamsson called together his opponents for a disputation. But even this did not produce any result. Afterwards, every single one of these combatants believed that he was the winner of the competition, and complained that the others refused to listen to reason.

MOTHER SIMPLE, who had been present among the ladies in the audience, found herself especially troubled by all of this. At one point, she had even been ready to jump up and speak her mind. And she probably would have done this, too, had not MR. BIBLE-BOUND tapped her on the arm and whispered to her the words: *let women keep silent in the congregation.*[141] But before the disputation had hardly finished, she hurried off to find Abrahamsson. Though, as it was her practice in these sorts of occasions, she did find time first to go to IMMANUEL and tell him what she was about to do. It had become a necessity for her, before she went anywhere, to first hear IMMANUEL's assuring words: *Go in peace!*[142] After she had spoken with him, she continued on her way to Abrahamsson's, who had himself only come home a few minutes before she arrived.

"What did you think about our disputation?" he asked immediately, so pleased he was with himself that he stood there eagerly rubbing his hands together. "You know, it really was a marvelous evening," he continued. But he managed to restrain himself, when he noticed that the expression that fell over the face of the little old woman communicated anything but satisfaction.

"Didn't you enjoy it," he asked, "because you are so quiet and look so displeased?"

"No, indeed," answered the little old woman.

"And why not? We were discussing rather important issues."

"Yes, so important," answered the little old woman, distressed. "So important, that IMMANUEL ought to have been included."

At first, Abrahamsson did not know how he should answer a response like this. He took up his handkerchief, blew his nose, coughed, scratched his head and thought: "This woman is indeed a peculiar old bird." But he was glad that he had not said this out loud. Finally he asked her outright, what she thought about the hard sayings in IMMANUEL's decree.

"Well," she answered, "I think that I would, of course, very much like to understand them. But after listening to all these dissertations, I did not become any wiser for it. So I went to IMMANUEL and asked him instead. His answer to me was that I ought to first go and practice and do the things that I did understand, and then I would find out about the rest eventually. For me, at least, I think this is the best way to arrive at a proper understanding of those hard sayings."

Once again, this answer was not what Abrahamsson had been expecting. However, he soon recovered himself and said:

"Yet, you must understand, dear mother, that it is of the utmost importance that we get this matter explained as soon as possible?"

MOTHER SIMPLE, who could see well enough where Abrahamsson was going with all of this, made up her mind at that moment not to let go of him.

"Is it of less importance," she asked, "to begin with practicing what one does understand? Or does the Squire believe that

IMMANUEL will be satisfied with us passing the time with disputations, when he really wants us to be accomplishing something?"

Abrahamsson became uneasy, as he now began to realize that the little old woman, in her usual way, was in the process of getting all too personal with him. And he remembered from long experience that MOTHER SIMPLE was not someone who allowed herself to be played games with or be teased. Thus he decided to try to shift the conversation to other matters. But MOTHER SIMPLE remained firm and unyielding.

"I have not come here," she said, "to waste any more of the precious hours that remain in this evening with vanity. The disputation you all held just now has wasted plenty of hours already. Therefore, I will get to the point of my errand. Tell me, how are things standing with the Squire *nowadays,* for it has been a long time since I have seen the Squire in SANCTIFICATION."

"Well, as you can see, I am doing rather well. But I have been so occupied with all this writing recently that I have just not had time to work in SANCTIFICATION."

"Be that as it may, it is written," answered MOTHER SIMPLE, "that *without sanctification, no one shall see the Lord.*[143] But nowhere is it written that no one may see the Lord without writing books."

A moment of silence ensued, as each one sat eyeing the other. Finally MOTHER SIMPLE said:

"Well, how are you doing now? The question is an important one."

"Well, dear friend," answered Abrahamsson in a lamenting tone, "I am in rather poor shape! A great sinner I have always been and it is still the case that I certainly deserve reproach. But IMMANUEL's grace is sufficient for all my misery – at least that is what you yourself have so often told me."

"So, does the Squire intend to use IMMANUEL's grace as a disguise for his own idleness?"

"No, but I certainly remember, and will never forget, those priceless words that you yourself once used to give me assurance in one of my darker moments. You said, so sweetly: *When you have sinned, then believe grace.*"

The little old woman understood, of course, that Abrahamsson was merely praising her as a means of coaxing her into leniency in order to get her to yield her firm position. But she did not allow herself to be fooled.

"Can it be," she said, "that the Squire remembers those words? He does well by that, for they stand more firm than mountains and apply without limitations. But I wonder, does the Squire remember just as clearly the other words that I also shared with him on that same occasion?"

"No, the rest I have forgotten, for it has been quite a while since we had that priceless conversation, as you know."

"Well, I went on to say these words: *And when the Squire believes grace, then be diligent in seeing to it that the Squire lives a holy and righteous life!*"

"Yes, yes, now I remember that rather well. But then, if I remember correctly, you also added, *that grace is not only supposed to be the first step, but also the last.*"

"Yes, I have said that many times. But just as it does no good to add a 'however' after IMMANUEL, neither is it acceptable to add a 'however' after SANCTIFICATION. Both need to remain in their respective places unaltered. One should not be going around here in EVANGELIUM saying, as they do in SELF-RIGHTEOUSNESS: 'IMMANUEL's grace is certainly great, *however,* all the same, one still must produce GOOD DEEDS.' But instead one should say: IMMANUEL's grace is great and limitless, *therefore* we also want to live holy and righteously, as is befitting his people.' In the same way, people should not say here, as they do in Loose Living: 'We ought to produce Good Deeds, *however* Immanuel is so full of grace, after all'; but instead: 'We ought to produce Good Deeds *because* Immanuel is so good.'"

Abrahamsson became deeply troubled as she spoke. Once again he stood there like a convicted criminal. So he took a seat at the desk, and with tearful, troubled eyes he asked:

"Tell me then, how can I get back on the right path; for there are times when I veer off to one side, and at other times, veer off to the other side. What is someone like me supposed to do?"

"Believe in grace," answered the little old woman, "for whenever one has gotten sidetracked, one always has to begin again from the same starting point."

This unexpected response made Abrahamsson feel rather disoriented. He could not say a word. At this point, the little old woman took him by the hand and led him along with her to Immanuel. There Abrahamsson tearfully confessed his sins, and Immanuel assured him of his unchanging grace.

As they left that place, Mother Simple said:

"Does the Squire now see, how good it is that there is true grace for true sinners?"

"Yes, dear friend," answered Abrahamsson. "I am beginning to believe now, that things just might have gone well for Fallen after all. And if that is indeed the case, then he is probably out-singing everyone else in Holiness right now…that is, until I get there."

It would have been good if Abrahamsson had faithfully held on to that peace, which he had again received undeservedly. It would have been good if he could also have remained still. But this time, as before, he would be led astray by his strong-willed nature. With energy and earnestness he did try to work for quite a while in Sanctification, the whole time rejoicing over the free grace, which provided him with all his assurance, and which demonstrated its power in and through him.

During these days, he also made it a regular habit to spend time with Immanuel and Mother Simple, who faithfully challenged him to continue on this path in reverence. But it was not long until he began to forget that this great power he was experiencing *was a grace*. He soon noticed that there were many others around him in Sanctification who went about their work sluggishly, as well as one or two other people who appeared to be satisfied with their weakness. This awoke the zealous spirit within him. He could not tolerate laziness like this, and so he now began to strongly and energetically preach against it. He carried on with this for quite some time. This once so peaceful worker had now become a preacher, and there were a fair number of other people who were awakened by his preaching to zeal and seriousness. Many a faltering knee was strengthened. But Abrahamsson had never actually been called by Immanuel to preach. Though his zeal was great, he was lacking in wisdom. Despite this, it seemed that his desire to preach grew with each passing day, and so gatherings began to be held regularly in a hall arranged specifically for this purpose.

This caused Mother Simple to grow awfully concerned about him. For at the same time as she was forced to admit that he did possess quite a bit of talent, she still could not discern in him the kind of meek and humble spirit that she considered essential for a preacher in Evangelium. Oftentimes she found his lofty speech and his dramatic expressions downright painful to endure. Once, within earshot of others, she quite ingeniously summed one of his lectures with the brief evaluation that "his mouth was simply too crammed with words." What is more, she also often found that he altered his voice in such a way that it seemed like he was trying to achieve a profound effect. In particular, this happened whenever he was about to pray. For it was then that she thought she could make out an artificial, sorrowful quivering in his voice, which she took as an attempt to express some deep emotion of the heart, but which she had every reason to suspect as evidence of quite different motivations. From time to time she would even mention these things to Abrahamsson, and one of these conversations in particular is worth recounting.

On this occasion, Abrahamsson had just finished giving a lecture. The audience had been quite moved emotionally by his speech and his prayer in particular. Abrahamsson had set out to make his way home when he suddenly encountered Mother Simple, who greeted him with a restrained curtsy, making no sign of wishing to stop and talk with him. Perplexed, he asked her what the reason might be for her unusual behavior.

"Well," she answered, "I think that the Squire has demonstrated a particularly self-satisfied attitude today."

"How do you mean?" asked Abrahamsson. "Why should I be prevented from being able to rejoice over the role that I have played today as an agent of blessing?"

"No, of course not. But how is it that the Squire is so certain that this blessing has been all that great? The Squire has, through this assumed persona, managed to stir the natural emotions of his audience, that is true. They have cried, and I have heard many people highly praise the spiritual upbuilding that they supposedly received from the Squire's lecture. But I would like to explain to the Squire one thing: that there is a great difference between the experience of sweet emotions and true upbuilding. And for me, both the Squire's speech and prayer this evening have left a painful impression. For this reason, I really do wish that the Squire had stopped preaching long ago – for the Squire has not been called to it."

At this they parted company. Abrahamsson did not give any answer. His joy had vanished, and he walked home downcast.

"That odd little old woman never allows people to be left in peace," he mumbled.

For her part, Mother Simple continued on her way to Immanuel in order to relay to him everything that had happened, and to beg him to see to it that Abrahamsson's preaching would soon see its end.

The next few days for Abrahamsson were spent in anxious deliberation about what he should do. Mother Simple's candid speech had left a deep impression on him. In the midst of his irresolution, he happened to receive a visit from a good friend, for whom he unloaded his troubles. This friend was highly perplexed over all this, but explained that Abrahamsson ought not to attach too much importance to these words.

"For," the friend said, "it is remarkable, all this with Mother Simple. She is a loveable human being through and through. But on occasion, she can be peculiarly arbitrary and biased. Yet, it is not surprising that she is clueless about this profession, as it is something with which she has no experience whatsoever."

Abrahamsson felt relief and encouragement from these words by his friend. When the day came for the next scheduled assembly, he set out on his way to the usual hall with renewed courage. Upon his entrance he immediately noticed Mother Simple and the bookkeeper Conscience sitting among the numerous people in the hall. Yet, he did not let this affect him, but instead began to speak with great defiance. After the lecture had ended, he encountered Conscience standing by the exit, seeming displeased.

"It will never do," he said, "for the Squire to keep on in this way. For I can tell that the Squire has become addicted to the praise of other people."

Abrahamsson was immediately silenced and felt uneasy. Yet, after a moment, he asked CONSCIENCE:

"Do you mean to say, that I should wish that people would speak ill of me, or that I ought to dislike it whenever they praise me? Besides, I am certainly not hoping that they will praise me, but simply the blessing that God is giving them through me. And *you* certainly ought to be able to figure out what is really going on here."

Passion just then overcame CONSCIENCE, and he attacked Abrahamsson violently and gave him quite a boxing. For CONSCIENCE had an anxious disposition and did not tolerate backtalk well, but instead quickly became irate. Fortunately, MOTHER SIMPLE soon arrived with help, and Abrahamsson was transported by her and some of our other friends back to THE FORGIVENESS OF SINS. He was altogether in despair. MOTHER SIMPLE spoke as soothingly as she could.

"IMMANUEL's blood cleanses from all sins," she said.

"I have heard that so often; it is not helping me right now."

"IMMANUEL's blood cleanses from all sins."

"Listen to what I am trying to tell you: it is no longer of any help to me."

This conversation continued for a long while, but MOTHER SIMPLE persevered in repeating the same thing. In the end, these words did begin to take root in his heart.

"What was that again?" he asked urgently.

"IMMANUEL's blood cleanses from all sins."

"Just imagine – I have never heard that before," exclaimed Abrahamsson.

He raised himself up in his bed, clasped his hands together and praised Justus All-Powerful.

At the next assembly, he came to the hall accompanied by Pastor Evangelist and appeared deeply moved. After offering a short prayer, he held a speech, in which he acknowledged before all of those present that he had in fact never been ordained by Immanuel to preach, but had done it out of an unwise zeal, mixed with a desire for the praise of other people.

"I have," he added, "never before been made so aware of my error and the danger I was in. But I can never be thankful enough for the fact that I, through the efforts of the dear Mother Simple and the bookkeeper Conscience, have now had my eyes opened to this."

He could not say a word more. Evangelist had to take over from there. Abrahamsson himself left the hall, overwhelmed with grief, and headed home in order to find peace in The Forgiveness of Sins. But with a glad spirit, Mother Simple hurried off to speak about all of this with Immanuel.

FOURTEENTH CHAPTER

Abrahamsson in Theology

After experiencing all these setbacks, and several others which will go unnamed in this tale, one would certainly be justified in the expectation that Abrahamsson would have, sooner or later, learned to be still. But he had yet to learn that art, which after his first conversation with MOTHER SIMPLE he believed he had learned so well that he would never forget it. One more example of this will be evident in this next regrettable account.

One of the greatest difficulties that he struggled against was an almost indomitable need to *accomplish something great.* He had difficulty being satisfied with lowly and modest accomplishments. Thus engaged with his lofty plans, he arrived at the conclusion that he really ought to become a resident of THEOLOGY. THEOLOGY was a camp that was set up along the walls of the city EVANGELIUM. In this camp, there could be found many soldiers and mighty warriors, who referred to themselves as THEOLOGIANS. They were a peculiar band, which was divided into two groups. The one group lived in tents outside of the city, and had in fact never tasted of the joys of living in the city. Yet they considered the city to be their territory and strove with an indomitable spirit to defend it against a mighty giant, whose name was HERESY, and who had in his employ an army of WINDS OF DOCTRINE.[144] These THEOLOGIANS had two weapons, one of which was called PEN and the other TONGUE. They sharpened and honed these weapons with two stones named ACUMEN and MEDITATION.

These they wielded with great strength and talent, which was certainly necessary, as the enemies never gave up any ground, but persisted in their attacks.

Now the THEOLOGIANS who did live within the walls of EVANGELIUM added to this arsenal a third weapon, which they called PRAYER. But this was despised by the others, as it was deemed to be too ordinary.

In order to get the lay of the land and see how things were going in EVANGELIUM, those who lived outside the walls made use of certain viewpoints, more specifically a kind of high lookout tower, which were called SYSTEMS, which they had raised, and from which they could view the area below. From these towers they claimed that they could get a general, organized, and honest assessment over the whole region. Yes, they even asserted that they knew the city better than those people who lived inside, because these people could never get a complete view of the whole area at once. It is indeed true that they knew the streets in the holy city rather well. But how people lived inside the houses, about this they were always clueless, although they had read many scholarly books about these topics, and even wrote their own books – in a somewhat a similar fashion as the blind might write about color. However, they considered themselves as rather eloquent authors.

It was this group that Abrahamsson eventually decided to join. Now it was merely a question of which of these two camps he should side with; either those who lived within the city walls or those who lived without. In the beginning, he thought it was a good idea to make his camp with the former. Here he came under the guidance of PROFESSOR CONSCIENTIOUS, who, for him, had become a faithful and tender-hearted father, who sincerely looked after him. Abrahamsson, for his part, also became attached to this new friend of his, who could not help but rejoice over his good behavior. MOTHER SIMPLE, too, took joy in seeing him under the care of the dear professor. As long as she had him in The Forgiveness of Sins and Sanctification, as well as in the school of Father Experience, she was satisfied and glad. In addition to this, it encouraged her much to see him increasingly come to trust Schoolmaster Faithful, as she regarded him as a particularly pious and endearing man. And furthermore when she saw him regularly begin to keep company with Mr. Meek, a son to the Spirit of Reverence for God, then she not only began to hope for a good conclusion for Abrahamsson's life, but she even began to expect this with confidence. In this, she was given more than a little encouragement by Mr. Hopeful, who visited her regularly.

This was how things went for a while, during which time people took particular joy in Abrahamsson and expected that he would become a great blessing to Evangelium. But Mother Simple and Professor Conscientious, who were old and experienced, almost appeared to compete with one another in their encouragements to him, as well as their warnings whenever they deemed it necessary. For Abrahamsson possessed such a nature, that he could become reckless, when things were going well for him, and equally often could become defeated when things did not.

Nevertheless, he began all the more to excel and make a name for himself. This caused Mother Simple great misgivings, in particular when she noticed that he more and more began to be drawn into the company of Mr. Bold and Mr. Dead-Sure, and also seemed to be forgetting his once close friendship with Mr. Meek. She now started trying to convince him of the dangers that he faced, but he refused to heed these warnings.

Yes, he even began to be more distant from this previously beloved little old woman. For partly, he felt that she had too great a need to get involved in other people's business, partly because he now felt that he had, due to his scholarly education, arrived at a vantage point which Mother Simple, with her lack of this kind of study and knowledge, would have great difficulty understanding. Thus when he would see her appearing worried, he would often grin to himself, as he thought that her anxiety was a result of a well-intentioned ignorance. He also thought that Mother Simple ought not to worry about or get mixed up in matters that she simply could not possibly understand from her vantage point.

This was how things had been going for a while, when among the friends of Evangelium there suddenly started to circulate a terrible rumor that Abrahamsson had not only gotten into an argument with Professor Conscientious, but even had decided to move and join the Theologians who lived outside the city. The cause of this argument, Abrahamsson explained, was that Professor Conscientious was altogether too weighed down by old prejudices. But those who knew the situation better confirmed that the disagreement resulted from the fact that Abrahamsson had become bitter toward Conscientious, who had warned him several times about Mr. Self-Wise and his friends. Conscientious had once even harshly chastised him for a mistake he had made. Conscience, who was also present during this episode, later told about how Abrahamsson had one time mumbled to himself the following statement, as he was leaving the house of Professor Conscientious:

"There is no reason for me to remain as his pupil. I am my own man, and that's what I ought to tell him."

Everyone who had been observing Abrahamsson lately also knew that he had acquired some pills, which made him act rather peculiar, despite the fact that he claimed that they had a rather positive effect on him. The name of the pill was By One's Own Power,[145] but they were commonly sold under the incorrect label: Treatment for Narrow-Mindedness.

What Mother Simple herself thought about all of this was not entirely clear or easy to coax out of her. She cried nearly all the time. Only one time did she break her silence on this subject, and that was on an occasion when Schoolmaster Faithful, in the company of others, pronounced a rather harsh judgment on Abrahamsson. Upon this Mother Simple was reported to have made the following response, earnestly and with sadness: *Let him that standeth, take heed lest he fall!*

That the reports of Abrahamsson's move were so inconsistent caused confusion for many. But those who were better acquainted with Abrahamsson reasoned that it was due to the fact that he had such a strong tendency to, whenever he came into an argument with someone, present the matter in such a way that the fault would always land squarely on his opponent.

Whatever the reasons were, it was a fact that Abrahamsson had moved out of the city and joined the ranks of the Theologians who had their camp out there. Here his reputation grew day by day, and soon he had distinguished himself in wisdom and assertiveness, to the degree that other people, as well as *he himself,* were of the opinion that they had never seen the likes of this warrior. Never did he rest. During the day, he went out to battle; at night, he sharpened his weapons. Wherever he went about, he strode like a lion, and even the giant Heresy himself trembled like an aspen leaf at the sight of his gaze. It was natural for everyone to look up to him as being truly superhuman. Almost everyone sought council from him; his recommendation was weighed heavier than other people's, and if someone's work was to be evaluated as good, it first had to be tested and corrected by him.

In an attempt to try to keep Abrahamsson in check and to mitigate the devastation brought about by his mighty blows, Heresy sent two of his elite warriors, Prideful and Partisan, out to meet him. These two were not so much known for their strength and their valor, as for their wise and shrewd strategy of carrying themselves in battle. Namely, they never let on that they were actually *enemies.* When they approached

Abrahamsson, they behaved *amicably and fueled his courage even more.* They presented themselves merely as Theologians. Abrahamsson could not help but see them as anything other than strong allies, and soon they became his *inseparable* companions and served as his pages in every battle. Poor old Abrahamsson would have been completely lost to this deception had it not been for Mother Simple, who came in once more to intervene. Abrahamsson was not worthy of this little old woman's help. This entire time she had been mourning his absence in The Forgiveness of Sins and had been petitioning Immanuel to remain true to his promise: *I will bring back that which was lost.*[146] In the end, she could no longer restrain herself. She hurried off to find him. When she discovered him, she found him in the company of the aforementioned enemies. Dismayed, she cried out to him:

"This is not all right! This will bring the Squire to disaster. Doesn't the Squire realize the kind of enemies with whom he is keeping company?"

"Oh, dear mother, they are certainly not enemies, but instead mighty allies," answered Abrahamsson.

"Oh, how can the Squire say that?"

"Well, it ought to be clear as day, since they help me, of course. Whenever I go out to battle Heresy, they fuel my courage, so that I am even willing to lay down my life for Evangelium. Calm down, now, dear little old woman. Take care of your own affairs, and do not assume you understand everything!"

Distressed, Mother Simple went away to Immanuel and poured out her troubles. He sent her back with the same message to communicate. She made her way back, defeated and anxious.

"Well, have you come back again?" said Abrahamsson, when she walked in.

"Yes, Squire. If I may just pose three questions, then I will go again."

"Ask as many questions as you wish."

"My first question will be this one, then: Whatever happened to that humble spirit, which hungered after grace, and which used to fill the Squire's heart and allow him thrive in grace?"

Abrahamsson blushed. The little old woman kept silent. She looked at him, and her gaze pierced like a sword through his soul.

"Where, Squire? Tell me. Where?" she repeated.

Abrahamsson sat himself down and wiped his forehead with his hand.

"It is gone," he sighed.

"And now, then, my second question: Where is the earnestness, with which the Squire used to go about his work in SANCTIFICATION, when he was glad and thriving in grace?"

Abrahamsson turned to look away.

"Gone. That is gone, too," he sighed once again.

"And now, the third question: Where is the deep love, which used to bind the Squire to all of the friends of IMMANUEL?"

Abrahamsson stared at the floor. He did not make a sound. After a moment, MOTHER SIMPLE continued:

"I will answer – it is gone. The Squire has abandoned that first love. Oh, what a dreadful transformation!"

Abrahamsson leaned forward and buried his face in his hands and sniffled loudly. This deeply moved MOTHER SIMPLE. With the help of CRY-FOR-MERCY, the wretched and destitute son of MOTHER PRODIGAL, she hurried off to IMMANUEL to inform him about how things had gone. He came immediately. Oh, poor Abrahamsson! He felt as though he wanted to dig a hole and hide in it. When he caught sight of IMMANUEL, he cried out in his distress:

"Depart from me, for I am a sinful man, O Lord!"[147]

But IMMANUEL transported him once again to THE FORGIVENESS OF SINS, where he was tenderly cared for.

Among the THEOLOGIANS camped outside the walls, there was much alarm over what had happened. Everyone expressed their sorrow. But deep down most of them were glad, for lately they had begun to be a little bit overshadowed by Abrahamsson. They assembled for a council meeting and decided that Abrahamsson should be issued a serious word of reprimand.

It was quite a while before Abrahamsson dared to believe that IMMANUEL was indeed showing him grace. But MOTHER SIMPLE said to him once, as he was worrying: "If IMMANUEL wasn't still showing the Squire grace, then he would not be so faithfully caring for the Squire, of course." Then he began to be glad again, and praised aloud his merciful lord with a full heart.

MOTHER SIMPLE could hardly function, so joyful she was at once again seeing her friend so miraculously saved. In her tears of joy and thankfulness, she did the best she could to join him in singing praises to the honor of IMMANUEL. And although her song was hard to hear for most human ears, everyone who did hear it was amazed. For it was generally known, and people often had held this against MOTHER SIMPLE, that she almost never sang. But this was a result of the fact that she had developed a large growth in her throat, which the doctor called CROSS. This growth had damaged her voice box, so that she could usually only squeak out a few off-key notes. Yes, sometimes it was so difficult for her, that only a few heavy sighs could escape. She herself felt as though there were times when she had altogether lost her voice. But she nevertheless had still managed to enjoy herself as long as she was able to live in Evangelium and eat her meals in The Forgiveness of Sins. And this, Immanuel had assured her, she would be able to continue doing *as long as she needed to.* Of course, whenever she had heard others rejoice and sing, she would often become discouraged and worried that Immanuel might no longer care for her, and so she had often begged him to remove the growth. But she had repeatedly received the response that she should be satisfied with his grace, as well as *the promise,* that when she one day arrived home in Holiness, then she would finally be rid of this impediment.

But we return now to Abrahamsson.

FIFTEENTH CHAPTER

Abrahamsson's journey to Self-Righteousness

Once Abrahamsson had calmed down and regained himself, he resumed his work in the previously mentioned "workshop for the redeemed," properly called SANCTIFICATION. Here he occupied himself at times, although under great fear, with composing brief texts for the spiritual upbuilding of the inhabitants of EVANGELIUM. He even authored texts to be sent out to THE WORLD, intended for the awakening of the people there. In all of these works, the centerpoint was IMMANUEL, whom Abrahamsson always exalted and praised. This was the beginning of each text, and it was to here that he always returned at the end. During these working periods, he constantly had VIGILANT in his company, for although he did not depend on him much these days, he still *did not ever want to be without him.*

And now the days drifted by, as they sometimes can do in EVANGELIUM. But one evening, Abrahamsson suddenly came into the room where his wife was, with his countenance dark, in low spirits and sighing deeply. Noticing this at once, she asked him if he didn't feel well. A deep sigh was the only answer she got from him, and her husband began gathering up his things to be packed.

"What are you intending to do now?" she asked him, frightened.

"I intend to move to the city SELF-RIGHTEOUSNESS, over there on the other side of the RIVER OF BLOOD."

"Poor man, are you leaving once again?"

"Yes. It does no good for me to stay here any longer. As long as I live here, it only ever amounts to misery for me, and I am only getting worse. I live altogether too close to LOOSE LIVING, and it is a fair question to ask, which side of the city line our house lies; on the side of LOOSE LIVING or EVANGELIUM? The residents in SELF-RIGHTEOUSNESS, on the other hand, have always distinguished themselves, and even enjoy a certain amount of respect, and deservedly so, for their diligence, firmness of character, and their seriousness. And so that is where I am planning on moving, for lately things have not been going well for me here."

"But tell me, how is it that you have arrived at an idea like this?"

"Well, listen here! When I was sitting in the workshop one day, I was informed that MOTHER SIMPLE was in bed, sick with a fever. Just then, there came a message for me from IMMANUEL, that I should go and visit her. I set out in a hurry to go there, but when I had gotten a ways down the road, I thought: 'This must be a mistake – I possess no skills or anything else that I can offer to help the little old woman. IMMANUEL can certainly send someone else there, with some wisdom to impart. This message must be the work of that sly enemy, SELF-RELIANCE.' Upon that realization, I turned back. But I ran into CONSCIENCE on the road. He verified that the message was in fact from IMMANUEL. Now terrified, I immediately turned around again, but when I arrived, the little old woman was no longer to be found. Right after I had turned around, the summons had come from JUSTUS ALL-POWERFUL that she should immediately journey to HOLINESS. By the time I had returned, IMMANUEL had already set out with her on the journey. And now I simply do not dare remain here!"

"I see. But tell me, what kind of fever was it, that the little old woman had come down with?"

"If it had been anything else, it would not have been all that serious. But in this case, it was that severe fever that the doctors call Mortal Anxiety."

"But remember, Immanuel has promised that you may remain here, as long as you need!"

"Yes, that was before. Now I *feel* that things are different, and that is also what Conscience told me."

Thus, they both made up their minds to move. While they are engaged in packing up their things, we will hurry on ahead to Self-Righteousness in order to have a look around for a minute.

Self-Righteousness was, in terms of appearance, a remarkably beautiful and well-situated city. It lay a good distance from Evangelium, several miles on the other side of the River of Blood. Admittedly, the city was a little bit crowded and enclosed by sturdy walls, but it had broad streets that were straight and level, and in general it was well built with grand, stately homes. The residents appeared to be unusually hearty, healthy and strong, and were also unbelievably productive and talented workers. The city was primarily a factory town, and wherever one went, one could hear the pounding of the machines. The people one encountered on the street seemed to have nothing else to talk about besides how busy they were and how they really ought to be getting back to work. The residents also held regular meetings, in which they discussed together how to arrange the factory so that production could be optimally streamlined and that out-put could be driven up to the maximum level, as well as other matters regarding the quantity and quality of their products. These gatherings were held in a great hall, called "Don't say 'Christ.'" The chairman of the board was the burgomaster and the highest official, whose name was Wages, a distinguished and especially engaging man, both through his way of being and his generosity. Universally beloved by his citizens, he had an amazing ability to keep all of the workforce in motion, as well as to be the *very spirit behind their work.* People claimed also with complete certainty, that if not for his considerable motivation, the city would long ago have gone under and all of the work at the factory ground to a halt. But at the present time, it had *him* to thank for its current state of affairs and blossoming economy. The burgomaster had as a colleague and a powerful coworker a municipal judge by the name of LAW PREACHER, who had the assignment to, in part, come to the assistance of the residents in terms of advice and enlightenment, and partly to supervise all of their work. And as an example of this judge's prudence and wise conduct, we will turn now to the following episode.

Immediately outside one of the city's gates, called TIREDNESS, lay a beautiful park, which had been named REST. Here there was a spring of striking beauty, called PRAISE OF VIRTUE, but which was actually called SELF-PROMOTION. It was here that the residents sometimes came to refresh themselves and gather their strength so they could return to their efforts renewed. Yet one might add that many people, to their great credit, seldom visited this place. Among the most honorable of them it was considered to be a bad sign, or at least a sign of weakness, for people to frequent this place of refreshment – or at least to do so conspicuously. Their great love for the burgomaster WAGES, whom they called "the hope of the city," was so strong, that they needed rest seldom at the most. And if they occasionally did need it, they usually made their way to the park in *secret.* Yes, there were even some people, who enjoyed the reputation of having never laid eyes on the place, which caused them to be held in high esteem and earned them the title ELDERS. Yet there were not many, who hoped or even attempted to achieve the same status as these people. Most considered them to be outstanding role models and brilliant lights, whose example one ought to try to come *as close to as possible,* without necessarily trying to be their *equals.* Partly, people would view with suspicion those who tried to imitate the ELDERS perfectly, and regarded them as presumptuous, especially when they allowed themselves to entertain the hope that they were capable of one day reaching that goal. More specifically, people felt that these efforts were in vain, which was why there were so few who attempted to accomplish this. It was in keeping with the good traditions of the city, and it was regarded that an essential sign of humility was to lower the bar a little bit.

"For," people explained, "when one cannot achieve perfection, then it is not worth striving just for that, per se. Of course, one should never, as the people in LOOSE LIVING do, completely abandon the goal of perfection. But *first and foremost* one ought to fix their sights on *some specific aspect* of perfection, something that *can be reasonably achieved.* Otherwise it could easily happen, that while one was striving to attain full perfection, as the people in EVANGELIUM do, one could fail and not achieve anything."

In this way, people thought it best to keep to the golden *middle way* between the two extremes, which were dominant in EVANGELIUM and LOOSE LIVING. On the one hand, one ought not to be too hard on oneself for not being *completely* perfect. But on the other hand, one ought not to allow for any laziness. But now we should return to the event that we were going to discuss.

On the lawn by the above mentioned spring, a factory worker had lied down one day, as he was rather exhausted in body and spirit. He was contemplating moving away, for he felt that it was so difficult to work like a slave all day long. He was just then debating the idea within himself, whether he should move to EVANGELIUM or to LOOSE LIVING. Back to THE WORLD he had no desire of moving. Deep in these thoughts, he was awakened by the sting of a switch. He turned around and saw at his side none other than LAW PREACHER.

"Why are you wasting so much time here?"

"I am considering moving to EVANGELIUM."

"Is this a betrayal of our dear burgomaster?"

"No, but I simply cannot stand to stay here any longer."

"Do you mean to deprive yourself of the grace and favor, which you have enjoyed here at the hand of JUSTUS ALL-POWERFUL, and bring his severe wrath upon yourself?"

"Is it so certain that one would lose his favor, though?"

"Yes! Apart from the expressed commandments of JUSTUS ALL-POWERFUL to that effect, you have seen yourself how glad the people have been who have come here from EVANGELIUM after they have had their eyes opened to the delusions that had previously held them captive. You have heard their testimony about how miserable it is to live there, constantly trying to rely on a grace, which is supposed to be free, while they themselves, rather than becoming better as they should be, are instead becoming worse and worse."

The factory worker was now convinced. With a deep sigh he returned to the city. But his spirits were raised by the information that he received outside the gate, that a certain Mr. Abrahamsson, with wife and children, had just arrived there by caravan from EVANGELIUM. It is difficult to explain the spirit of joy that this produced within the city. This addition was considered to be an important achievement for their side. For people were quite familiar with this well-known hero from the camp of the THEOLOGIANS. And so our factory worker clasped his hands together and thought:

"We must be in the right, after all, since such a learned and respected man has come here from EVANGELIUM with the intention of settling here. He certainly must know what he is doing!"

Many other tired souls thought along roughly these same lines. The enchantment was universal.

While they are fluttering about as cheerful as can be, we will take a quick look around the various roads into the city. From the cities of THE WORLD and LOOSE LIVING there only was one road that led to SELF-RIGHTEOUSNESS, which ran rather close beside EVANGELIUM and was usually referred to as REPENTANCE, even though it was nothing more than MORAL IMPROVEMENT. This road was very long, such that it split into a number of winding paths. Furthermore, it was uneven, steep and bumpy, to the degree that did not allow for any smooth train travel. Instead, people usually traveled with oxcarts or even on foot. Naturally it took a considerable amount of time to complete the journey, especially for those who were suffering from any severe disabilities. From this road, one entered into SELF-RIGHTEOUSNESS through a very narrow gate which was called FAITH, but in reality was known as CONVICTION. This road was joined by a railway, the name of which was DESPAIR, and which led away from EVANGELIUM. At the place where the roads joined, people would disembark from the train and continue the journey, as mentioned, either on foot or by oxcart. From SELF-RIGHTEOUSNESS there was yet another train that led away to LOOSE LIVING and THE WORLD, which was called IRRESPONSIBILITY. The name of the road itself was NOT-SO-CAREFUL. Besides that, there was also another road that led off to the north from the city, which the residents called SANCTIFICATION and was often speculated to lead to the city HOLINESS, where LORD JUSTUS lived.

We shall now return to our travelers.

SIXTEENTH CHAPTER

Abrahamsson's return to Evangelium – The move to Holiness – The fate of Evangelist

As soon as Abrahamsson had arrived in SELF-RIGHTEOUSNESS, his re-entry was documented at the office of the burgomaster, to whom he swore his faithful allegiance, and at this point adopted the name HAGARSSON.[148] He was greeted warmly, and also admitted as a novice (or, as he was also known, "new Christian") in the factory school, where LAW PREACHER served as an instructor. To be sure, he was rather frequently treated harshly here. But nonetheless, he remained calm and glad, for he had found the peace that he had long been seeking. It was here that he learned about the importance of the factory, the necessity of being a diligent worker, and many other essential lessons, such as the proper way to maintain a factory, as well as how to distinguish between good and bad nutrition, and so on. After this period of training was over, he was granted his own factory, where he began producing many things, all of which were labeled CHRISTIAN VIRTUES. It was not long before he was counted among the most highly respected citizens of the city, in terms of his entrepreneurial spirit, his talents and diligence. And since he also possessed an academic education and a knack for writing, he also began to hold public lectures in the aforementioned hall, DON'T SAY 'CHRIST', on topics such as *"The only true peace; which is won by diligence and faithful work according to the word of All-Powerful."* In addition, he also distributed miscellaneous texts on various factory products, which he had manufactured, and which the residents of SELF-RIGHTEOUSNESS referred to as

Godliness, Seriousness, Prayer, and several others. These were deceptively similar in appearance to the fruits of faith that one could find in Evangelium, and which bore the same names. But despite these similarities, they were of a markedly different nature and composition, which is why they were regarded by the inhabitants of Evangelium as imitations. In Self-Righteousness, by contrast, they were regarded highly and even coveted as though they were of great worth.

Furthermore, Hagarsson began to publish a journal, in which he attempted to prove that, on this point, Immanuel showed himself to be ungracious toward the inhabitants of Evangelium, since he withheld from them all assistance and forced them into bankruptcy. This had the end result of keeping them in such a state of anxiety that they finally were forced to the realization that they had to move to Self-Righteousness.[149] That this was preached and written by a man like Hagarsson, made it seem that this message ought to be heard and read with the greatest urgency, and it was soon apparent to all that he deserved to be ranked among the Elders. People began to have an extraordinary degree of confidence in him, and claimed that everything that he said or wrote was masterfully crafted and spiritually upbuilding, strengthening people in their faith. He did make that qualification, however, that it might be possible for the residents of Evangelium to make it to Holiness, although these people's work needed to be first consumed by fire, as hay and straw. In his explanations, he would often point to the example of Mother Simple, who he believed was now at home with Justus. And as long as Hagarsson was of this conviction, and kept speaking and writing about it, then the rest of the city was of a mind to agree. But when his concern for true doctrine eventually caused his thoughts to wander to their logical extreme, such as to see in Mother Simple a terrifying example of Beelzebul's cunning, then the others also changed their minds. Yet, one had to admit that the description he gave of both Mother Simple and Evangelium, and in particular of the district called The Forgiveness of Sins, actually inspired many a tired factory worker to up and move there, in search of the peace they hoped to find for the remainder of their days. But those who heeded Hagarsson's warning hoped with all their hearts that they would never allow themselves to be misled like these people, who had furthermore become the subject of general sympathy and pity.

However, Hagarsson's misadventures were not yet over. His earlier departure from Evangelium had set that whole city abuzz. Also contributing to this were all the reports that came back to the city from workers who had moved there from Self-Righteousness, who described Hagarsson and his new business ventures. Mother Prodigal informed Immanuel of all of this. At once, he sent word to his father Justus All-Powerful, describing the course of events. Lord Justus became indignant, but yet he was of a mind to keep his patience and wait. Time passed – several years, in fact – but everything remained the same. Then one day Justus All-Powerful summoned his faithful old servant Moses. When he arrived, Lord Justus said:

"You remember Adamsson, don't you?"

"Yes, Gracious Lord, you must mean that man who received the name Abrahamsson from Immanuel way back when?"

"Yes, the very same! He calls himself now 'Hagarsson' and lives in the city Self-Righteousness. He has now taken up living on his own, has established his own household and seeks to earn his income by means of a factory. Go to him with this certificate of debt and demand payment on the spot!"

"As my Gracious Lord commands," answered Moses, and he departed.

Hagarsson was just then sitting in his office, quiet and reserved, and one could see that within him there brewed a dark inner turmoil. In a heap by his side, lay his wife, with her face hidden in a handkerchief, which was soaked through from a torrent of tears. What had prompted this? Well, a terrible accident had occurred.

While Hagarsson had been taking a midday nap in the park by the aforementioned spring, SELF-PROMOTION, a fire had broken out in his factory. By the time this was detected, it had already spread to the point where it was impossible to even consider attempting to put it out. With terrifying strength, and in no time flat, it devoured that beautiful factory and reduced it to a heap of ashes.[150] While husband and wife sat there, sunken in their sorrow over this pitiable turn of events, there came a loud knocking at the door.

"Come in!" yelled Hagarsson, with a faltering voice, though his face began to lighten once again. For he thought that it just might be IMMANUEL, who had so often before come to his aid in difficult circumstances. But to his great horror, he recognized the visitor as the very person he had least of all wished to ever look in the eyes again. It was MOSES. Trembling, Hagarsson received the letter, and he read aloud for his wife the following stern words:

> *Untiring has my patience been with you, all the time that you lived in my holy city EVANGELIUM; and as long as you owned nothing, you were allowed to remain under a constant and unwavering grace, through my son IMMANUEL, despite all of your many debts. Everything that you owed me, I granted to you. But now, when you have grown tired of my love, as well as found it desirable to move to SELF-RIGHTEOUSNESS – and there assume another name and establish a new home and source of income – then it follows that I am demanding that you immediately pay your debt of 10,000 talents, or risk your eternal imprisonment!*[151]
>
> *For holiness on the day of reckoning,*
>
> – JUSTUS ALL-POWERFUL

Hagarsson remembered all too well his previous time of imprisonment, and so he had no desire to trifle with his master again. With his poor wife in hand, he rushed out of the gate through which he had entered that unfortunate city, and set out for EVANGELIUM. But as we remember, the road of MORAL IMPROVEMENT was difficult. On that day, there was not a single oxcart available. What is more, it was raining, such that the road was muddy and slippery. It also was beginning to get dark. Oh, this unfortunate man! What was he to do? It was with all his energy that he made his way, and at every moment he was on the verge of collapsing. Finally, he simply lost the path, and was forced to stop. His wife broke into heavy sobs of despair. His own heart was altogether too heavy for him to even cry.

Now this poor man would soon have been completely lost if it had not been for the willing assistance provided by CRY-FOR-MERCY, who entered just at the right moment. Like lightning, he darted off to IMMANUEL in order to report on this dire situation. Sweaty and panting from exhaustion, he was so tired when he arrived, that without asking for admittance, he rushed straight up to IMMANUEL. Unable to say a word, he fell down at his feet, sighing heavily. BANKRUPT FAITH, who had also been following behind, was harassed the entire way by DOUBT, who was trying to hinder his progress.

"Where are you headed?" he asked.

"To IMMANUEL; do not get in my way!"

"Keep this in mind, though: he who sows to his flesh will of the flesh reap corruption![152] Hagarsson has ruined himself, and now he must bear the consequences of his actions."

FAITH became deathly pale with fright and trembled like an aspen leaf.

"But IMMANUEL has certainly said..." he stammered.

"Said what?!" interrupted Doubt. "Nothing more than that for those, who have once tasted of grace, but fallen away, there is no more grace to be had, but instead they shall await a terrible judgment and fire of fury, which will consume all those in its path."

Faith just stood there, unable to respond, while Doubt continued:

"Immanuel does not allow himself to be mocked.[153] Abrahamsson could have, for all eternity, been happy and blessed if he had stayed in Evangelium. But by this assumed identity as Hagarsson, he has branded his soul and become a terrifying example of All-Powerful's righteous wrath. Oh, how horrible it is to fall into his hands! But this he brought on himself, and as the proverb says, 'he that makes his bed shall lie in it.'"

What would have become of poor old Faith is hard to say, if Schoolmaster Faithful had not come upon the scene. Bankrupt Faith was on the verge of dying from anxiety, but Schoolmaster Faithful encouraged him with some profound verses from God's Word, such that he could in fact continue on his way, though weakened and shaking as he was. Yet, Doubt was relentless.

"Who knows," he exclaimed, "whether or not Hagarsson has been judged to perdition!"

These words might have fatally wounded poor old Faith, if Schoolmaster Faithful had not countered Doubt with this response:

"It is Immanuel's will that all may be saved."[154]

Upon this, Bankrupt Faith began to approach Immanuel, but was so powerless that he collapsed before he had crossed the threshold, and in his weakness he could move neither hand nor foot. Those standing by believed that he had simply run himself to death. However, Immanuel understood at once what needed to be done. He hurried off to the place where Hagarsson was and carried this half-dead man back along the above-mentioned road, Despair,[155] and into the city Evangelium. There he restored him to his proper name, Abrahamsson, and got him settled in that old familiar room, The Forgiveness of Sins. Here he lay now, sick and wretched, the chief of sinners.[156]

"Oh," he sighed, "poor creature that I am! What shall become of me? Oh, if only Mother Simple was still with us!"

Just then, he heard sniffling coming from another bed. He listened, and his heart began to beat louder, and he thought he recognized the voice. He listened closer, and could make out the following:

"My life is spent with sorrow, and my years with sighing: my strength faileth because of mine iniquity, and my bones are consumed."[157]

Abrahamsson could no longer keep still. He jumped up and raced to the bed, from which this melancholy lamentation had come. There lay his old acquaintance, Depraved, having recently been returned to Evangelium. And so we will leave Abrahamsson here for a moment, while he is moved to tears, and while the glad news of his return races around the city like a wildfire, prompting a commotion of thanks and praises throughout the whole city. Present during this reunion with Depraved was none other than Mother Prodigal and Bankrupt Faith, and they confirmed that a meeting like this was simply not possible to describe.

Immanuel informed his father immediately about how everything had gone. And there was great joy in the city of Holiness.

The one who rejoiced the most was JUSTUS ALL-POWERFUL himself. He had the glad news published in handbills and distributed throughout the city, announcing that there was to be a great banquet for Abrahamsson, who had at last returned. In jubilation, everyone gathered around his throne. It was as though people didn't have anything else to talk about besides the rescue of Abrahamsson. Songs of praise resounded in honor of IMMANUEL, and people were in general agreement that this was one of the most marvelous celebrations that had ever been held in HOLINESS. And all this was because Abrahamsson had so often gone astray, but each time had been searched for and found. Everyone saw this as proof of a bottomless love and a limitless patience. It was as though, in this event, one could peer just a little bit deeper into the heart of JUSTUS ALL-POWERFUL.

At this point, we should not neglect to mention that among all the voices, which joined in these songs of praise, there were few that were as clear as MOTHER SIMPLE's. She had now, as IMMANUEL had promised, been freed from that troubling growth, which she had suffered from while she lived in EVANGELIUM. Next to her, one could also hear the resounding voice of yet another familiar person, who in this tale has been known by the name of FALLEN. He and several others were singing their praises, as well. They did not sing all the words, but only the first and the last word in each verse. All the verses began with the word *grace.* When that came, they joined in with lungs full of air, and each wailed on a great drum. The last word in each verse was *honor.* When the choir came to that word, FALLEN and the others joined in there too, as though enraptured, and their voices became like the roar of a waterfall.

After some time had passed, people in HOLINESS were beginning to fear that Abrahamsson would find some way to go astray again, if he was allowed to remain any longer where he was. It was about that time that JUSTUS ALL-POWERFUL sent his orders to IMMANUEL that Abrahamsson should be saved from this dreadful possibility of being completely lost, and instead be transported home. It was with trembling that Abrahamsson heard this summons, for all of the times he had gone astray now came back to haunt him, and this seemed so overwhelming, that he feared that the summons was actually going to lead to his final judgment and banishment. Immanuel tried to assure him; and certainly Abrahamsson did not believe that Immanuel wished to be cruel and mislead him. But he was afraid anyway, and fell into the same fever, which had plagued Mother Simple in the end. Nevertheless, he committed himself, with tears, into the hands of Immanuel, who transported him through a deep dark valley, which was called the Valley of Death.

"Where does this lead?" Abrahamsson asked, terrified.

"To Holiness," was the answer.

"But how is this possible?"

"It is as *I* have said."

Abrahamsson kept silent, but probably wondered how all this could be, for everything appeared so strange to him. He clasped his hands tight around Immanuel's neck, and in response, Immanuel tightened his embrace around Abrahamsson.

When he had arrived at the gate, Abrahamsson saw none other than Evangelist, who in despair was wandering alongside the outer walls.

"Why don't you go in?" asked Abrahamsson.

"Woe, woe. I may not!" was the terrible answer.

"Well, but you have certainly always been pious, preached mightily and helped to transport many people to Evangelium with your faithful prayers and your perseverance."

"Yes, it is true. And Mother Simple, who is now at home in there, was among those in whose salvation I was able to play a role. Now she is rejoicing, while I must despair for all eternity."

"Why is this?"

"Well, I lived happily for a long time in EVANGELIUM, but, oh, woe is me! I began to take pride in myself and seek my own honor. I abandoned EVANGELIUM and moved to SELF-RIGHTEOUSNESS. It was there that I lost this first love and became all the more blinded. Then a summons came for me. With great presumptuousness, I shouted out: 'I have fought a good fight, I have finished my course, now there is laid up for me the crown of righteousness,'[158] but when I arrived there, I found myself sorely mistaken."

Abrahamsson shuddered, and buried his head against IMMANUEL's chest. They then entered into HOLINESS. How things went for Abrahamsson after that, it is not possible to know. But those, who will one day go there themselves will surely find out. May God help us all through his son IMMANUEL!

Now to him who relies on works, the wages are not counted as grace but as debt. But to him who does not rely on works but believes on him who justifies the ungodly, his faith is accounted as righteousness. Amen.

THE CHARACTERS, IN ORDER OF APPEARANCE

(This Translation)	(1938 Swedish Translation)	(1928 English Translation)
Squire Adamsson / Abrahamsson	Brukspatron ...	Squire Adamson / Abrahamson
Mrs. Adamsson / Evasdotter	Fru Adamsson / Evasdotter	Mrs. Adamson / Daughter of Mother Eve
Mrs. Praise	Fru Beröm	Mrs. Flatterer
Mr. Admirer	Herr Beundrare	Mr. Admirer
Mrs. Admirer	Fru Beundrare	Mrs. Admirer
Pastor Shepherd-for-Hire	Pastor Legoherde	Pastor Mercenary
Mother Pious	Mor Andäktig	Mother Devoutness
Mother Simple	Mor Enfaldig	Mother Simplicity
Conscience	Samvete	Conscience
Mother Capricious	Mor Lättrörlig	Mother Emotional
Mother Wounded-Hip	Mor Höftlam	Mother Invalid
Heart-For-Children	Barnkär	Child-Lover
Mother Prodigal	Mor Förlorad	Mother Forsaken
Mother Penniless	Mor Utfattig	Mother Penniless
Kind-Hearted	Godhjärtad	Kindheartedness
Complacent / Humble	Självbelåten / Ödmjuk	Self-Satisfied
Miss Unwilling	Jungfru Ovillig	Maid Unwilling
Lord Justus / All-Powerful	Justus Allsvåldig	Justus Almighty
Moses	Moses	Moses
Hateful	Hatfull	Hate
Bitter	Bitter	Bitterness
Immanuel	Immanuel	Immanuel
Mr. Doubt	Herr Tvivel	Mr. Doubt
Bankrupt Faith	Utfattig Tro	Poverty-Stricken Faith
Beelzebul / Lucifer	Beelsebul / Lucifer	Beelzebub / Lucifer
Mrs. Sensible	Fru Förståndig	Mrs. Sensible
Bold / Confident	Stark / Förtröstansfull	Strong / Trustful
Dead-Sure / Straight-Forward	Tvärsäker / Frimodig	OverConfident / Fearless
Self-Wise / Enlightened	Självklok / Upplyst	Conceit / Enlightened
Professor Conscientious	Professor Redlig	Professor Honest
Schoolmaster Faithful	Magister Trogen	Instructor Faithful
Pastor Evangelist	Pastor Evangelist	Pastor Evangelist
Father Experience	Fader Erfarenheten	Experience
The Spirit of Truth	Sanningens Ande	Spirit of Truth
Mr. Must	Herr Måste	Mr. Must
The-Class-of-the-Wretched	Ömklighetsklassen	Miserable Class
Old Mrs. Love	Kärlek (äldre fruntimmer)	Love
Miss Busy	Fröken Verksam	Miss Energetic
Mr. Listless	Herr Olustig	Mr. Reluctant
Mr. Weary	Herr Trött	Mr. Weary
Mrs. BackStabber	Fru Baktalare	Mrs. Slanderer
Mrs. Gossiper	Fru Skvallerbytta	Mrs. Gossiper
Vigilant	Vaksam	Vigilance

(This Translation)	**(1938 Swedish Translation)**	**(1928 English Translation)**
Drowsy	Sömnaktig	Drowsy
Conscience-Peace	Samvetsfrid	Peaceful-Conscience
Have-Enough	Haver-nog	Have-Enough
Need-Nothing	Behöver-intet	Need-Nothing
Weather Cock	Väderdriven	Weather-Driven
Dean Orthodox	Prosten Renlärig	Dean Orthodox
False Assurance	Falsk Tröst	False Comfort
Good Natured	Fromsint	Good-Natured
Primitive Piety	Naturfrom	Naturally-Pious
Self	Jag	Ego
Will	Vill	Will
Shall	Skall	Shall
Freethinkers / Thoughtlesslings	Fritänkare / Tanklösingar	Free-Thinkers / Imbeciles
Liberally-Minded	Frisinnad	Liberal-minded
Watchman	Väktare	Watchman
Professor Worldly Wise	Världsvis	Worldly-Wise
Mrs. World Enamored	Världskär	Mrs. Worldly-Wise
Miss Immodest	Fröken Otuktig	Miss Unchaste
Promise	Löften	Promise
Miserable	Olycklig	Unfortunate
Depraved	Fördärvad	Depraved
Fallen	Sjunken	Degenerate
Doctor Godly	Doktor Gudelig	Doctor Godly
Vile	Usel	Licentious
Wretched	Eländig	Wretched
Councilman Cautious	Rådman Försiktig	Councilman Discreet
Mr. Bible-Bound	Herr Bibel-Trogen	Mr. Bible-True
Theologians	Teologer	Theologians
Heresy	Villfarelse	Unorthodoxy
Winds of Doctrine	Mångahanda Lärdomsväder	Diverse Heresey Blasts
Mr. Meek	Herr Ödmjuk	Mr. Humble
Spirit of Reverence for God	Herrens fruktans Ande	God-Fearing Spirit
Mr. Hopeful	Herr Hoppfull	Mr. Hopeful
Prideful	Högmod	Pride
Partisan	Partisinne	Dissension
Cry-for-Mercy	Nödrop	Cry-of-Distress
Self-Reliance	Självförtroende	Self-Confident
Wages	Lön	Hireling
Law Preacher	Lag Predikare	Law Preacher
Elders	Fäder	Fathers

PLACES

(This Translation)	(1938 Swedish Translation)	(1928 English Translation)
The World	Världen	Worldliness
Industriousness	Arbetsamhet	Industriousness
Self-Centered-Piety	Självfromhet	Self-Righteousness
Selfishness	Självviskhet	Mount Selfishness
Self-Activity	Självverksamhet	Self-Activity (later conflated with Industriousness)
WorldChurch	Världskyrkan	Worldly congregation
Holiness	Helighet	Holiness
Evangelium	Evangelium	Gospel City
Pious Street	Fromgatan	Pious Street
Sinai	Sinai	Sinai
Gehenna	Gehenna	Gehenna
New Birth	Nyfödelse	Regeneration
Narrow Gate	Trånga Porten	Narrow Gate
Golgotha	Golgata	Golgotha
River of Blood	Blodsälven	Blood-River
The Forgiveness of Sins (Room for the lost)	Syndernasförlåtelse	Forgiveness of Sins
Sanctification	Helgelse	Sanctification
Theology	Teologi	Theology
Self-Righteousness	Egenrättfärdighet	Self-Righteousness
Loose Living	Lösaktighet	Looseness
Prayer-Closet	Bönevrå	Prayer-Chamber
Emptiness	Tomhet	Emptiness
Carnality	Köttslighet	Carnality
Freedom	Frihet	Freedom
Own Bootstraps	Eget Arbete	Own Labor
The rock of Offense	Förargelseklippan	Rock of Offence
Broken Heartedness	Förkrosselse	Contrition
Moral Improvement	Förbättring	Reformation (later Improvement)
Hypocrisy	Skrymteri	Hypocrisy
River of Life	Livets Älv	River of Life
Kingdom of Darkness	Mörkrets Kingdom	Kingdom of Darkness
Paradise	Paradis	Paradise
Fear of God	Gudsfruktan	Godliness
The Church	Kyrkan	The Church
Adultery	Hor	Adultery
Fornication	Boleri	Fornication
Impurity	Orenlighet	Uncleanness
Idolatry	Avguderi	Idolatry
Witchcraft	Trolldom	Witchcraft
Enmity	Ovänskap	Hatred
Quarreling	Kiv	Variance
Zeal	Nit	Emulations
Wrath	Vrede	Wrath

(This Translation)	(1938 Swedish Translation)	(1928 English Translation)
Strife	Trätor	Strife
Discord	Tvedräkt	Seditions
Partisanship	Parti	Heresies
Jealousy	Avund	Envyings
Murder	Mord	Murders
Drunkenness	Dryckenskap	Drunkenness
Gluttony	Fråsseri	Revellings
Vanity	Högfärd	Pride
Greed	Girighet	Covetousness
The Hidden District	Det Hemliga Kvarteret	The Secret Quarter
Don't Say 'Christ'	Tig med Kristus	Speak not of Christ
Tiredness	Trötthet	Tiredness
Rest	Vila	Rest
Praise of Virtue/ Self-Promotion	Dygdens lov/ Självberömmelse	Virtue's Praise/ Self-Praise
Repentance	Bättring	Repentance
Faith	Tro	Faith
Conviction	Övertygelse	Conviction
Despair	Misströstan	Despondency
Irresponsibility	Lättsinnighet	Frivolity
Valley of Death	Dödens Dal	Valley of Death

MISCELLANEOUS

(This Translation)	(1938 Swedish Translation)	(1928 English Translation)
Good Deeds	Goda Gärningar	Good Works
God's Love	Guds Kärlek	God's Love
Bible	Bibeln	Bible
Philosophy / Logic / Proud Delusions	Filosofia / Logiken / Fåfängt Bedrägeri	Philosophy / Logic / Vain-Deceit
God's Word	Guds Ord	Word of God
Enlightenment	Upplysningen	Enlightenment
Indolence / Convenience	Maklighet / Bekvämlighet	Ease / Comfort
Desire of the Eye	Ögonens Begärelse	Lust of the Eyes
Desire of the Flesh	Köttets Begärelse	Lust of the Flesh
Prideful Living	Högfärdigt Leverne	Vainglorious Living
Devotion	Andakt	Devotion
Worship	Gudstjänst	Worship
Pretensions	Skrymteri	Hypocrisy
Pen	Penna	Pen
Tongue	Tunga	Tongue
Acumen	Skarpsinnighet	Sagacity
Meditation	Begrundning	Reflection
Prayer	Bön	Prayer
Systems	Systemer	Systems
By One's Own Power	Inbillingar om egen Kraft	Illusions of own Power
Treatment for Narrow-mindedness	Piller mot Ensidighet	Pills against Narrowmindedness
Cross	Kors	Cross
Mortal Anxiety	Dödsångest	Death-Agony
Not-So-Careful	Icke Så Noga	Not-So-Particular
Christian Virtues	Kristliga Dygder	Christian Virtues
Godliness	Gudsfruktan	Godliness
Seriousness	Allvar	Earnestness

NOTES

1 The titles of the translations are *Squire Adamson, or Where Do You Live?* (English), *Brugspatron Adamsen eller Hvor bor du?* (Norwegian), and *Brugspatron Adamsen eller Hvor boer du?* (Danish).

2 Harry Lindström, *I Livsfrågornas spänningsfält; Om P. Waldenströms Brukspatron Adamsson – populär folkbok och allegorisk roman.* (Stockholm: Verbum Förlag 1997), p. 10.

3 Gunnar Hallingberg, *Läsarna: 1800-talets folkväckelse och det moderna genombrottet* (Stockholm: Atlantis 2010), p. 340.

4 Ibid., p. 354; For example, one of Waldenström's books, *Herren är from,* sold out in the 1870s even though it was printed in approximately 50,000 copies, whereas Strindberg's *Röda Rummet* only sold about 7,500 copies during the same decade.

5 Ibid., p. 343.

6 William Bredberg identified *Squire Adamsson* as reflecting "Rosenius' own melody" and served as "a useable compendium in Rosenian dogma." William Bredberg, *P.P. Waldenströms verksamhet till 1878; Till frågan om Svenska Missionsförbundets uppkomst.* (Stockholm: Missionsförbundets Förlag 1948). pp. 55-56.

7 For instance, even after controversies in 1872 alienated him from the Church of Sweden, Waldenström maintained his ordination until 1882, and remained active as a layman representative in the church's governing body, the Church Assembly *(Kyrkomötet)*, as late as 1910.

8 Zinzendorf's concept was that each individual church is a "trope" that completes the diverse whole that is the greater church. Eric W. Gritsch, *A History of Lutheranism.* (Minneapolis: Fortress Press 2002). p. 155.

9 Waldenström, *Paul Peter Waldenströms Minnesanteckningar* 1838-1875, Ed. Bernhard Nyrén (Stockholm: Svenska Missionsförbundets Förlag 1928), p. 85.

10 John Bunyan, *The Pilgrim's Progress; From this World to That Which is to Come.* Introduction by W. Clark Gilpin, (New York: Vintage Spiritual Classics 2004), p. 195.

11 Lindström, pp. 135-141.

12 Bredberg, p. 145; Oloph Bexell, *Sveriges kyrkohistoria vol. 7; Folkväckelsens och kyrkoförnyelsens tid.* (Stockholm: Verbum 2003). p. 110.

13 Quoted in Bredberg, p. 144.

14 Waldenström, "Sjuttio år" *Pietisten* 22 Dec. 1911, p. 375.

15 Waldenström, *Genom Norra Amerikas Förenta Stater; Reseskildringar,* (Stockholm: Pietistens Expedition 1890), pp. 591-592.

16 Journal entry. Umeå, 29 May 1866. Waldenström, "Några ord om quinnans intellektuella bildning." Riksarkivet, Waldenströmska släktarkivet, del I, vol. 9; Letter to Svenska Morgonbladet and Jönköpings Posten. Stockholm, 11 Dec. 1913. Waldenström, "En liten tripp igen." Riksarkivet, Waldenströmska släktarkivet, del III, vol. 3.

17 Advertisement. *Pietisten.* 8 Mar. 1916. Back cover.; Apparently with the purchase of a special print *Räddningsbåten går ut,* "Departure of the Lifeboat."

18 *En Christens Resa genom werlden till den saliga ewigheten, framställd såsom sedd i en dröm af John Bunyan predikant i Betford.* (Stockholm: Isaac Marcus 1853.)

19 Lindström, pp. 37-38.

20 Ibid., p. 28.

21 Bunyan, pp. 62-64.

22 Lindström, p. 15.

23 Ibid., p. 66.

24 Ibid., p. 16.

25 Gritsch, p. 193.

26 Karl A. Olsson, "Paul Peter Waldenström and Augustana" in *The Swedish Immigrant Community in Transition; Essays in Honor of Dr. Conrad Bergendoff.* Ed. J. Iverne Dowie and Ernest M. Espelie (Rock Island, Illinois: Augustana Historical Society 1963). p. 110.

27 Lindström, pp. 170-175.

28 Translation by Safstrom.

29 Zinzendorf articulated this supremacy of experience in "Thoughts for the Learned and Yet Good-Willed Students of Truth," in which he states, among other things: "Religion must be a matter which is able to be grasped through experience alone, without any concepts." *Pietists: Selected Writings.* Ed. Peter C. Erb (New York: Paulist Press 1983), p. 291; Johann Arndt, *True Christianity,* (New York: Paulist Press 1979), p. 127.

30 Bredberg, pp. 25-26.

31 Søren Kierkegaard, *Fear and Trembling.* Introduction and notes by Alastair Hannay, (New York: Penguin Classics 1985), p. 153.

32 Waldenström, *Gud är min tröst,* Fifth edition (Stockholm: Svenska Missionsförbundets Förlag. 1938), p. 9.

33 Bunyan, pp. 98-102.

34 Bredberg, pp. 4-12.

35 Stanley E. Fish, "Rhetoric" in *Doing What Comes Naturally; Change, Rhetoric, and the Practice of Theory in Literary and Legal Studies.* (Durham, North Carolina: Duke University Press 1989.) pp. 471-477.

36 Richard Rorty, "Truth without correspondence to reality" in *Philosophy and Social Hope* (New York: Penguin Putnam Inc. 1999), pp. 36-39.

37 Lindström, p. 221; Lindström concludes his evaluation of "The Hidden District" with this summary: "Waldenström's literary action on behalf of those who were condemned sexually, who were oppressed by their own consciences and self-loathing, this was bold and purposeful, characterized by his own experiences, new evangelical faith in grace, and pastoral-psychological intuition. He brought a storm of indignation upon himself and initiated an intense theological debate. He appeared to many to be a new evangelical iconoclast, a preacher of loose-living, and a dangerous author. For young people who were struggling with these sexual questions, he became an understanding friend and a helper who brought liberation." (p. 242).

38 Mark Safstrom, *The Religious Origins of Democratic Pluralism: Paul Peter Waldenström and the Politics of the Swedish Awakening 1868-1917.* Dissertation (University of Washington 2010).

39 Waldenström. *Squire Adamson; Or where do you live?* Translated by Ruben T. Nygren. (Chicago: Mission Friend's Publishing Company 1928).

40 Lindström, p. 143.

41 Ibid., pp. 120-22.

42 On the various names of Adamsson, see I Cor 15:45-47; Gal 4:24; Lindström points out that in this latter passage, St. Paul himself has made an allegorical reading of the Old Testament, as he has interpreted Abraham's children with Sarah and Hagar as symbolizing two different covenants between God and the Israelites. Waldenström demonstrated awareness of this convention in his own commentary on this passage in his annotated translation of the New Testament, explaining that it represented an ancient tradition of allegorical readings of scripture (Lindström, 70). Allegorical readings of scripture were quite common in 19th century Pietist circles, demonstrated notably in the commentary on scripture by Peter Fjellstedt, which in turn seems inspired by Luther's own allegorical explanation of scripture (pp. 40-42).

43 (Waldenström's own note in Swedish editions.) Rev 2:2-3.

44 It is worth noting that all non-Lutheran confessions were referred to as "foreign" doctrines in Sweden.

45 Jn 10:12; Lindström points out that the word *Legoherde* was used by Rosenius to refer to sometimes well-meaning clergymen who have questionable priorities at best, and at worst, can be harmful and misleading "wolves" (p. 249).

46 Heb 3:7-4:11, among other places.

47 *'Och när jag levat, som jag bort, du för mig öppnar himlens port.'* From a hymn that appears in the "Wallin Hymnal" from 1819, edited by J.O. Wallin (1779-1839), a central figure in Swedish hymnody. The line appears in psalm 202 *"O Gud, som även räckt din hand"* attributed to C.A. Kock (1788-1843). Waldenström is suggesting that this hymn represents flawed theology.

48 Lindström suggests that it is unclear whether Waldenström meant this as "the world-wide church" or as a "church that had become worldly." When this accusation was leveled against the Church of Sweden, it usually referred to either "Catholic tendencies" or worldly attitudes and practices among the clergy (p. 251).

49 Mt 7:16.

50 "Simple" *(enfaldig)* is used in its most positive sense, reflecting the sincerity of the heart *(hjärtats enfaldighet),* as in Acts 2:46, and the revelation of spiritual wisdom to those who are like children *(de enfaldiga),* as in Mt 11:25. However, Lindström suggests that Waldenström's choice of "Simple" for this character's name was made with full awareness of the difference of interpretations of this word. In new evangelical circles, being "simple" was a positive trait, whereas among cultural elites, being "simple" was a pejorative and associated with ignorance and anti-intellectualism. Mother Simple is "simple" in her maintenance of first principles, but she is far from unreflective, as evidenced in her temptations in Chapter 9.

51 Wounded-hip is an allusion to Jacob wrestling with God in Gen 32:30-31.

52 Mk 12:42; Lk 21:2.

53 Lindström explains these two lads thusly: "Kind-hearted symbolizes Adamsson's humanitarian and Christian goals and his desire for community. Complacent represents all those incessant and unavoidable expressions of pride and satisfaction, which selfishness manages to create from charitable activities" (p. 126).

54 Mt 5:16; "...and glorify your Father in heaven" is conveniently left out.

55 "Holiness" is presented drawing references from a number of places in the Bible that refer to heaven, and as Lindström notes, especially Rev 21-22, as "a collage of heaven imagery" (p. 104).

56 (Waldenström's own note in Swedish editions.) "Justus is a Latin name that means righteous."

(Translator's note) It is important to point out that while Justus appears in many ways to be God, the characters refer to God in addition to Justus, indicating that they are not one and the same. God, and even Christianity itself, seem to operate independently of the allegorical world that Adamsson inhabits and, in many ways, has created for himself. Adamsson's punishment by Justus primarily represents Adamsson's understanding of justice.

57 Mt 18:24.

58 The choice of bankruptcy is not only convenient as an allegorical image, but also seems partly inspired by recent events in the 1850s and 60s. Lindström notes the following:

"Immediately prior to the writing of the book, a series of economic crises had struck Sweden. People in all classes were ruined, cotters, deans, factory workers and factory owners. Especial attention was drawn to the plight of brukspatron Paul Adolf Tottie of Olofsfors factory and estate in the parish of Norberg, which was hit with bankruptcy toward the end of 1861" (p. 129).

59 Gehenna is the allegorical mask for Hell, drawing from among other places Matthew chapters 5, 18 and 23, in Mark chapter 9, Luke chapter 12-13, and Rev 20:10. "Gehenna" also seems to appear more frequently in historic Swedish translations of the Bible, whereas this is translated mostly as "Hell" in English.

60 Lk 15:20.

61 Mt 7:13-14; Lk 13:24.

62 Mt 27:33; Mk 15:22; Jn 19:17.

63 Isa 11:1, 27:6, 35:1, 60:21.

64 Mt 28:20.

65 Mt 6:30; Lk 12:28.

66 Isa 43:1.

67 Rom 4:3-5.

68 Lindström points out that there are no churches or allegorical equivalents in Evangelium, and neither are there any corresponding allegorical figures to new evangelical leaders – all spiritual activity is conducted by lay people. The activities of the residents of Evangelium are independent of formal church structures, while communal Bible reading is a centerpiece of life in that city (p. 107).

69 Phil 4:7.

70 This is a common critique made by Pietists concerning the clergy of the Church of Sweden, who seemed to them mostly interested in shutting down conventicles, while at the same time showing little concern about alcohol and the culture that surrounded it.

71 Jn 10:28.

72 Ps 2:11.

73 Lindström notes that "Evangelist" may refer to the Baptist newspaper of the same name (p. 106).

74 Mother Simple's suspicion of logic is not to be confused with anti-intellectualism but a general skepticism of claims to objectivity. Arne Fritzson has theorized that Waldenström's championing of simplicity *(enfaldighet)* served to keep his own theology in balance. "In analyzing the methods for theological argumentation that Waldenström employs as he lays out his understanding of Christ's atonement activity, one can thus find an interesting duality. [...] Simplicity *[enfaldighet]* is a theological or spiritual virtue that Waldenström

champions, which appears, among other places, in the fact that the heroine in Squire Adamsson is called Mother Simple. In this way, tradition/revelation becomes a corrective for the universally human way of thinking. The method of theological argumentation that Waldenström uses here can be characterized as orthodox. On the other hand, he argues against the objective atonement motif by referring to universal human experience. He talks about how inappropriate we would regard it if a human being were to act in the same way as God acts, according to the objective atonement motif. Here Waldenström uses methods for his theological argumentation that can be called integrating/correlating *[integrerande/korrelerande]*." "In the Mission Covenant Church of Sweden there is both a tradition of "simply" *[enfaldigt]* reading what is written *[som det står]* and of using integrating/correlating methods for theological argument." Arne Fritzson. "En Gud som är god och rättfärdig" in *Liv och rörelse: Svenska missionskyrkans historia och identitet.* Hans Andreasson, et al. (Stockholm: Verbum 2007), pp. 360-372; The conclusion that one can gather from this is that in crafting his character of Mother Simple, Waldenström is testing where the balance lies between orthodoxy and experience. However, Mother Simple should not be seen as pure "orthodoxy," as Fritzson seems to suggest, since she is vocal in her opposition to the characters who represent legalism, and since she too encourages Adamsson toward an experiential understanding of grace (attending the class of Father Experience, as well as accepting the residents of the Hidden District). I would suggest that Mother Simple demonstrates a similar duality as the one that Fritzson sees in Waldenström overall.

75 Rom 7:15; Bredberg explains that Waldenström is directly referring here to the comments made by Rosenius on this passage in *Pietisten,* which was then featuring a series on the Book of Romans. By the time this chapter was added, Rosenius would have gotten as far as the 7th chapter of Romans. Rosenius says about this chapter, "This Bible passage is directed in particular at offering assurance to those who are oppressed by a frightening state of depravity, a fierce inward struggle, which no one knows except for those people themselves and the one who searches the heart." Schoolmaster Faithful is likely a model for Rosenius, as well (Bredberg 59, 62).

76 Jn 6:37.

77 Lk 19:10.

78 Isa 1:18.

79 Isa 54:10; In Waldenström's Swedish, it reads "grace" instead of "kindness."

80 Isa 46:4.

81 Isa 31:5; In Waldenström's Swedish, it reads in the first person and refers to the "Holy City" (instead of Jerusalem).

82 Mt 24:35; Mk 13:31; Lk 21:33.

83 Jn 7:38. Instead of "heart," it reads "life."

84 Rom 5:20.

85 Rom 6:2.

86 Jn 15:9.

87 Throughout this chapter, the word for temptation is *anfäktelse,* which indicates an existential crisis, rather than a simple temptation *(frestelse).* See discussion of temptation in introduction.

88 Ps 6:6.

89 Mother Simple's vision of Gehenna/Hell draws from typical medieval and renaissance depictions of the last judgment, which can be found all over Sweden in church paintings. Perhaps the most famous of these hangs in the Great Cathedral in Stockholm, an enormous, floor-to-ceiling painting with life-size subjects called "The Last Judgment" *(Den yttersta domen)* by David Klöker von Ehrenstrahl 1695.

90 Jn 6:37.

91 Lk 19:10.

92 Ps 88: 1-3.

93 Ps 88: 4-5, 8-9, 14-15.

94 Mt 11:28.

95 Ps 143.

96 Jer 29:11.

97 Mt 9:18, 24; Mk 5: 23.

98 Isa 54:8.

99 Mt 6:6.

100 Job 1:12.

101 Isa 54:10.

102 Rom 5:20.

103 Ps 103:11-12; In the Swedish it reads 'grace' (not 'mercy'), and Waldenström has added the last sentence.

104 Mt 9:2.

105 Lindström explains that the "loose-living" in question is not of a sexual nature, but instead indicates that the residents of this city "placed emphasis on peace, love and harmony, but they were not so particular about either doctrine or life. [...] The people in the city seemed relaxed and happy" (p. 107). Later he notes that Waldenström gives a surprisingly positive presentation of life in Loose-Living, indicative of a willingness to present a realistic sense of the relativism that is a part of the modern experience. "[Loose-Living] is characterized by a relativism that liberates people from the existential complications that are involved in living in Evangelium. Here there is no conflict between

grace and distress, between faith and temptation [*anfäktelse,* or existential crises]. The culture of Loose-Living seems to be free and unthreatening, it is an open-minded place, life is easy, it involves no difficult life decisions, no ethical struggles" (p. 113). One can also add that it is in this regard that Waldenström again resembles Kierkegaard, in that he seems to be advocating a lifestyle that involves an intentional choice of the suffering that is associated with facing one's doubts and embracing despair. This choice involves leaving the relatively carefree existence of The World and Loose-Living, and entering into a less comfortable, but more genuine existence in Evangelium.

106 Lindström notes that critics of the revival movements have characterized the suspicion of worldliness among Pietists in a way that does not take into account this nuanced relationship. "It was not so much a matter of the culture [of worldliness] in its various forms, but rather the content, that is to say values, attitudes toward life and religion, motives for ethical action, and a prioritization of spiritual needs over material. One can perhaps say that the revival movement's cultural interests were great, but often critical." (p. 110)

107 Gal 6:7.

108 Lindström notes that in earlier editions of the allegory, *liberaler* (liberals) was used here, whereas in later versions this was changed to *frisinnade* (p. 107). *"Frisinnade"* translates to liberal-minded, and was also a terms used by the liberals in Swedish politics. Waldenström himself tended to align with the liberals in his early years as a member of parliament, beginning in 1885, so this is in some respects a self-critical reflection.

109 Ps 103:11.

110 Heb 12:14. Waldenström's Swedish reads 'sanctification' *(helgelse)* instead of 'holiness' *(helighet).*

111 Gal 5:1.

112 Gal 5:13.

113 Ibid.

114 The "Rock of Offense" is Jesus Christ (Rom 9:33). The later attempts by the learned to roll away this rock resemble the discussion in Swedish academic circles (including Uppsala), in which the divinity of Christ was being challenged in an attempt to rationalize faith, reform church structures and do away with extraneous miracles, etc. Prominent in this discussion was the commentary by Viktor Rydberg (*Bibelns lära om kristus,* 1862).

115 I Tim 1:7, in the Swedish *skriftlärare,* teachers of Scripture.

116 Lindström describes this trio of *"Jag," "Vill,"* and *"Skall"* (Self, Will, Shall) as three parts of a whole, "a kind of troika of necessity, a system of selfishness, methodicalness, and complusion" (p. 106).

117 Lindström has noticed that there were significant revisions to the text after the atonement controversy in 1872, which appeared in the 1874 edition of *Squire Adamsson.* These changes are slight, but reflect the main point of Waldenström's atonement theology,

which is that God and Christ are of the same mind and both reflect grace. This was in contrast to the doctrine in the Church of Sweden, based on the Augsburg Confession, which indicated that God was reconciled to humankind through the crucifixion, rather than that humankind was reconciled to God. Thus, in the prevailing Lutheran understanding of the Swedish clergy, the nature of God is in opposition to the nature of Christ and the result is a state of tension in which Christ shields the believer from God's wrath. Here in the statements of Justus All-Powerful it is being made clear that God is indeed also the agent of grace through Christ's actions (p. 271).

118 Probably a provocative reference to the low-church newspaper, *Väktaren* ("The Watchman"), which was critical of Waldenström's allegory (Lindström 63).

119 Lk 9:62; Gen 19:26.

120 II Tim 1:8.

121 Ezek 34:16; Lk 19:10.

122 Mk 10:51 (note the contrast with Mk 10:36); Lk 18:41; Jn 5:6.

123 Lk 10:30-36; here it is striking that Immanuel is the Good Samaritan.

124 Gal 5:19-21.

125 As noted in the introduction and drawing from Lindström's research, the sin impied here is likely masturbation *(onani /självbefläckelse)* specifically, as it was a prominent topic in the debates about sexual health in the late 1800s (Lindström 221). However, the scriptural taboos against this refer to Genesis 38:9 and the displeasing actions of Onan, who refused to impregnate the wife of his deceased brother. So more generally this is an expression of sexuality that is not reproductive and conflicts with the duty to build families. Most important to note here is that this is a sin that is so shameful that it is never spoken of, causes general revulsion, and precludes membership in the congregation. This is in contrast with the long list of sins mentioned just prior, which grave as they may be, are not stigmatized to the same degree since they can at least be discussed. Waldenström was criticized by the Church of Sweden's journal *Swensk Kyrkotidning* for having contested articles 3 and 4 in church doctrine, which were: 3.) "The forgiveness of sins has the unconditional and immediate power to keep the law," and 4.) "Although the carnal nature of the righteous person causes many lapses and weakness, even so, faith and sanctification cannot remain in the person who obeys evil desires and falls openly into sin" (p. 228). Lindström sees both Waldenström and Rosenius as reflecting the new perspective that masturbation was evidence of a disease or medical condition, rather than evidence of sinfulness, which was the traditional perspective (p. 235). Furthermore, Waldenström was opposed to the treatment prescribed for this condition by medical professionals like C.S. Kapff, who attempted to discourage this behavior, as Waldenström explained it, "by inspiring anxiety" in the patients. Waldenström warns that this risks driving the patients to suicide, and gives the example of one such 16-year-old who tragically ended his life in the hospital after such treatment. In keeping with the theme of this novel, on this issue Waldenström preferred to emphasize assurance over anxiety. (See: *Om Ungdomens Farligaste Fiende)*.

126 Rom 5:20.

127 In Swedish, the word for 'all,' or 'everyone,' is *alla*, which is a palindrome.

128 Ps 103:11.

129 Gal 6:1.

130 Isa 42:3.

131 Rom 7:14-25; instead of "mind," Waldenström's Swedish reads "spirit." One of Rosenius' only criticisms of the allegory was that he wished that Waldenström, in writing this chapter, would have gone further by including excerpts from Romans 8 (Bredberg 64).

132 I Cor 5:6-8; Mt 16:6-12; Lk 12:1.

133 Lk 23:39-43.

134 Mt 26:33-35; Mk 14:29-31; Lk 22:31-34; Jn 13:37-38.

135 Mt 26:69-75; Mk 14:66-72; Lk 22:54-62; Jn 18:15-27.

136 Lk 18:13; the Swedish reads 'gracious.'

137 Mt 10:22, 24:13; Mk 13:13; Lk 21:36.

138 Rom 4:4-5.

139 Jn 11:25-26.

140 Lindström speculates that this could refer to the exposition on the book of Romans that Rosenius began writing in *Pietisten* in 1860 (p. 205).

141 I Cor 14:34.

142 Mk 5:34.

143 Heb 12:14. Waldenström's Swedish reads 'sanctification' *(helgelse)* instead of 'holiness' *(helighet)*.

144 Eph 4:14.

145 Acts 3:12.

146 Ezek 34:16; Lk 19:10.

147 Lk 5:8.

148 Gal 4:21-31; Gen 16:1-15.

149 This (mis)conception of the role of the law is one that Waldenström wished to correct. Lindström explains the situation thusly: "The role of the law as an agent of discipline, one that will drive people to seek Christ, to the gospel and to grace, this was an important motif in Lutheran theology, even in the new evangelical version. [...] It is possible that Waldenström in this way wanted to intensify the novel's message that the law does not

have a role to play for the person who is already experiencing the state of depravity. Then it is only Immanuel and grace which are operative" (p. 193). Throughout the novel, characters have viewed Moses and Justus All-Powerful as chastising with the law (payment of debt, bankruptcy) in order to bring people to Holiness. However, Hagarsson here is missing the point that once the individual is experiencing his wretchedness, like the residents of Evangelium do, then there is no function for the law. Lindström has noticed that in earlier versions of the novel, Waldenström made allusions to the traditional Lutheran understanding of the three functions of the law, but gradually removed these references in order to strengthen his assertions of the primacy of grace in the state of depravity. This made him vulnerable to accusations of antinomianism from both high- and low church circles (p. 200). Waldenström may have been particularly influenced by Luther in this matter, thanks in part to a new edition of Martin Luther's exposition on the book of Galatians, which came out in 1861, published by none other than A.P. Falk, editor of the *Stockholm City Missionary* and Waldenström's friend. According to Luther, "The law has its appointed time, namely up until Christ, as Paul explains in [Romans] chapter 3:24. But when he comes, Moses has to yield with his law, circumcision, sacrifices and sabbaths, yes, even all the prophets" (pp. 201-202).

150 1 Cor 3:13.

151 Mt 18:24.

152 Gal 6:8.

153 Gal 6:7.

154 I Tim 2:3-4.

155 (Waldenström's own note in Swedish editions.) It was by despairing of grace that he had entered into self improvement and self righteousness; and through despair in all of his own being and doing, he came once again to belief in the gospel and peace.

156 I Tim 1:15.

157 Ps 31:10.

158 II Tim 4:7-8.

ABOUT THE AUTHORS & CONTRIBUTORS

Paul Peter Waldenström (1838-1917) was a clergyman, revival preacher, educator, prolific author and editor, and one of the foremost figures in the 19th century spiritual awakening. Born in Luleå in northern Sweden, he attended Uppsala University, where he earned a doctorate, as well as completed the examination for ordination in the Lutheran Church of Sweden, which was the state church. His primary occupation was as a teacher at several upper secondary schools *(högreläroverk)* where he taught theology and classical languages (in Växjö, Umeå and Gävle). In 1868, he assumed the role of editor for the devotional journal *Pietisten* ("The Pietist"), following the death of his mentor and predecessor Carl Olof Rosenius. Decades of dissatisfaction among Pietists in the Church of Sweden resulted in 1878 in the formation of the Swedish Mission Covenant (*Svenska Missionsförbundet*, now part of *Equmeniakyrkan*), also inspiring the formation of the Evangelical Covenant Church in North America in 1885 among Swedish emigrants. Waldenström's writings and theology played a pivotal role in the formation of both these denominations. A lifelong avocation as an itinerant preacher took him on extensive preaching and study tours, including numerous tours of North America, Europe, the Middle East and China. He was awarded an honorary doctorate in theology from Yale University in 1889. He also served in the Swedish parliament, *Riksdag*, from 1884-1905 as a representative for the city of Gävle.

Mark Safstrom is lecturer of Swedish and Scandinavian studies at the University of Illinois at Urbana-Champaign. He has written on various topics in the history of Pietism and the influence of this movement in 19th century Scandinavian politics and literature. Since 2010 he has served as chief editor of the journal *Pietisten,* which regularly features his translations of texts by authors such as P.P. Waldenström, Carl Olof Rosenius, Carl Boberg, and Lina Sandell. His dissertation explored the political implications of Waldenström's career in the Swedish parliament.

Jeffrey T. HansPetersen is a freelance artist who specializes in ink sketching, watercolor painting, oil painting, wood sculpture, and digital media. His primary occupation is practicing family medicine as a doctor on Vashon Island, Washington. Original artwork by Jeff has regularly been featured in the journal *Pietisten*.

Gracia Grindal is professor emeritus of rhetoric at Luther Seminary in St. Paul, Minnesota, having taught there since 1984 as a professor in pastoral theology and ministry, communications, and rhetoric. Prior to this, she taught English at Luther College, in Decorah, Iowa, beginning in 1968. She has been a consultant for several American hymnal committees and translated many Scandinavian hymns, and has written on a variety of topics relating to hymnody and Pietism, including *Preaching from Home: The Stories of Seven Lutheran Women Hymn Writers* (2011).

ACKNOWLEDGMENTS

Illustrations by Jeffrey T. HansPetersen.

Cover design and manuscript layout by Sandy Nelson.

Editorial assistance by Stephanie Johnson Blomgren and David Nelson.

Publisher, Karl Nelson.

ABOUT PIETISTEN

Pietisten, Inc. is a 501(c)(3) non-profit and the publisher of the twice-yearly journal of the same name.

Pietisten is ecumenical and does not formally represent any institution, but it draws heavy inspiration from the collective heritage of Lutheran Pietism, as represented in a congenial flock of historically-related traditions: the Evangelical Covenant Church and the Mission Covenant Church of Sweden (Equmeniakyrkan), the Augustana Lutheran heritage (ELCA), the Evangelical Free Church, and the Baptist General Conference, and epidemics of Pietism within the Congregationalist and Methodist folds. *Pietisten* is the spiritual heir of a Swedish devotional newspaper of the same name, published between 1842-1918. www.pietisten.org

www.ingramcontent.com/pod-product-compliance
Lightning Source LLC
Chambersburg PA
CBHW020559310726
48979CB00008B/1274/J

* 9 7 8 0 9 9 1 3 5 0 6 2 9 *